A

READING

AT                                    THE

BEACH

Library of Congress Control Number: 2021940133

ISBN: 978-1-7371255-5-6

Wild Pansy, an imprint of Armin Lear Press Inc
215 W Riverside Drive, #4362
Estes Park, CO 80517

# A READING AT THE BEACH

a love story of vengeful spirits
and novel couplings

## BRYCE HARTE

# TABLE OF CONTENTS

# PROLOGUE

## *PSYCHOMETRY ON THE BEACH*
### *Saturday Afternoon, August 1973*

Psychometry (from Greek: ψυχή, psukhē, "spirit, soul"
and μέτρον, metron, "measure"), also known as token-
object reading, or psychoscopy, is a form of extrasensory
perception characterized by the claimed ability to make
relevant associations from an object of unknown history
by making physical contact with that object.

Kyle Wilson and his Aunt Rebecca had walked to Henlopen beach from the nearby Wilson family home. The angle
of the sun and the thin morning mist gave the place and the
people the look of an Edward Hopper painting. A casual observer would see an elderly woman in a sun dress and floppy straw
hat and a muscular young man in a tie-dyed t-shirt and purple

Speedo - enjoying the sea air and morning sunshine. A deceptive appearance.

Seated on the big old driftwood log, they each had a lot on their minds. She needed information her nephew could provide, so getting him away from a house full of relatives in town for the funeral was helpful. Unaware of his Aunt's motives, Kyle was happy for this brief escape from his new "grownup responsibilities." Besides, that spot on the beach had always brought him solace of one degree or another.

His Aunt Rebecca needed information Kyle's father, her brother, John Wilson, Sr., had kept from the rest of the family, and now he was dead.

But when Kyle told her of his newly acquired psychic ability, Rebecca Wilson heard opportunity knock.

Sitting there, Kyle stared up the beach at a group of college students tossing a Frisbee. He was grateful for the distraction. Rebecca Wilson Thompson watched him staring and waited to continue their conversation. She was fingering a double eagle - a twenty-dollar gold piece from the 1800's. She switched it from one hand to another. Finally, she spoke.

"So far, your readings have been accurate," he told him. She then held out the gold coin as she instructed, "take a deep breath, clear your mind and hold out your hand."

Kyle did as told and she placed the shiny gold coin in his palm asking, "Can you-"

But Kyle couldn't hear her. The pain and anguish were overwhelming. He heard screams and he saw blood. He pushed the coin off his palm and covered his ears with both hands.

The gold coin fell into the sand.

"Kyle? Kyle, are you all right?"

He dropped his hands to the driftwood log to steady himself. "Headache," he lied. "a powerful headache. Whoa. We better try this again later." He stared at the breaking ocean waves for a moment, then stood up, kicked off his sandals and removed his t-shirt. Without a word to his Aunt he ran to the shoreline and dove into the surf. When he surfaced, he swam very hard until he was a hundred yards from the beach.

He stopped, rolled over, spread his arms and legs and floated. He hoped somehow the ocean would cleanse him of what he had seen.

"But it was so real," he yelled to the sky. "I saw it!"

The rest was too difficult to shout out loud. He whispered, hoping saying it out loud would diminish the horror. "I saw it. I saw a beautiful woman get half of her face ripped away by a shotgun blast. I heard the screams, I heard the gunshot, I smelled the stench, I saw flesh and blood fly, I could feel a man's anguish." He took a couple deep breaths. He watched a gull swoop past high above his head and then told himself, "this new talent is way too trippy."

He continued to bob in the surf, not wanting to go back to the family, to the house, to the complications. He wished he could undo everything that had occurred since Thursday two days ago. It was Thursday when his twin brother Johnny spoke two words to him: "it's time." Those two words reminded Kyle of his brother's warning from years ago. "When Dad dies, Norman's business dealings will destroy the family. You're going to have to stop him, Kyle, even if you have to kill him, because if you don't, he will kill you."

Norman was their very much alive older brother. Kyle's twin Johnny had been dead since he and Kyle were 14 years old.

Kyle had never shared that information with anyone. And with the events of the past 48 hours, he wasn't sure he could trust anyone with it now.

# CHAPTER ONE

## *MULTIPLE VISITATIONS*
### *Two Days Prior in Henlopen, Delaware*

On that Thursday morning in August 1973, peculiar things would happen to four people that would draw them together in a lethal entanglement before the weekend was out.

Kyle Wilson was asleep. Just days prior he had closed up his apartment in Boston, moved most of its contents into a storage facility outside Washington, DC and then, last night arrived at his family's summer home in Rehoboth Beach, Delaware. Law school was done, all loose ends tied up in Beantown and he was looking forward to what he expected would be a restful three-week vacation with his family and friends. But of course, as with many things in this or any other lifetime, it wasn't going to work out the way he wanted. He didn't know it at the time, but it was as if the Gods, the whatever it is that runs the universe, was looking down on the boyishly cute young man asleep in the room in which he had spent so many of his formative years, read his mind and proclaimed, "no way, my friend."

He had arrived in the little seaside community of Henlopen Acres at almost midnight. The only ones still awake were his stepmom and his older sister. They were watching Johnny Carson. Kyle begged off having the invited nightcap.

"I'm wicked sleepy," he averred. "Why waste good scotch?"

He gave each of them a peck on the cheek. "I will see you at breakfast," he explained. "I hope you will lavish course after course of your Thursday morning specialties on us."

This got him the expected laugh. Weekday mornings at the summer house meant a wide selection of cereals and toast. Eggs? Sure, but only if you cooked them yourself. It was vacation and no one wanted to cook.

Upstairs in his room, he dropped his duffle bag in a corner. He immediately shed his street clothes and slid on one of his nylon Speedo swim briefs and a faded tie-dyed tee-shirt. Then he hopped into bed. For as long as he could remember his summer uniform was a swim brief and a t-shirt or sweatshirt.

He felt very content nestling amid the linens on the familiar bed in his familiar clothes and in his old room. The place had plenty of good memories.

There used to be twin beds in here, he remembered, *twin beds for us twins*. Back then, he actually thought they were called "twin beds" because they were used by him and his twin brother.

"Johnny," Kyle sighed out loud.

The twin beds were still in the room the summer after

6

Johnny died. *Norman was home from military prep school. He would come in here to sleep so he wouldn't be alone (though he would never admit that.)*

As young boys often would, they talked about a hundred and one things until each dozed off. One night they got on the topic of ghosts and monsters.

"Did you ever get a feeling that our home up in town was haunted?" Kyle asked him one night before dozing off.

"No. But you think there's a boogieman in the basement. You stupid shit. I heard mom telling dad that's why you run up the basement stairs all the time. There's no such thing as ghosts, Kyle."

"What if there were? Can you imagine? Johnny coming back to haunt us!" That made Kyle laugh.

Norman didn't even smile. He simply growled, "Go to sleep, asshole."

Lying there then, so many years older, Kyle reexamined the memory and thought *that was so Norman. He would come in here for comfort and companionship, but he would still have to dominate. Norman always had to be the biggest dick in the room. That was Norman. Huh. Still is.*

Kyle turned this way and that and pushed his pillows around to get comfortable. Something was unsettling. He murmured, "Medicine." He flicked on the bedside lamp, hopped out of bed and crawled under it.

*Whoa. No dust bunnies. They must have cleaned especially for me. Cool.*

He pressed down on the top edge of a section of the baseboard molding and drew it towards him. It disengaged from the wall allowing him to reach inside and withdraw a small wooden box. He quickly replaced the wood, slid out from under and hopped back up on top of the bed.

He was not disappointed. His old stash box still had a small foil square.

*Blonde hash if I remember correctly. And, whoa, that looks like about a quarter ounce of weed in a baggie, papers, pipe and even a Bic lighter. I am so anal.*

"It is always good to plan ahead," he whispered to no one in particular and then drew two rolling papers from their little cardboard sleeve. "Of course," he continued telling the empty room, "the only other person who knows about my hiding place is Daniel Mason and he certainly hasn't been around for a while."

Kyle rolled a fat joint then opened the bedroom window wide and sat on the sill so he could blow the smoke out. *A little harsh*, he thought after a couple tokes. And after taking a few deep breaths of nighttime ocean air he realized —*still potent.*

As he headed back to bed, he couldn't help but stop in front of the door mirror. He lifted the t-shirt and looked at himself. "I still can cut it in a Speedo. Time in the gym never fails. Not bad. Still pretty tight." He whispered to his image in the mirror. "Yes. I would do me," he continued as he ran his hand down his stomach and gently massaged the bulge of his purple nylon Speedo. "I am so conceited!" he admonished himself. "Then again, you did just graduate Harvard, made law review, caught no STD and did not get anyone pregnant in your three years in Boston. That's got to account for something." And with that, he switched off the bedside lamp, jumped back into bed and enjoyed the floating feeling the weed induced.

Staring at the ceiling, he recalled good memories of his bedroom.

There were the late-night bull sessions with the guys: Mason, Henderson and other friends who'd stay with them for days at a time during the summer. Daniel "Moose" Mason was the handsomest of the three, a fellow swimmer & gymnast and best friends with Kyle's twin brother Johnny. Henderson, as much a jock as the other two, was the smartest of the group. He was always coming up with theories tying to apply logic to an illogical world. One particular bull session with Mason and Henderson came to mind. It was the night Henderson gave his memorable and infamous "p-c speech."

"It's all about pussies and cocks," Mike Henderson exclaimed one night as only a 16-year-old sex-obsessed male could.

"Right," Mason agreed, "it's all about getting laid."

"No, my good friend, not at all," Henderson admonished him. "I definitely am not referring to the orgasm," he expounded in his best professorial voice. "When I say it is all about pussies and cocks, I refer to the very physical nature of pussies and cocks. The shape of the organ predetermines a human being's behavior. Men deal with outward shit, women with inward. Thus: cocks and pussies." He took another swallow of beer then continued. "Take money. Women save, men invest – inward: saving. Outward: put money to work."

"Or buying great shit like cars and boats," Kyle chimed in.

"Precisely!" Henderson exclaimed with a deep bow to Kyle's wisdom.

"What about breasts?" Mason exclaimed with an air of discovery. "They're outward."

"Shut up, Mason, I am making a point about sexual organs, not a baby's food source."

"Or Kyle's obsession," laughed Mason.

"My point is thus," Henderson explained, unzipping his fly and producing his flaccid, yet long penis. "Men want to put their dicks into things." and thrusting his hips forward with each word he shouted, "Invest! Gamble!" Then he stuffed his meat back into his shorts as if demonstrating his next point, "Women desire to gather stuff close to them." And he zipped shut for emphasis. "No young man alive has a hope chest," he continued with great earnestness, "yet girls do. Why? Because women are savers. They are collectors! Mason, I bet your mother has some of your baby clothes in a cedar chest in the attic."

"Yes! With my baby book and this stupid little fucking sailor suit she made me wear."

"See! Gathering stuff! Collecting! Holding on to stuff! Holding on to time! Women want to be filled. Men want to spread their seed! Outward!" He chugged the rest of his beer, then added, "cocks and pussies my friends! I rest my case!" He then let out a very long and loud belch.

*And we applauded. I remember we applauded!*

Kyle rolled over on his side and enjoyed the "rush" the quick head movement created.

"Nice," he whispered to the darkness around him. "Vacation. Time for pondering."

For three weeks he didn't have to think about case law. He could simply ponder other things like the ocean. Even on those relatively calm days he loved standing at the shoreline and letting the expanse of the ocean embrace him. For Kyle Wilson, it was like being enveloped in the arms of a lover after a very satisfying encounter, a sense just about as consuming and wonderful as when he and his partner would be staring deep into each other's eyes and climax together. The ocean held that kind of erotic power- the power of being connected. Whether on the shore or in the water, it always provided a feeling he was a part of the world not just someone walking around on it and taking it for granted.

His mind continued to wonder as it often did prior to surrendering to sleep.

*"There is energy all around us all the time," she told me, "it's when you're near the ocean it's more obvious."*

"She?" *Whoa. Haven't thought about her in a while.*

This bed and lovers? Of course, Cyndy Weaver.

Why her? Such an easy answer. There had been no long relationship since Cyndy. Why is that? Because no one before or after was ever as challenging or exciting as Cyndy Weaver. Maybe Daniel Mason, but the relationship with him was doomed from the start. But with Cyndy? Then he remembered why they broke it off.

*That. Yeah, that. That visitation from Johnny and his warning about how when Dad died, I had to kill Norman or Norman would...*

He wouldn't let himself finish.

Kyle could never bring himself to tell Cyndy any more than he had an encounter with his brother. No matter how hard she tried to get more information from him. So, he shoved her further away and avoided any additional psi research.

Kyle sighed and forced himself to focus on happier thoughts of their times together in Henlopen, and how they defied his parents by sleeping together, and making love, in his bedroom.

*In this bed*, he remembered happily.

*Beds.* Recently beds seemed to be triggering as many (if not more) memories than old pop tunes. *Is that a sign of aging?* he wondered. *A sign of maturity? Or promiscuity? Obviously, the latter,* he decided and almost laughed out loud.

As he was drifting off, he wondered aloud (as he found himself doing more and more), "what the hell would she think of this new respectability?" Hearing his own voice intruding on the nighttime litany of crickets and locusts, he was startled a moment, and he shivered.

He settled back into his pillow and continued his assessment. *Would Cyndy go for my being so legit?*

Their ghost-chasing days were behind him by a little more than three years now. The family expected more from him, and he'd shown them he was up to it. Soon he'll take the bar and easily enter a K Street firm. He'd be 26 years old, he'd have a career and yes, respectability.

*Would becoming a respectable Washington lawyer mean I'd have to go straight?*

He yawned.

*Not something to decide tonight. Right now, it is just damn good to know there are three whole weeks before I start clerking and preparing for the bar. For right now, sleeping is the greatest idea ever.* And with that thought, he rolled over on his stomach and fell into a deep, dreamless sleep.

It was almost dawn when it happened.

The sparsely clouded sky was pale blue through the pines beyond the double window at the foot of the bed. The white sheer window curtains framed the specter of a teenage boy.

Kyle stirred. Outside the window, a bird call to its mate.

"Kyle?" The young boy's unearthly voice broke the silence in the room.

Outside the birds called to one another.

A shiver started at the base of Kyle's spine and raced to the nape of his neck. He quickly rolled over, wanting to speak to his brother, but was unable to. It was too wild and too incredible.

Then, in a moment Kyle would remember for the rest of his life his brother Johnny told him, "Kyle, it's time."

His voice was so clear. Kyle sat bolt upright. He wanted to speak, but his brother was suddenly gone. There was only the sound of the birds and the sight of the sky beyond the trees becoming light with the new day.

Kyle knew exactly what Johnny meant.

He wanted to scream.

\* \* \*

### That Same Morning in Chicago, Illinois

Hours before Kyle was startled by his visitor his aunt Rebecca also experienced a "visitation."

Rebecca Thompson was asleep beside her husband in their lakeshore apartment. She was dreaming of her childhood. It was a comfortable dream of Nuns and Catholic School and the playground at Sacred Cross Academy. Then the dream abruptly changed as dreams usually do. She suddenly found herself in a void, and, of all things to have happen, she heard her brother calling to her.

"It was so damn real," she would later tell her nephew, Kyle Wilson. But at the time she was positive it was a dream.

*My brother John? Nah. Must be a dream,* (she thought at the time) *for John to be speaking to me! Hadn't it been three, what, four years since we fought?*

"Rebecca, honey."

She opened her eyes.

*Funny, she thought, why bother? It's just a dream.*

But there on her left, beside her bed, stood her brother John Wilson.

"I've come to say I'm sorry, Rebecca, and to say goodbye. I need you to watch the boys for me. Watch out for them, please."

Her mouth and throat were dry as toast yet she managed to whisper, "John?" She wanted to reach out, but her arms seemed paralyzed. She needed a witness to this encounter. She was desperate to wake her husband, Nick.

The figure beside the bed seemed to lean towards her. She finally managed to gain control of her arm and land a punch on her husband's beefy shoulder.

The specter of her brother continued to lean closer, as if to kiss her cheek, but her husband stirred and the specter of John Wilson vanished.

"Huh?" he managed to groan, "why'd ya-"

"Nick, it's John. Something's wrong."

*　*　*

## That Same Morning in Washington, DC

At just about that time, Kyle's older brother Norman Wilson was awakened by a phone call. He was pissed. No one was supposed to call him at home. Not about this, anyway. His wife, Susan, luckily, was sleeping soundly, and Norman was spared the usual questions. *Christ, she asks so damn many questions,* he thought as he paced the large living room of their duplex apartment. *And there are going to be questions. Damn!*

It was quite a call all right. He got the message loud and clear. It was information that would keep him awake through the period of time when his brother and his aunt each received their strange visitors. And it made him worry. Why wouldn't it? The call was from Turlino in New York. The crates had been searched and seized and Norman's $50,000 investment was suddenly the property of the United States Customs Agents at Kennedy Airport.

"I can grease the skids and get your cargo released, but it's going to cost you ten grand," Turlino explained to Norman.

While Kyle and Rebecca were contemplating their mysterious visitations, Norman had more serious things on his mind. *Just how the hell am I ever going to repay the fifty grand I borrowed before Dad finds out I pulled such a stupid stunt? I wish I never heard of fuckin' pre-Columbian artifacts.*

But, at the time he got involved, it was such a sure thing. At the inception of the deal he was positive he would never get caught short nor have to come up with his own cash. *Damn.*

Damn voice inside his head wouldn't let him go, either.

*"Sure thing?" Yep, that's what Dad'll say. And "Don't you know there's no such animal?"*

It goaded the hell out of Norman to think he would have to talk to the old man about it, and it would have to be soon, too. *Damn!* He grabbed his jock and jogging shorts off the chair and hurled them towards the front door. *Shit. He's going to ream my ass over this deal,* he realized, as he crossed the living room. *He'll rip me another one,* Norman decided, snatching up the garments and quickly pulling them on.

"Shit. Shit. Shit." he continually muttered as he put on socks and his running shoes, "Shit! Carloads of shit!"

He left the apartment at dawn's first light, careful not to slam the door as hard as he wanted to because it would tip off Susan that he was pissed and cause her to ask her stupid questions at breakfast.

The sounds of the city coming awake surrounded him as he crossed Q Street and headed towards Rock Creek Park for his morning run.

"What the fuck," he wondered out loud, "am I gonna do now?"

*There's always that freak at the bank. He'll give me the ten grand. He better.*

\* \* \*

### That Same Morning in Denver, Colorado

Cyndy Weaver was just heading towards her bedroom and a welcoming empty bed. Her Denver apartment was a mess. It had been a good party. She had finally ushered Ron out the door at 2 a.m. She wasn't up for what he had in mind.

She had just turned off the last light, figuring she'd clean up the mess in the morning, and was headed towards her bedroom when it hit her - an overwhelming sense that someone was in trouble.

"Who?" she asked herself out loud.

The first person to come to mind was Kyle Wilson. *Kyle*

*Wilson? Really?* And she realized she hadn't thought about him since-

It didn't matter. The feeling was too strong to bother with any such calculation. *Kyle's in trouble. Gentle, loving, stupid, Kyle Wilson. Damn. Just when I thought I was done with him.* But she couldn't shake it. The concerns, even the old affections were all there, and they were deep. Deep and sure as the knowledge he needed her.

Odd, she thought, (having quickly figured it was too early in the morning to call and knowing they'd all most likely be at the summer house in Henlopen, Delaware) how odd that this talent of mine, the very thing that led to our parting is suddenly drawing me to him again.

She made a mental note to phone him at 5 a.m. her time, and went back into the living room. Suddenly, she wasn't sleepy. In fact, she decided she'd best clean up the place and then pack.

"Pack?" she thought aloud once more. "But where am I going?"

\* \* \*

### That Same Morning in Henlopen, Delaware

The sun was up as Kyle donned a pair of sweatpants and slumped into the old rocker by the window.

"So much for plans of sleeping the day away," he mumbled -- then thought, *maybe later on the beach.*

At that moment, he had to take some time to think.

The extraordinary nature of the supernatural experience didn't frighten him. He'd had several in the past, including appearances by others who had "gone over to the other side."

17

But years prior, in yearning for his former twin, Kyle had success-fully contacted the boy. That time he received a far more specific message from Johnny. That devastating prediction was what ulti-mately drove Kyle away from the psi studies and Cyndy Weaver.

"But," Kyle told himself, out loud this time, "here he is again."

The old yearnings had been stirred. Kyle missed his brother more than ever that Thursday morning, and, at the same time, was a bit annoyed. For the past three years he had done nothing in the area of psi studies. He'd returned to school and followed his father's every wish. He had done everything to suppress old curiosities and restrain his longings for his former best friend and confidant.

"But here you are again, telling me `it's time!' I need to forget that stuff Johnny! I need to be doing things for myself now!" Then, looking down at his hands folded in his lap, he added, "Don't I?"

"Could have asked how I am. You could have said hello first. Jesus, Johnny, what a way to start a vacation! Does Dad know you're running around playing cosmic hide-and-seek this morning? Run into him lately?"

At that point the curtains by the open window stirred as if a gust had just blown into the room yet everything outside was perfectly still.

"Oh Jesus, what made me say that?" Kyle wondered out loud. "This is getting too creepy for me. I need company."

With that, he grabbed his sweatshirt off the bureau, headed out of the room and downstairs in hopes his nieces would be in the family room watching early morning television. Anybody for company right now was his feeling. Even kiddie cartoon shows would be a welcomed distraction.

He turned off the hallway and into the large family room at the back of the house. It was deserted.

"Great family. Lazy. All of them sleeping in."

He headed on to the kitchen as he shoved his chilled arms through the sleeves of the sweatshirt.

"Johnny, if you can hear me and I know you can-go away! Just go away. Got it?" he pleaded in a whisper as he filled the tea kettle at the sink, keeping his eyes locked on items immediately in front of him. As he turned to the stove and switched on the gas burner, he kept his vision restricted to the kettle. He wasn't about to look anywhere else for fear of seeing his brother again. But it didn't entirely work. Kyle could feel a presence behind him. No matter how hard he tried, he couldn't ignore it. He placed the kettle on the burner and turned around to dress down his invisible visitor when the phone rang.

Kyle literally jumped off the kitchen floor. Nothing of Olympic proportions, but his bare feet did, for a moment, leave the ground.

He caught up the telephone handset on the second ring hoping not to wake the rest of the house. His "hello" was in tandem with his stepmother's.

*She must have grabbed the phone by her bed*, Kyle figured. *I hope this doesn't wake Dad.*

"Hello?" they called together.

"I've got it, Vicki," Kyle continued.

"John?" she asked sleepily.

"No ma'am," answered the stranger on the other end of the line.

"Oh-"

"I got it, Mom."

"Mrs. Wilson, this is officer Paterson of the Delaware State Police."

"Oh?" She snapped awake.

As Kyle stood there beside the doorway to the deck, staring out beyond the pool and the lawn slopping to the lake so calm and still, a stream of warm air seemed to pass through him. Before the officer could speak another word, Kyle knew. He knew what it was. And he knew it was true -- as true as gravity. He knew Johnny was right. His father, John Wilson was dead, and Kyle knew horrible things would happen.

# CHAPTER TWO

## *A DEATH IN THE FAMILY*
### *Along the Road in Delaware*

Only eight hours prior to the phone call from the Delaware State Police, John Wilson was cruising along Route 80, driving from the Washington suburbs to his Eastern shore home for a long weekend with the family.

He had a touch of indigestion and was feeling tired but satisfied as he drove his Ford LTD across the Eastern Shore of Maryland. He had every right to be very proud of himself. It had taken a hell of a lot of time and attention, not to mention all the company's assets to close the deal. He now had the controlling interest in the biggest housing project he'd ever attempted. It would mean years of work for his company and what he liked to call his "extended family." It would also mean healthy profits for everyone involved.

*Things are going so well.*

The more he thought about it as he drove eastward, the more he found himself smiling.

*Kyle will be here for the next three weeks. Maybe I'll hire a charter on Monday so Kyle and I can go for marlin.*

It gave him pleasure to have witnessed such a turnaround in each of his two sons over the past couple of years.

*Norman is treating the clients better —he's being more courteous in his dealings with the workers. Norman's maturing. That's the key. Maturity. I'm betting the boy will be all right.*

Wilson nodded and repeated himself, aloud this time, "The boy will be all right."

His thoughts shifted to Kyle.

*Talk about a one-eighty. I'm sure glad he stopped wasting his time with all that spiritual crap. It will be good to have him with us for the rest of the summer. He's actually finished law school. Law school. I knew he could do it! Soon as he's passed the bar, we'll steer the company's legal work to Kyle. There's a sense of dynasty to it ... Norman managing the business and Kyle seeing to the legalities of it when I'm gone.*

*Wait a second. Gone? Gone? Where am I going? Not anywhere anytime soon.*

And his mind wandered back to the business as he automatically slowed down for the flashing light in the little town of Bridgeville.

*Was it wise to tie up all that money in the new housing development? It left the company with very little cash. Forget it. If we get into a tight situation, there's Grandfather's stash. Never had to use it, of course, but what if I had to? What would those old coins be worth now?* And he unconsciously reached his right thumb under his right palm and stroked the underside of his ring that held a gold "double eagle" coin.

He continued cruising down the road. On his right there were endless fields of tall corn, acres of low rows of soybeans on his left, and in the distance beyond he could see the lights from the laying sheds of a chicken farm. *Not too far now*, he figured. And his thoughts returned to his grandfather's "stash."

*When was it? Yes. It was early Spring of 1936, about a year before the old man passed away.*

*What a cantankerous old goat he could be! And downright mean sometimes. I was lucky he took a liking to me.*

"Now there's me being too modest," he told the windshield.

I saved his bacon with a couple simple letters- stopped the Feds from seizing everything he owned by selling all that timber to a paper company- rescued him from that Federal lean. That tax bill was a whopper."

* * *

In 1932 John Wilson hopped freight trains and generally worked his way across the country, leaving his family and Montana in hopes of finding his grandfather, Jonathan Wilson- and better opportunities in the East.

*What a grilling he gave me! It was weeks before he believed I was family. Made me look after the livestock and sleep in the barn.*

Eventually old man decided the boy living in his barn was truly kin. So, he let the boy move into a bedroom in the main house.

*Then there was that meeting in 1936.*

The old man had retired for the night and John Wilson was sitting out on the front porch letting his thoughts wander from one subject to another. He could see the headlights of an occasional automobile on the Bladensburg Road through the evergreens that fronted the lawn. An old rattle trap was chugging up the road just as he heard the old man call to him.

"John? John? Haul yer ass in here, boy!"

Being ordered around by the old man didn't much bother John Wilson because he usually did it with a bit of a smile for his grandson.

John crossed the living room, the screen door slamming behind him as he pushed the large oak door closed tightly. He tossed his coat on the easy chair.

"On my way, Grandpa."

He crossed down the narrow hallway, pausing in the doorway and looking in on his grandfather.

It had been four years since he had first arrived on the Wilson farm, and he usually marveled at how much energy his eighty-six-year-old grandfather had. Usually. But not that night. That night it was different. His grandfather was lying there, his head almost lost amidst two feather pillows. The quilt was neatly spread out over the bed and pulled halfway up his chest. His hands were neatly clasped at his waist, grasping a small coin purse. He looked very frail.

"Yer a smart boy, but damn slow sometimes, you know that? Come in."

"Yes sir."

"Don't stand there gawking at me. Come in and sit down. I have something-" and he paused. A coughing fit got the better of him. "Damn cold!" he cursed, then spit a wad of phlegm into his handkerchief. "Damn nuisance," he continued. "Listen to me. I need you to know something and it's only because you've taken good care of me that I'm telling you. Sit. Sit down, damn it!"

"Certainly." John took a seat in the rocker next to the bed. It was the first time he had been in the room. It was the old man's sanctuary and John respected that.

Jonathan Wilson didn't speak for a minute, just stared at his twenty-two-year-old grandson who was looking around the room, seemingly more interested in the wallpaper than his grandfather.

The young man figured his grandfather would get to the point when he was ready. But he was feeling very self-conscious as he waited.

"You keep this to yourself, you hear?"

"What, grandpa?"

"Don't cross me, boy. Not on this. Ever."

"I promise whatever it is, I will never tell anyone. I promise."

"There's some money I put away. Hope never to touch it." And he held up the coin purse for John. "Here. Take it. Open it up."

He did as he was told, taking three $20.00 gold pieces, Double Eagles, from the purse. They were very shiny and seemed very new. The government hadn't issued coins like those in years. Turning the coins over he saw they were date stamped, "1886."

"You want me to keep these for you?"

"You can have them. But the rest you should never touch unless you absolutely must. It's bad money, son."

"Why's it bad?"

The old man stared deep into his grandson's eyes the same way he did the first day John showed up announcing he was the man's grandson.

"S'not important right now," he snapped. The old man sighed and then added, "best you never know."

"All right, Grandpa, you tell me what it is you want me to know."

"You take those three gold coins there, keep two for yourself. Never spend them unless you have to. Keep them and you'll never be broke in your life. Take the third and send it to your sister, Rebecca. Don't know much about her, but from her letters I think she's real smart. She's getting married she tells me. You send her that as a gift. She's the only one 'sides you ever to speak to this old man. Her father – your father - hasn't been around these parts since 88. He's a damn runaway. You know that, don't you? Never mind. You send her a thousand dollars in a check for a wedding present. You write it, I'll sign it. Want both mailed tomorrow, understand?"

"Send her one of the coins and a check for a thousand dollars. Yes, sir."

"And when I die. Listen carefully to this now boy because I arranged it with the bank and my lawyer yesterday. Don't let them try and pull no fast nonsense on you or let anyone of my kids, if they're alive, give you trouble in this. When I die, I am leaving everything to you, boy. You understand? You know how to manage it. You're damn young, but you're smart."

"Thank you, Grandpa."

"Damn brothers of mine all gone. Children all run off. You and Rebecca are family. You have yourself a family. You have a big one and move into the lodge over on the northeast tip of the property. It's yours. Have a family and take good care of 'em."

"I will sir."

"You know the old lodge?"

"Yes sir."

"In the lodge, under the flagstone hearth, there's a metal strong box. Over a thousand of those coins there. Made that money when my brothers and I were young- had a business restoring things down south after the war. It's bad money- best you should know it's there."

"All right. But why's it bad?" he asked again, staring at his boots then looking up again at his grandfather.

The old man paused. Then not looking at his grandson, he explained, "the money's rightfully mine, there is no doubt, but people died over it, you understand?" He paused and then added, "There's blood on that money, boy, so you just let it be for now. And don't cross me on this. You understand?"

"Yes sir. I want you to know I deeply appreciate everything you've done for me, sir."

"Good. Now get out of here."

"Goodnight, Grandpa."

And the old man coughed and waved the boy out of the room as he reached to turn off the bedside light.

* * *

As he drove through Delaware toward his own home that hot August night 37 years later, John Wilson recalled his excitement after the meeting with his grandfather. He was set to inherit a massive estate- and he was not yet 25 years old.

"That was $20,000 in 1936!" John Wilson shouted to his empty car, and laughed out loud.

*Back then few Americans could make that amount their entire career. It was 1936- the damn depression. Damn. What could those coins be worth today?*

Then noticing the sign, he read it out loud, "12 miles to Georgetown. Getting closer and closer. It will be very nice to get some sleep."

\* \* \*

It was in the late fall of 1939 when Jonathan Wilson died. Six days later, John Wilson went to the lodge to look for the coins and found them right where the old man said they would be- a total of 1,023 coins. There was also a scribbled note.

"You found it, boy," the note read, "Now put it back and don't use them unless you must. You're a good man who will always provide for his family. There's blood on this money. Just put it away until its need is absolute."

He replaced the strong box and the flagstone hearth and left the gold there until 1955. By that time, he cleared the land across the highway from the lodge and built a new home for his family. In '55 he put in a terraced garden behind the new home. The construction of the new garden walls gave him the perfect opportunity. He secretly moved the chest to the bottom terrace of the garden near the patio where it would be safe. Every year he would plant marigolds in that part of the garden. His own private joke.

*Truth is,* he thought as he slowed his car automatically while approaching the little town of Georgetown, Delaware, *it has been very nice to know all these years that the money was there. I really should tell the children about it. Which one should I tell? Trish? Norman? Maybe Kyle.*

But his thoughts were interrupted momentarily when he as he drove around the at the square in the center of Georgetown.

Someone, he thought, was calling his name.

*Kyle? Damn. Sounded more like Johnny. Johnny? Oh boy, I am getting tired.*

The drive continued quietly, farms passing, as he got closer to home. Then, when cruising past Anderson's horse farm, it began. It was as if someone had taken a baseball bat and hit him square on the back. He had trouble breathing and began to panic.

"Oh, dear god not on the highway. This is the worst timing ever."

With that thought he swerved and brought the car to a stop on the gravel shoulder.

*Breathe in. Breathe out,* He silently reminded himself. *Think of something comfortable like curling up with Elizabeth right after we were first married. We were so in love.*

And he thought back on his first wife; of being loved and the belonging.

"Is this it, Elizabeth? No offense, but I didn't expect a reunion so soon."

The pain hit him again. He desperately wanted air, but it wouldn't come. Nor would it do any good. His body slumped over on the front seat of the car, its eyes permanently fixed on the star-pocked sky through the windshield.

Everything was very still.

An MGB sped noisily by.

Across the way an owl let out a screech and flew from its perch in an old elm tree to the grove of pines across the horse paddock.

Then, for John Wilson, there came a new sensation. He could feel the movement of the earth as it traveled its prescribed orbit. It was about to leave him gradually behind.

It was as if he dissolved through the back window of his automobile and watched the idling Ford LTD move away from him. Then he watched the earth continue to move, taking the car, the road, the farmlands away from him. The entire countryside was receding before him. He watched as the peninsula, the Chesapeake Bay, the continent, the entire planet tumbled away, leaving him serenely still and suspended in a void. Silence surrounded him as the world he knew dissolved into the distance.

Then, as if carried on the wind, he was everywhere; in every moment of his life at one time. Every sensation, memory, desire, emotion and encounter of his lifetime occurred in an instant. And then that experience seemed to expand, elongate into a massive ribbon of images that circled around him. The swirling cinematic-like montage comfortably enveloped him, and for a moment he was at peace within the vortex of his every experience.

He blinked.

Everything dissolved into a warm mist.

There was silence. And then peaceful blue light. And a voice.

"Pop?"

"Johnny?"

And then a soothing and affectionate woman's voice stated joyfully, "Jonathan."

"Elizabeth."

And he felt a loving embrace unlike any he had ever experienced.

# CHAPTER THREE

## ADULT RESPONSIBILITIES
*Thursday Morning in Henlopen*

Kyle entered the large glassed in breakfast room and set the two mugs of coffee on the large table. He looked around.

*The draperies are all closed. The wicker furniture, the bookcase, the lamp shades, everything looks so fucking dismal. It's a Miss Havisham special, and not what I need right now.*

So, one by one, he opened the draperies that covered the floor-to- ceiling windows. Morning sunlight filled the room.

*There. Safe. Perhaps. Maybe. I hope.*

He took a seat facing the doorway and waited for his sister, the oldest of the Wilson children, to join him.

"Kyle?"

He could see her in the kitchen.

"Here."

"Oh, good." she uttered, crossing toward him.

"Trish, coffee. Coffee, Trish." he said pointing from his sister to the mug across the table and then back at her.

"Thanks."

She smiled weakly and took a seat.

They sat there quietly for a short while. Kyle figured she'd start when she was ready.

A long time ago he had tried to envision what this day would be like. Who would shoulder the arrangements?

*Does that thought hit all kids? 'Someday I'm going to have to arrange a funeral for my father.' Probably not. I've always been just a little morbid. Or is it normal?*

He looked across the table at his sister who was staring into her coffee mug.

*Poor Trish. Just moved East since Jeffrey dumped all over her and now, she has to handle this.*

His sense of humor was about to got the best of him. He considered telling her, 'Well Johnny seems to be hanging around lately, let's let him do all the work.' But he decided against it.

"Kyle, what are you smiling about?"

"Huh?"

"You were just smiling. What's so funny? Tell me. I could use a laugh, even a chuckle, believe me."

"Lawyer humor," he lied. "It would take too long to explain."

"Oh."

"So, Trish, you okay?"

"Vicki's very upset, which is understandable. We will have to make a few decisions on our own," she explained between sips of coffee. "We're going to have to make some choices for her about the relatives like who stays in the house here, who stays in the carriage house and who is on their own. Family politics is the last thing she needs to deal with."

"I've never done anything like this before," he told her. "I mean it's Dad!" He felt his cheeks getting hot and the sting of tears forming in his eyes. Above all, he experienced an overwhelming need for comforting.

"Whoa, boy. Save that for later. We've got dozens of people to call. Hang on for now, okay? I know what you mean, but we can fall apart later, all right?"

"Yeah," he muttered, choking it all back in.

*She makes a better adult than me. Can't I just run from the house?*

*Wouldn't work. I'd run to the beach and find Johnny sitting there with his morbid instructions.*

So, he sat quietly as she jotted down a list of tasks they would have to perform over the next several days.

"I've called Norman. He's got business to take care of then he is flying over. I've got to remember to arrange a rental car for him at the airstrip. We'll go to the florists together this afternoon. Then we'll have to go to the funeral home when the hospital releases Dad's body."

Kyle listened quietly. She had talked to their stepmother. The funeral would take place there in Delaware.

"I tried to reach Mr. Rosenberg, Dad's lawyer, to set up a meeting to clear up all the legal matters, but they're not opened yet. Something about "summer hours." His service will have him reach us. In the meantime, we should get all the papers together. There are three safety deposit boxes in Woodmoor. I found a set of keys here. I have no idea what's in them, but probably everything we need. You can drive over to Suburban Trust Company or you can take Mom to the funeral home to make the arrangements."

Kyle felt like doing neither.

"Johnny, are you listening to me?" Trish asked a little too sternly.

This startled Kyle. He abruptly looked away from the window and into his sister's soft brown eyes.

"What did you call me?"

"Oh, my God. I called you Johnny, didn't I? That's so-" And then she lost it. Suddenly her businesslike composure was gone, and she began weeping.

Taking a chair on the other side of the table, Kyle sat down beside her and put his arm around his sister.

"Trish. Come on hon, Trish. It's hard. I know. I know. Just, I dunno, hang in there, Trish."

"I want him back, Kyle. I never … I thought we all had more time with him."

"Me too, Trish. Me, too. But sometimes-" But Kyle couldn't quite finish. His face grew hot again and the tears came for him, too. It was a needed release for them both. They sat there holding each other for several minutes, each lost in their grief.

She was the first to speak as they regained their composure.

"I suddenly got this strong memory of Johnny. I didn't realize how much I still missed him, I guess. I guess? I do. I do. Poor Johnny. Oh God. His funeral. His funeral was so horrifying for me. I was so scared. There was Johnny. Poor Johnny. Johnny laid out in that box. Oh, it was so barbaric. And that's what we are going to have to do for Daddy."

She was quiet for a moment. Then she softly continued. "She wants an open casket, Kyle." And she took a sip of coffee, staring blankly into space and then blurted out, "I don't want to get old and die." And the tears began once more; heavy wracking sobs. Kyle held her once again, and she clung to him.

*That's what it all came down to, didn't it,* he thought. *Our mortality? That's it, isn't it? The unspoken grief at every funeral, with each loss, is the unspoken fear that we'll all wind up as meat in a box? All of us except Johnny, of course. Damn. If she only knew what I knew. Hah! Even though I know what I know, death is pretty scary.*

Once he sensed she was regaining her composure, he released her from his embrace asking, "More coffee?"

She nodded, wiping away her tears with the shredded napkin she'd been holding on to for the past ten minutes.

"Um, and another napkin."

He crossed into the kitchen for more coffee, stopping and tossing back a box of napkins as he passed the counter.

"Catch."

"Thanks."

"You call Aunt Rebecca yet?"

"Yes, I did. She said to be sure to say hello to you and send you her love."

Trish blew her nose then wiped it.

*She's the only one who can blow her nose and look very lady-like about it,* he thought.

"Aunt Rebecca and Uncle Nick will arrive from Chicago tonight. Uncle Benjamin might not be able to make it from New York until tomorrow."

"It'll be nice to see Rebecca again. Don't know about Uncle Ben," he observed as he brought their refilled coffee mugs to the table and took a seat opposite his sister.

"Out of respect for your father, I hope you'll behave yourself around your Uncle Ben."

They both turned. Their stepmother had entered the kitchen unnoticed.

"Even though," she continued, "he is such a hopeless stuffed shirt. Good morning. No, don't get up."

"Are you-" he started.

"I am managing to keep it under control. Sometimes I surprise myself."

"Good."

"Coffee?" asked Trish.

"No." She paused, looking from one of her stepchildren to the other. "Trish?" she asked. "Promise me one thing? Promise me that you and the girls will continue to live here. At least for a while?"

"Sure, Mom."

"I'll be around for the next three weeks at least," Kyle chimed in.

"Splendid. I am going to need the company. So. What's the drill, children? Did you get breakfast? Kids fed? How about a Bloody Mary? I know I could use one. Excuse me."

And with that she went into the family room and to the bar.

"What's it to be?" Trish asked her brother. "Stick with Vicki or drive to Woodmoor?"

"Neither. I want to go back to bed."

"Wrong answer. So you drive to Woodmoor. I'll stick with Vicki. Oh, by the way, your old drinking buddy, Daniel Mason, is now manager of the bank."

"That'll make this easier," he told his sister while thinking, *Easier? Awkward more likely. She must know that we became more than drinking buddies during sophomore year.*

"I am sure he will take good care of you," Trish responded with an ironic smile.

*Yep. She knows.*

Kyle finished his coffee, showered and hit the road. Off to the Washington suburbs called Woodmoor.

As he sped up the highway his thoughts wandered back over the morning's events. He wasn't sure what to do next.

*Help the family get through the next few days, I guess. And avoid Johnny.*

"Got that, kid?" he called, shivering from a sudden chill. "Next time you call, don't call collect!" And with that he turned up the tape player and let The Grateful Dead fill the car with their music.

As he drove across the Chesapeake Bay Bridge and looked down on Sandy Point beach. Once again, he thought of Cyndy Weaver.

*They're everywhere. Signs. Reminders. Someone trying to tell me something? Is that it? Last night and now; remembering a romance from years gone by. Oh boy. She was right. Gotta admit it.*

"Whenever you cross this bridge, you're going to think of me," she had said.

*Right you are, Cyndy. Right you are.*

# CHAPTER FOUR

## *MEMORIES OF CYNDY WEAVER*

He had to meet her.

On a Friday afternoon in the Spring of 1968, Kyle was lounging on a bench under one of the flowering dogwood trees on the University quad. He had seen her pass several times before. The problem was he couldn't decide which was the best way to introduce himself. He wanted it to happen naturally.

On that particular day, Kyle wasn't alone. He was hanging out with his buddy, Mike Henderson. Mike found Kyle's reaction to the approaching female trio to be very humorous.

"Far out, man!" Henderson commented. "I would do any of them. Maybe the trio. A foursome, yeah. Ask 'em if they want to toke up with us."

"Cool it," Kyle quickly shot back.

"Which one's your favorite?"

"Green leotard and blue bell bottoms. Cool it."

"Hey man, you're drooling."

Kyle didn't respond. He just kept watching as the slender brunette in the body-hugging leotard, low-cut bell bottom pants and white cardigan came closer.

"Why hide such a fine body?" he whispered.

"Hey man," Henderson giggled, "your tongue is hanging out."

"I'm in love," Kyle hissed in his friend's general direction not wanting to take his eyes off her.

"You're stoned and you're horny."

As the trio of girls were passing, Kyle could hear she was embroiled in a discussion about palmistry with her two classmates.

"Who is that vision of sensuality?" he asked his friend shortly after the little group had passed.

"Name's Cyndy Weaver. She's in Lucille's parapsychology seminar. I'm meeting 'Cille after class. You can come with me and we'll talk to 'Cille. I am sure she would be happy to introduce you."

"No thanks." Kyle rose to his feet still staring off at the three girls. "See you later." And he walked away without looking back at his companion. His eyes were fixed on Cyndy as followed her across the quad and into the Marvin Center a couple blocks away. He caught Lucille in the hallway about to enter the classroom just behind Cyndy.

"Lucille," he almost whispered as he reached out and steered his old friend away from the classroom doorway.

"Kyle, hi! What's happening?"

"Um. Nice shirt."

It was a baby blue silk cassock shirt hanging loosely from one shoulder. "It makes your eyes sparkle."

"You are so full of shit." She said with a smile. "What do you want, sweetie?"

"I need a favor, okay? If anyone asks, I'm with you, okay? I want to audit this class here, okay?"

"Who is it this time?"

"Please?"

"Oh Lordy, come on."

"Thanks."

They entered the classroom and took seats in the large circle of desks. It was perfect. He was just opposite Cindy Weaver.

She took off her sweater revealing the perfectly proportioned torso Kyle had imagined. Swimming, maybe some gymnastics? But not too much. Just enough.

*Now*, thought Kyle, *I know I am stoned, but I also know I am awake and really seeing this. She is the most beautiful girl I have ever seen who did not intimidate the hell out of me. Far out. Far fucking out.*

Being stoned, Kyle worked a little too hard to look interested in the discussion. But mostly he was intent on watching Cyndy. She kept fingering a single bead hanging from a short chain around her neck.

*Turkish Blue Bead, thought Kyle. To ward off the evil eye? What's she afraid of? Don't go there,* he told himself and focused on the seminar.

The students were discussing poltergeist phenomenon. He

noticed Cyndy was staring straight ahead, holding the bead and looking like she was considering every word they were saying.

*Nice high cheek bones. They give her a kind of bold look.*

She scribbled a note in her spiral notebook every now and then but did not participate in the discussion right away. She finally joined the conversation when someone mentioned "the bell witch." It quickly became obvious she could concisely explain the details of the "the only clearly documented case of a poltergeist phenomenon in the United States."

Kyle drank it all in. Her intelligence and self-assuredness made her even more attractive.

*I would bet she has a photographic memory. No one remembers details like those without a photographic memory. Do they?*

He sat there starring at her and marveling at her presentation. He was so lost in considering her explanation and mulling it over in his mind that he didn't even realize the seminar was over.

He felt a gentle punch on his shoulder.

"Huh?"

"So?" Lucille asked in a not so quiet voice, "You want me to introduce you to her?"

"Who?"

Lucille nodded in Cyndy's direction.

"You are no slouch, 'Cille."

"Yeah. Like it takes ESP to know she's the reason you followed us here? You're interested, and she's single … and she's right behind you."

Kyle first instinct was flight, but for some reason he turned around abruptly. He was immediately entranced by her eyes (one blue, one green) but managed to blurt out, "you have a photographic memory, don't you? Is it the green eye or the blue one?" *That was so stupid*, he admonished himself silently.

Cyndy did not react immediately. "Very clever," she said finally and smiled.

*She's smiling at me. Thank you, Lord.*

"Or maybe it's both eyes?" Kyle added, giving her his best boyish grin. "Kinda like 3-D glasses. Oh. Those glasses are blue and red, aren't they? 3-D glasses, I mean- and I think I will shut up now."

"I don't think I know you," Cyndy replied in a very simple way that was not an invitation for an introduction nor was it a brush off so Kyle replied-

"And you are very direct, aren't you?"

Lucille spoke up. "Kyle Wilson, Cyndy Weaver."

"Yes," Cyndy stated simply.

"Yes, to possessing a photographic memory or to being very direct?" Kyle teased with a smile. *Damn. I am totally flirting with her.*

"Yo, Weaver!" came a husky voice from the classroom doorway.

They turned to see a rugged young man wearing a work shirt and wrinkled chinos and sporting a big beard. "You ready?" he asked Cyndy.

"Certainly. Be right there." She turned to Lucille. "I promised I would sit for him. He's the only artist I know who likes to be on time." Then, re-shouldering her satchel, she told Kyle, "See you around, Wilson." And she headed to the door.

"I certainly hope so," Kyle said a little bit too loud.

But it made her stop, turn and look at him without

comment before finally going out the door. The way she looked at him gave him no indication of what she was thinking, but he could feel it.

*She has just taken a picture of me.*

He turned to Lucille. "So 'Cille, who is Paul Bunyan?"

"Sculptor. She's been trying to avoid him, but he's pretty persistent. A really good sculptor, too. Says he has a block of marble with her name on it whatever that means."

"From the look of him," Kyle observed, "you'd think he wishes he had a lily pond somewhere. Could his outfit be any more Monet?"

"Rodin and Lipchitz are his idols."

"Figures. You think she likes me?"

"Kye, you are so fickle."

"What?"

"What do you mean, 'what' Kye?" What about Daniel Mason?"

"He met a BPA major who swept him off to Key West for spring break. Then he dumped me."

Lucille shook her head. "I guess when you're a saloon door swinging both ways you have more to choose from, don't you?"

"Who can explain affairs of the heart?" he sighed looking towards the empty doorway.

"An affair of the heart or another part of your body?"

"Unfair, 'Cille." He admonished her, then added, "There's just something about her that beckons me."

"'Beckons me'? 'Beckons me'? Damn, boy, you got it bad."

"Could be, 'Cille, could be. So, you think she likes me?"

"From that short encounter? Please, Kyle. She is single, but are you ready to have your heart broken? Really? Twice in one year"

"Do you have to bring reality into this?"

"I thought you liked 'direct'."

"Hmmm, got me there."

"Come on. Henderson and I are doing the Tombs. First round is on me."

"Far out."

\* \* \*

Kyle returned to audit the class the following week. She participated in a discussion about ghost hunter Hans Holzer. She was a good listener as well as an informed participant during the ninety-minute seminar. When the session came to a close and others were filing out of the room, she took her time rearranging her spiral notebooks and note cards in her satchel. To Kyle, it seemed to be a rather thin reason for sticking around the classroom and took it as a sign she was waiting for him to say something to her.

The classroom had just about emptied when he finally approached her.

"Nice haircut. Very feathery," he offered along with a boyish grin.

"I thought I would try short for springtime. My roommates started calling me 'Peter Pan.'"

"I was thinking more Mia Farrow in 'Rosemary's Baby.'"

"Not creepy, though, I hope."

"Very becoming."

"Thank you."

"No sitting for Rodin today?"

"He's got pictures of me. Besides, it turned out to be some kind of ridiculous cubist thing so he couldn't exactly make a case for my presence being mandatory. Oh, crap. Did I just say that?"

"S'okay. I don't like cubism either."

She laughed slightly then explained, "No… 'make a case for my presence being mandatory.'"

"Yeah. You did. You said it. So, you're a classics major?"

"No. I think you make me nervous, Wilson." It was more a statement of discovery than a complaint. Then she added, "I'm on a pre-med track."

"A pre-med with a photographic memory. That makes me nervous. I can truly see us nervously getting together and being nervous with each other sometime."

"You can, can you?" she asked with a smile.

"I think it's in the cards."

"Cards?" she asked, latching the strap on her satchel.

"You read Tarot, don't you?" This stopped her. She simply stared at him. "Come on," he continued, "in your bag there. Your cards are wrapped in a burgundy scarf."

"Oh?"

"I am a keen observer of people. The photographic memory thing was an educated guess because of the details you cited about the Bell Witch when the spines of your books are not well-worn."

"Give me your hand," she suddenly asked.

He held out his right. She took his left hand and she started writing on his palm with a ball point pen. "My roommates are having a party tomorrow night. Starts at eight. This is the address."

"Do I get your phone number?"

She didn't answer right away. She was staring at his palm where she had written the address.

"Forget your zip code?" he asked with a chuckle.

"Huh? Oh. No. Just something …" and she made a little circle next to a line on his palm as if doodling.

"See something interesting?" Then, with his other hand, he pointed to his palm and explained, "Right there- a space for you to write your phone number."

She shook her head. "Nope."

"What? No phone number?" he whined comically. "Come on!"

"No phone number, Wilson. That way you cannot call me at the last minute and say you can't make it."

"What if I get hit by a car and have to call you from the emergency room so you can come and apply your gentle healing hands to my profusely bleeding body?"

"Look both ways when crossing the street, wise guy."

"Would you? Would you apply your healing hands to my body if the opportunity presented itself?"

Without giving away what she was thinking, she simply told him, "That may or may not be in the cards."

"You saw something in my palm. You saw something, didn't you?"

"Nice hand." And with that, she turned and walked out of the classroom calling over her shoulder, "see you tomorrow night, Wilson!"

Kyle took a seat on one of the desks and stared at his hand.

*She reads palms. She saw something that stopped her. Something? Some things?*

He continued to stare at his hand. What is that doodle? Is that a smile? Whatever it was, Kyle felt very happy.

"You're pretty slick, Wilson," he heard a girl's voice from the corner of the seminar room.

*Damn,* he thought, *weren't Cyndy and I alone in here?*

"I considered slipping out the rear door and leaving you alone, but it's fun to watch you in action."

She stared at him and he at her for almost a full minute. Hippie chick, cotton shift, no bra, water buffalo sandals, bunches of wild curly red hair tied back with a scarf of many colors and she was smiling at him.

"Alice?"

"Yes. Alice. I was wondering how long before you noticed me. Cigarette?" She opened a beaded cigarette case and offered it to him.

"Well, you're —yeah, look at you." He took the case, removed one cigarette and handed it to her and took one for himself. "You always were a free spirit, Alice, but you look —"

He lit both cigarettes before continuing. "I mean —"

"S'okay for you to say it, Kyle." She retrieved her case, clicked it close and took a long draw on her Marlboro.

"Been a few years," he said. "Whoa. You're a young lady now."

Exhaling, she observed, "and not the pimply faced geek who used to sneak cigarettes with you and Johnny outside St. B's on teen club nights."

"You were a good dancer."

"Still am. And I am not surprised you didn't see me. You've been so focused on the Weaver lady. Hold on to your heart, Kyle.

I overheard you telling 'Cille about Mason. You're not finished with him. You, Cyndy Weaver, Daniel Mason– it's going to get very interesting."

"Have you been stalking me?"

"No. I check up on old friends in the crystal ball now and then."

Kyle was amused at how comfortable he felt being with his childhood friend and how easy it was to revert to a time when the two could talk about anything.

"You're looking good, Alice. It is very nice to see you."

"Thank you."

"Have you been here all year?"

"New England's not a quiet place for a psychic, so I transferred here at the start of the semester. I'm just slow in reconnecting with the old gang- 'The Happy Huggy Wolf Pack' of old."

"T-H-2-W-P. How could I forget."

"That was us."

"You ever do séances and all the stuff you said you wanted to learn?"

"You betcha."

"Do you talk to Johnny?"

"Do you want to know?"

"No."

"He has a message for you. It's a warning. S'all he'll tell me. He only wants to talk to you."

"Does the crystal ball tell you if I will ever swing one way over another? No, don't tell me, Alice. I've got such a jones for that Cyndy Weaver lady. I got it bad, Alice."

"It will be a very bumpy road for you both if you pursue it past this weekend. Always tell her the truth. She'll sense a lie real fast."

"Yeah?"

"Like a duck on a June bug, Kye."

"You know that as a fact?"

"I know people Kye and you know I know people. You are a good soul. Johnny watches over you. Did you know that? I would prefer you not be hurt. You're too stoned right now to appreciate what I am telling you and it is something you do not want to hear, Kye. Sometimes we have gifts that aren't well used. Use yours wisely."

"What gifts?" Kyle asked her with a grin.

"You haven't discovered them yet, have you?" she asked as she dropped her almost spent cigarette into her coffee cup.

"Alice, you are weird."

"So are you, Kye," she told him as she rose and shouldered the strap of her very colorful embroidered tote bag adding, "more than you know right now."

Kyle suddenly found himself saying, "Johnny loved you very much you know," which brought a lump to his throat. "I mean you do, don't you? Know he did?"

"And I still love him," she purred, cutting him off. "It's cool, Kye. It's all cool. Enjoy the weekend. I will be seeing you again.

* * *

Next evening, he toked up before the party and arrived around 8:30 not wanting to seem too eager. But he was.

The door to the apartment was unlocked, so he let himself

52

in, and stood on the edge of the living room checking out the scene. The place was pretty packed, and from the conversations he figured the crowd was pretty much made up of theatre majors. The original cast recording of *HAIR* was on the stereo and a bunch of hippie wannabes were recreating part of the show in the living room.

Getting all "touchy feely," seven or eight students did all they could to eliminate any space between them whatsoever as they swayed to the music. One reached out and took hold of Kyle's hand and drew him into the scrum.

"Come on, Tex, join us," purred a cute boy with long curly blonde hair. "This is a free love zone." And he and another young man drew Kyle further into their group while pressing their hips against either side of him. A very busty girl student in a rawhide vest that hid very little mashed her body against Kyle's back. The writhing was getting pretty intense. The bulging crotch of the blonde kid's very low-cut bellbottom jeans was getting very familiar with the front Kyle's button fly Levi's. Then the music shifted to "Aquarius," and, as if on cue, the intertwined bodies began singing the lyrics with gusto. They slowly disengaged and danced around with their arms waving high in the air. Kyle took this as his cue to move on and, as he backed away from the group, the blonde kid held his arms out to Kyle.

"Someone wants a hug?" Kyle shouted which the kid took as some kind of a signal and he danced over to Kyle. "Sorry my friend, but not tonight. I am otherwise engaged." As the kid threw his arms around Kyle, he figured what the hell and he returned the embrace holding the kid very close as he loudly whispered in his ear. "Yes, you are beautiful and yes, I could eat you with a spoon my friend, but I am not traveling that road tonight. I have a previous commitment and I would never cop out on my promise to her." And with that he pulled away, grasped the boy's shoulders, turned him and gently shoved him back towards the rest of the dancers.

Kyle escaped to the kitchen. *Damn,* he thought, *reminiscent of the back room of that bar in Berkeley last summer.*

"Beer?" a very red faced muscular guy asked. "I'm Jones, the de facto bartender. I can offer you a Rolling Rock or a Rolling Rock. Not an extensive beverage menu here at chez Harmon."

"Well, Jones, I think I'll take a Rolling Rock."

"You got it," Jones responded, popping the cap off the bottle and handing the familiar green bottle to Kyle.

"I heard the stuff makes you piss green," Kyle commented then took a swig.

"A totally unfounded rumor. You a friend of Dorothy's?"

"A friend of Cyndy Weaver's," Kyle responded side-stepping the not so veiled gay reference. "But thanks for the beer," he added putting a couple bucks into the "beer fund" jar Jones displayed prominently on the counter.

As he moved through the kitchen and into the dining room, he practically tripped over a gaggle of students seated on the floor having a heated discussion about "art" with a "small a" and "art" with a "capital a."

He continued moving through the crowd. He kept his fringed jacket on in case he couldn't find her and needed to split. Then, turning into a hallway beyond the dining room, he spotted her. She was wearing those wonderfully low cut and snug blue jeans and a fringe vest over a wine-red sleeveless leotard. As Kyle grew closer, he could see she had been cornered by the Rodin wannabe. And he was talking a blue streak.

*Damn. Doesn't that guy have anything other than work shirts and chinos?*

As he grew closer, he realized the guy was expounding on Lipchitz, Picasso and cubism.

*Oh boy.*

Cyndy noticed Kyle and waved him over. "Hey. Over here."

He slipped past two fat girls who were giggling and unsuccessfully trying to drink from a wine skin.

"Hi, Kyle," she half-shouted above the din, and then smiled a very welcoming smile.

"What's happening?"

"Kyle, this is Bradford."

"'lo."

"How's it going?" But before the guy could answer, Cyndy chimed in.

"Excuse us, Bradford, all right? Kyle is an old friend of the family who I haven't seen in some time."

"Understood," he replied, looking highly disappointed, but managing a smile for the two of them. "Wanting to catch up, huh?"

"Come on," she said, taking Kyle's arm and steering him away down the hallway. "Talk to you again later, Bradford."

*My god,* Kyle realized, *he's following us.* So, he leaned close and whispered into Cyndy's ear, "we're being followed."

She stopped and faced the pursuing sculptor. "This is family stuff, Bradford. It'll bore you to tears," she said with some finality.

"Oh. Later then?"

"Probably not. This will take a while."

"Uh, right." And he turned and headed for the living room where someone had put *HAIR* back on the stereo.

"Jesus, if I hear that cast album one more time, I might pour super glue on the turn table. What do ya say we get out of this noise?"

"Fine by me."

She ushered him out on the balcony and closed the glass doors behind them. "I'm sorry about the family thing. God, I hate to lie! A little lie, but he's been after me for the last hour and I had to get rid of him."

"S`okay."

"Thanks." She laughed and leaned up against the railing.

Kyle liked the laugh.

"I'm really not hyper like this very often."

"S`okay. Loosen up. Breathe."

"Good idea." And she took two deep breaths.

"That help?"

"It's just he was coming on to me and being so covert about it. Drives me crazy at these things, ya know? Oh god, I hardly know you and … um, you want something to drink?"

"Got a beer from Jones, thanks." he answered, leaning back against the brick wall to her right.

"Oh yeah. Sure. Good. So. How you doing?"

"Fine. Nice party."

"Don't lie, Wilson. Theatre majors are- well, I'm lucky to find a place that's so roomy and the boys are sweet and they share the chores. Jones is also a great cook. Are you into the arts?

"The art of motion."

"Come again?"

"Gymnastics. And in the summer, I am quite the pool rat - on the swim team."

"Ah. That's why you're so in shape."

"You should have seen me when I was competing." And he reached out and touched her leotard covered waist saying, "I used to have plenty of these. Very comfortable."

"Really?" she observed, looking down at his hand. He could tell she was intrigued. She definitely didn't object to his touch, but he didn't want to move too fast so he withdrew his hand.

"I use them instead of pajamas. I kept all my gymnastics stuff. How about you?"

"No gymnastics. Swim team winter and summer. I wasn't the greatest, but just good enough to fill my age bracket. I hated the swimming part but loved the camaraderie and the speedos."

"Me too."

"That's kinda hot," she replied with some innuendo.

"You still swim?"

"Three or four times a week."

"We should do it together."

"I am not competitive."

"Each at their own pace, Fine. So. You think this has possibilities?"

"I beg your pardon?"

"You and me. We could get that out of the way and just enjoy the company without all the 'will he - won't he - will she - won't she' tension shit."

"Okay, Wilson. Sure. You could be more than a one-night stand."

"So, I get one night?"

"That's the plan, Wilson. Happy we got that out of the way?"

"Oh, more than you know!"

"But I have to ask. What got you interested in psi studies? I'm thinking of making it my field of study. My parents would be crushed if I told them right now, but there's so much more about, well, about our being here than meets the eye. Literally. It fascinates me. What turned you on to it?"

"Actually," he began, then cleared his throat, "it was you."

"What?" she quickly asked with a suspicious glare.

But with a 'what the hell' kind of courage, he continued with the truth. "I'd seen you pass on the quad several times and wanted to meet you."

"You're putting me on now, aren't you?"

He looked directly at her. "I can't lie to you." Then he looked at the floor. *She's not reacting very well to my explanation right now, is she?* He straightened up and looked at her sheepishly "You want me to leave?"

"No! I mean … you're not joking, are you?"

"No," he replied being totally honest. Of course, what he wanted to say was I think you are the most beautiful person I have ever met in my life and I am madly in love with you. But for some reason he didn't have that much nerve at the moment. So, instead, he asked-

"Are you, like, attached to the sculptor?"

She just looked at him.

"Are you, um, pissed at me? I mean for using the seminar to …"

"I know what you mean," she interrupted him as she tried to stifle a smile unsuccessfully, so she turned, leaned her elbows on the balcony rail and stared out over the street. "And I'm not attached."

"Hey far out!" he cried with just a little too much enthusiasm. "Sorry, I get a little carried away sometimes. You don't seem real, ah, involved, you know, in this party. Want to go for a drive?"

"To where?"

"The ocean would be nice. It's not too far a drive. My family has a place on the Delaware shore."

"Way over there?"

"What the hell? It'll be a grin. We can get to know one another. Wanna go?"

"Wait here." And with that she went into the apartment, leaving Kyle to revel over their conversation. He couldn't believe he was so fortunate and ... suddenly she was back. She had her satchel and a sweatshirt.

"I am prepared," she announced.

"Bringing school with you?"

She patted the satchel as she explained, "Tooth brush, toothpaste, couple of change of clothes and a swimsuit."

"One or two-piece."

"One."

"Oh, the best," he purred.

"Then let's split."

\* \* \*

They headed east out of Washington and toward the Chesapeake Bay.

As they neared the bridge and he saw the Sandy Point State Park cutoff, he asked, "Tired of riding?"

"I could do with a stretch."

"How about we stop here? We could take a walk on the beach here."

He pulled off the highway and up the long road to the State Park. As they were getting out of the car, she stopped him. "Can I see your left palm?"

He complied then asked, "Whatcha see?"

The car's dome light wasn't too bright so she leaned in close as she studied his hand.

"Hmmm." She uttered and then gently placed his hand down on the console between them.

"Am I gonna live, Doc?"

"You should take up psi, you know."

"Anything you want."

"Don't be a smart ass. You've many important stars and lines on your hand. You have talents you don't even know you have."

"Yeah, but I prefer THC over ESP."

She frowned at him, but even in the faint glow from the light in the car, Kyle could see a glint in her eyes was unmistakable. She liked him.

"Okay. I'm just kidding," he added. "Come on, let's take a hike and talk about you for a while."

As they walked along the beach, he encouraged her to tell him more about her psi studies, which she did enthusiastically. It peaked his interest in the subject, especially when she explained about a recent experience with a trance medium.

*I could possibly make a long-distance call to Johnny,* he thought. But he didn't bring it up.

"Could someone put themselves in a trance and communicate with the, uh, other side as you call it?"

"A very experienced medium can, but it can be dangerous. You should have a control, someone who is conscious who can talk to your spirit guide. Of course, there have been a lot of people who've perfected automatic writing, even on a typewriter."

"Oh?"

She went on to cite a few incidents where automatic writing was successful, then returned to the subject of hauntings. His mind, however, went elsewhere. He began to think of his brother as he walked along the shore with Cyndy. He had been having pangs of nostalgia and feelings of loss were recurring recently. The possibility of contacting Johnny was very tempting.

"Have you ever had a premonition that came true?" she was asking him.

"Huh?" and he left his thoughts of Johnny and returned to the present.

"Are you listening to anything I'm saying?"

"Sorry." And he smiled his disarming smile at her. "I just flashed on something a moment ago, but I'm back. A premonition that came true? Yes, now and then. I had a twin brother who knew what I was thinking a lot of the time. It was kinda trippy. I always knew when he was in trouble. Does that count?"

"Of course, it counts! That's a great example of having a sense above and beyond the normal ones. I think you have it. Jung had a whole theory about the collective unconscious, you know. I haven't studied enough to be certain, but I think it has something to do with that. Symington is doing terrific work in studying twins and extra sensory perception up at Harvard. I'm thinking of taking his summer seminar. Would you be interested?"

"It's a long time from now."

"Ten weeks."

"Ten weeks is a long time. I'll have to see about what happens after exams."

"Where's your twin brother? He at the university?"

"Nope. He was killed when we were fourteen."

"Oh, I'm sorry. Is that a touchy subject? I mean, do you mind if I ask you about him?"

"You? Nah. You, Cyndy Weaver can ask me anything."

"Did he ever contact you?"

They continued walking silently as Kyle considered her question. He looked out over the Chesapeake Bay and watched the lights of a massive oil tanker gliding through the water towards Baltimore. He looked up and watched the automobile lights streaking east and west along the bridge. Without looking at Cyndy he finally replied. "For a whole year after he died, I used to talk to him all the time. We carried on long conversations, actually."

Kyle turned to Cyndy. *Why*, he asked himself, *am I able to tell this to her?* Then he found himself adding: "But after a while, I had to finally admit I was making up his responses and really talking to myself. Ya know?"

He stopped walking and looked up at the bridge and the

flow of car headlights again. "You're the first person I ever told that to."

She turned so they were facing one another and asked, "You still miss him very much don't you?"

He studied her face a moment once again marveling at how easy she was for him to talk to. He pierced his lips and let out a noisy sigh then told her, "You can't imagine."

"No. No, I can't," she replied and took his hand. "I'm an only child. I have no idea what it must have been like losing someone you love like that. Someone as close as a twin."

"If we were any closer-" he began, but then stopped himself.

He squeezed her hand and started walking again. She readily followed letting go of his hand and placing her hand in the back pocket of his jeans. Neither made much of the gesture but continued walking as if having such intimate contact was simply normal.

"Let me tell you- once Johnny and me – we were what? - nine years old. Anyhow, he's telling me one day he can remember being in mom's tummy. I couldn't recall it at all. So, he talks me into recreating our being inside our mother."

"Back to the womb."

"Exactly. We were standing in the shallow end of the pool– we scrunched up and held on to each other in a kind of fetal position and sank like a lump to the bottom of the pool while exhaling every bit of air from our lungs."

"Did you pass out?"

"There was this blissful feeling- just floating- holding on to each other, not breathing, slowly rotating- we were only in about three feet of water, but we had exhaled all of our air and we were hovering near on the bottom of the pool not breathing. That scared the hell out of the family. Our brother Norman jumped in and pushed us to the surface. Picture this - I'm gasping for breath, but Johnny? He's doing this whole waa, waa, WAA! crying thing like an infant just being born. Then he starts laughing hysterically. We had to promise Mom we'd never try that again. Never did either, not without snorkels anyway."

"Boys will be boys, right?"

"In so many ways! Well, look at that. We're just about out of beach here. Let's walk back the other way. "

"Good idea."

They turned and retraced their steps up the beach. They were both silent for a period. Cyndy was touched by the feeling of loneliness she detected in that confession of his. She was also somewhat amazed at how opened he was with her.

*Who is this man? Why is he being so honest? I mean, unless he's a damn good actor. This doesn't seem like a line of crap. I could really get used to him real fast. This is all very interesting.*

They continued to walk silently, then finally she asked, "I imagine it still hurts a lot, doesn't it?"

"Uh huh."

"I can't imagine what it would be like staring at yourself in a casket. Oh. I'm sorry. I didn't mean to say that out loud. Oh shit., Kyle, I am sorry to bring that up. Fuck! That's the wrong thing to say from any angle I am so sorry!"

"No. No. It's okay. It really is nice to have someone to talk to about it. How about taking a seat over there? I'm getting tired of walking."

"Fine with me."

They walked over to the point where the beach starts its curve around toward the Magothy River, and took a seat on the grass at the edge of the sand.

"Wanna get high?"

"Sure." And she laughed as he brushed back his long brown hair and withdrew a joint from behind his right ear. "You always keep marijuana cigarettes behind your ear?"

"Gotta be prepared."

"Aren't you afraid someone's going to catch you?"

"Can't be seen, so it's no big deal. Here. You do the honors."

She took the joint and he lit it for her.

"This'll make your toes twinkle, believe me."

And they smoked and laughed and talked for the next hour about their pasts and mostly about the curiosities of psychic phenomena, hauntings and poltergeists. He listened, as interested in her as he was with the dark world of hauntings which fascinated her so.

She enjoyed being with him and his sense of humor was a pleasant relief from her usual companions and dates. And she was nuts for that smile of his.

*The rest of him ain't so bad either,* she thought.

"Wanna do another joint?"

"No. No. Ah, I'm doing just fine, thank you very much. What have you got? Another one behind the other ear?" She reached over, her slender hand weaving and twirling the hair on the left side of his head and then playfully pinching his ear.

Taking the cue, Kyle drew her close and kissed her; focusing his full attention on her and on the kiss. He wanted her to know he meant it. And she got the message. Her lips slowly parted and she warmly welcomed his tongue with hers. It was a long, slow, passionate kiss, the kind that causes time to disappear. When their lips parted, she rested her head on his shoulder. Without fully understanding it, they both felt that the moment was a victory of sorts for both of them.

"I was wondering how long you were going to wait before doing that," she said, pecking him again on the lips and looking deep into his eyes.

"So was I," he grinned. And she laughed.

"You've got a great smile, Kyle."

And he kissed her again, sensing it was exactly what she wanted.

Her lips parted invitingly, and he slowly extended his tongue to meet the tip of hers as they drew each other closer and tumbled over on their sides. Then she pulled him over on top of her as they came up for air.

"Whew! I like that," she said, smiling up at him.

"Wow!" And he grinned again.

"Wow."

"Un huh." And then he had to laugh.

"What's so funny?"

"We're wonderfully articulate, aren't we?"

"We're doing all right."

"Wanna ball?" he asked.

"You betcha. But we have to have a blanket or something `cause it's getting cold on this here ground!"

"I got one in the car," he said, rising to his feet and drawing her up against him for another extended embrace.

"Let's get it," she cried, breaking away from him and running towards the parking lot.

"All right!" he sang out, running after her.

Their laughter echoed through the empty parkland as they raced to the car where he caught her and pulled her to him.

She kissed him as he reached around her and slipped his hands into her back pockets, drawing her hips tightly against his.

"I like that," she breathed and nibbled at his earlobe as she reached down and gently massaged the bulge in his Levi's. "That, too."

"Ah, ah, ah," he laughed, and pulled away, circling around to the trunk of the car. "Mustn't get too anxious!"

Laughing, she ran around to him as he popped the trunk. She hugged him around the waist, then dropped her hands down and stroked his thighs.

"Carry blankets all the time?"

"Believe me, no. This is a lucky break." he laughed as he snatched the army blanket from the trunk, slammed the lid and leaned around to peck her cheek. "Come on! Back to the beach you evil temptress!"

She grabbed the blanket from him. "Catch me!" and off she ran back toward the bay with Kyle in close pursuit.

They both reached the edge of the beach at the same time and tumbled laughing onto the grass.

They spread the blanket on the grass and were on top of it in an instant. She was on her back and he was leaning over her, kissing her deeply as her hand guided his to her breast.

"Oh my god," she intoned slowly and passionately, "Kyle get your damn pants off I want you inside me."

Normally, Kyle was the aggressor when it came to sex. This time, however, he was determined it would be different. He wanted it to be love-making, not simply a quest for orgasm. His goal was to take his time, to pleasure her.

It didn't exactly work out that way.

After several minutes of slow, passionate love making, Cyndy tightened her legs around Kyle's hips and rolled them over.

On top of her new lover, she got quite aggressive. She controlled their pace and led them to reach a glorious conclusion together. They stayed still for several minutes panting, holding each other close and enjoying the post-coital sensations.

"Whew," she breathed.

"Wow," he agreed.

They both laughed.

"We," Kyle observed, "are so articulate!"

Cyndy then rolled over so Kyle was on top. She held him tight and kissed him tenderly.

"That, my dear Kyle," she purred, "was a fantastic start."

How long they laid together catching their breaths, he would never be sure.

It was Cyndy who eventually broke the silence. "You know, Wilson, you will never ever again cross that bridge over there without thinking of you and me and what we've done here."

"We've defiled government land."

"From now on, whenever you cross that bridge you are going to think about our making love here on this night."

"How could I not?"

* * *

Kyle marveled at the memories of their affair. "Or was it an entanglement?" he asked aloud. "It lasted more than two years, so maybe it could be chalked up as a 'romance.'"

"Oh shit!" he yelled, realizing he was about to miss the exit off Route 50 to the Capital Beltway. He floored it and the Tempest lived up to its "Le Mans" name and shot across two lanes of traffic and down the cloverleaf.

He sighed. "The summer of 1968 was kind of like that; a wild ride."

Actually, for Kyle Wilson it was a hedonistic wild ride. But then, being 21 years old with a student deferment from the draft, there really wasn't much at stake. *Even when she had a fling with the sculptor. That was a strange turn of events. Why was that? Oh yes. I was sleeping around with the guys. But we got together again. Oh god, it was almost five years ago to this very date. Freaky.*

With his right hand, he reached down into his cassette file, rummaged around and found an old tape he hadn't listened to for quite a while. Never mind rewinding it. Just pop it in wherever. Loud, too.

"He stands like a statue, becomes part of the machine . . ." -- the pulsing beat of The Who's rock opera, *TOMMY.*

*If I'm going to play 'let's remember,' I may as well have the right background music.*

The good and some not so good memories of days gone by flipped through his mind as he sped west on I-495 toward his childhood home.

He remembered their first two months of bliss. They spent as much time as possible together some nights at his place, some nights at hers. They nursed each other through the remainder of the academic year. She did the cooking while he typed their papers because he was the fastest typist and she hated typing as much as she loved cooking. After successfully completing all of their exams they headed off for a week in Henlopen

Kyle's folks were not happy about the sleeping arrangements. In fact, while Cyndy was in the shower their first morning, Kyle was cornered by his stepmom and his dad. His step mom made it very clear she would prefer they slept in separate bedrooms. His father agreed vocally, but as soon as his wife had turned back to the waffle iron, he gave his son a very obvious wink. Kyle had to stifle a laugh when his father continued sternly, "When you and your girlfriend are with us keep the kissy huggy thing to a minimal – especially when your sister's around this week, understand?"

And later, when then two men were taking their plates to the sink and Vicki and Cyndy were talking over coffee, John Wilson whispered to his son, "She is on the pill, isn't she?"

"Yes, dad."

"Good. I have no problem with your being intimate with her, just don't flaunt it around Vicki."

"I get it, Dad."

And the subject never came up again.

Back in D.C., they settled into a new summer routine. Both had jobs for the summer and when they weren't working, they expanded their study of parapsychology.

About half way through the summer, Cyndy went out of

town for a weekend with her cousins and Kyle simply stayed at her house; spent time reading and working out. One Sunday morning he went for a nice long jog way up Rock Creek Parkway and back into Georgetown. Arriving home, he thought he'd found the place very quiet, so he figured he was alone and by the time he reached for the bathroom doorknob he had ditched his t-shirt and shorts and was only wearing a tight Speedo he was using instead of a jock.

Stepping into the bathroom, he quickly closed the door behind him and then realized he was not alone. Standing in the shower toweling off was Cyndy's very athletic and handsome housemate, Jones. Kyle couldn't help but stare.

"Nice run?"

"Um, Yep."

"I'll be done in a minute," Jones said with a smile as he stepped out of the tub and stood directly in front of Kyle whose appreciation for the man standing naked in front of him was readily demonstrated by the obvious expansion in his swim briefs.

The heat between them was measurable. Jones reached out, cupped and then stroked Kyle's bulging Speedo explaining, "I would suggest you take care of that. Unless you'd like some assistance."

Suddenly their lips were locked and their hands were all over each other.

"Weaver wasn't exaggerating about your meat. It is impressive."

"It's hard for me to keep my hands off you," Kyle sighed.

"Any time, sport, any time. I would never kick you out of my bed."

* * *

Next night, in bed with Cyndy, he told her about his encounter with Jones. From her reaction, Kyle figured she was either unconcerned or she could be the greatest poker player ever.

By the end of the week, she had had revenge sex with Jones (who knew he would?)

Being very casual about it all, she explained "Kyle, lover, ours is, I am sure you appreciate, an open relationship is it not?"

"Well, I guess."

... and she started seeing sculptor Bradford and they returned to living separately.

Time moved easily by them and suddenly it was two weeks before classes were to resume so he quit his job and headed north for some time on the Vineyard with his Aunt Rebecca who maintained a summer home there.

The train ride.

The memory gave Kyle a little chill.

He had grabbed several books and figured a long train ride to Boston would be just the right thing to clear his head and transition to a vacation state of mind. But he had just opened a book when he heard her voice.

"Of all the gin joints in all the world she had to walk into mine."

Kyle looked up. The sunlight was hitting both the green and the blue eye just perfectly. The overwhelming feelings of affection that hit him four months prior washed over him once more.

"Hello Cyndy."

"Hello Wilson," she answered in her noncommittal fashion

72

"I'd call this a happy coincidence," he offered with a big smile. "Have a seat?"

She tossed her duffle bag up on the overhead shelf and gracefully took a seat next to Kyle telling him, "I guess someone somewhere has determined we see each other."

"So," he asked, "Are you off to Boston or somewhere in between?"

"The Cape. The parents took a place in Harwich Port."

"Ah. Then I have between here and Beantown to convince you to blow off Harwich Port and fly with me to Martha's Vineyard?"

She simply smiled.

* * *

The ten days on the Vineyard were awesome, Kyle remembered as he continued around the Capital Beltway toward Woodmoor.

How different it would have been if the sculptor had held on to her. Kyle might not have gotten so involved with the relationship and the psi studies that came with it. He had to admit he was very much in love. It was just a shame it didn't work out.

Returning from the Vineyard they found an apartment for themselves in Foggy Bottom. They were nearly inseparable for the next two years during which time they readily handled their academic load while spending increasing amounts of time conducting their research on paranormal activities in the Baltimore-Washington area. They kept extensive notes in preparation to writing a book about it. They were, at one point, on the verge of signing a book contract when things started falling apart.

It was a fascinating experience for Kyle, yet it caused problems with his family. His father threatened to disown him when Kyle's interest in parapsychology grew into obsession. It especially rekindled his desire to speak with his brother Johnny. That desire grew stronger and stronger until one weekend when he felt he was ready.

It was April, 1970. A student strike had temporarily shut down the university, so Cyndy took the opportunity to follow a lead of a reported haunting in Ellicott City, Maryland. Kyle begged off claiming he wanted to pound the typewriter all weekend.

Cyndy had a bad feeling about leaving him alone for the weekend, but she reluctantly hit the road Saturday morning with her notebook and cassette recorder.

Kyle felt a guilty about not telling her the truth, yet Cyndy going to Ellicott City was a lucky break. Additionally, his parents were going to be out of town so the house in Woodmoor would be empty. He had to try it.

* * *

Kyle went into the house that Saturday afternoon and for the first and last time successfully put himself into a trance and made contact with his dead brother. It was something he had wanted to achieve for a long, long time. And it was a great reunion- at first. But ultimately it was disturbing beyond anything he could have possibly anticipated.

He did, in fact, cut his cosmic visit short, returned to the apartment and went to sleep.

He heard Cyndy return late that night saying something

to the effect that her entire trip was a waste of time because the initial report was made by two senile old ladies who were both starved for attention.

Kyle mumbled his condolences and slept through until Sunday afternoon.

When she asked about his typing, his inability to lie to her got the best of him and he admitted he had been to his house. It excited her and she wanted to hear all about it. They had documented all of their work and she wanted to put down some notes before the memory of the experience faded. But he refused. Adamantly.

She pressed him, but his final refusal was so passionate and sad, she let it go and retreated to write up the story of the wasted time in Ellicott City.

For weeks she did not bring it up. Nor did she press him when he would refuse to go into the field with her. Eventually he totally refused to participate in any psi research with or without her. His behavior began to strain their relationship.

She was getting into it deeper and deeper and wanted to see his interest rekindled. About five weeks after the incident, they were sitting at breakfast and she decided it was time they confronted whatever it was.

"So. I'm glad the Orioles are doing well. But I want to know once and for all, Kyle, just what exactly did happen in the basement of your parent's house?"

"Might even have a chance at the pennant this season."

"Kyle. Don't."

"You never did like baseball, did you?"

"Kyle, please."

He sipped his orange juice and looking hurt, not even attempting his disarming smile, he nearly whispered, "I asked you never to ask me about it."

"I have to ask, Kyle. It is my business. Our business. What happens to you is very much my concern, Kyle!"

"You're shouting."

"Damn right! You're making me nuts about this! I just have to shout, okay?"

"No. It's not okay."

"What happened to you?"

"Don't ask!"

"I'm asking!"

"I was in touch with Johnny," he explained quietly. "There. Now. That's all. Don't ever ask me again." And with that he grabbed his jacket and left the apartment, taking a long walk down Virginia Avenue to the Mall, and spent the rest of the day in the museums.

Cyndy never brought up the subject again. Neither did Kyle. But things never healed between them. She made an attempt. He tried. There were several false starts, periods of domestic tranquility, but each in their own way maintained some distance.

Several times, when she took the time to think about it, Cyndy would sit alone in Kyle's rocking chair and cry, marveling at the fact that someone so honest and so open could possibly shut her out so completely.

Without neglecting his academics, Kyle added as many hours as he could to his schedule at the bookstore and spent a lot of time reading the classics and listening to music with his headphones.

It was on the same day their book contract fell through that Cyndy was offered a position at a hospital in Denver.

She was going, she told him, with or without him. It would have to be without him he told her because he still had to pick up six more credits to graduate.

He wished her well, she did the same, and with much left unsaid, they parted shortly after she graduated.

Of course, she was hurt for quite a while and threw herself into her research work. She could never understand what had happened and figured she would never be able to.

Kyle worked very hard to convince himself that Cyndy Weaver and paranormal activity studies were strictly bad news and not to be messed with. He avoided the subject of ghosts, of hauntings, and of his entanglement with the sexy brunette who was once his only passion. He returned to the fold, as it were, rejoined the family, copped his bachelor's degree and even got into Harvard Law as his father wished. Both made the entire family very happy. He even got a haircut.

# CHAPTER FIVE

*REUNIONS*
*Midday Thursday in Woodmoor*

The Who's rock opera, *TOMMY*, was blaring from his car speakers as Kyle took the exit off the Capital Beltway.

"Damn it, Johnny!" He shouted to no one in particular, "I missed you so much! What a bummer. What an absolute bummer! Maybe I should have gone to Denver. Maybe Cyndy and I could have gotten it together somehow."

He snapped off the tape player, grabbed the cassette and tossed it hard into the open case on the floor to his right. The old feelings of abandonment came to the surface. He was angry, he was sad and he was lonely. But most of all, he was amazed that he was still naïve enough to be looking for fairness in an unfair world.

He parked the Tempest in the lot behind the Woodmoor shopping center near the rear entrance to the bank. Turning off the engine, he slumped back into the seat.

"Johnny. Listen up kid." Kyle told the empty bucket seat next to him. "You're half of me. I love you. But as soon as we put Dad to rest and I can get my money I am going to disappear to the other side of the world. Time for what, huh? What you predicted? It's definitely time for me to split this very freaky scene."

Again, Kyle got a chill and sensed he was not alone. For no reason whatsoever, the glove compartment door fell open with a clunk!

A chill run up his spine, causing his shoulders to spasm, "Holy shit! What the hell? Beat it! Split! Get the fuck out of here, Johnny!"

He grabbed his briefcase, hopped out of the car, slammed the door and stopped. He turned and slumped against the car. He hadn't realized it, but he had been crying. "I miss you so much you little fuck," he whispered to the parking lot.

He turned and put the briefcase on the roof of the car then checked his pockets for a Kleenex or something. The t-shirt would have to do. He wiped his face dry then, looking down on the t-shirt realized it was wet with tears and snot.

*Ugh.*

So, he exchanged it for a clean sweatshirt from his beach bag.

"Baggy old t-shirt verses snug Harvard sweatshirt? Tell the truth, Kye. You want to impress him."

When he stepped into the bank lobby he had to stop.

*Suburban Trust Company. What a throwback to the fifties. This place even smells old.*

The bank was empty of customers- only the young bank manager behind an old mahogany desk and a couple tellers at their windows.

"You guys ever going to remodel this dump?" Kyle called across the lobby.

The bank officer, a very handsome young man in a well-cut gray three-piece suit rose and walked towards Kyle explaining, "the 'classic look' is in."

The two young men stood and grinned at each other.

"Hello Mason," Kyle finally spoke and extended his hand. "Nice suit."

Mason took Kyle's extend hand and pulled him close half-whispering, "I am so sorry about your dad, old buddy."

"Thanks."

Kyle wanted to receive the embrace that the young man was so reluctant to offer in this public place.

"Is there anything I can do? You know I would do anything for you and your family," he told him as he guided Kyle over to his desk.

"I gotta get into the safety deposit boxes. I'm not sure if I am signatory."

"Like that would stop us? Have a seat while I pull the cards. Sit. Sit."

Kyle watched as Mason opened a wooden card file on his desk and flipped through several cards. Kyle was mesmerized. *He is still so fucking handsome.*

"Kyle?"

"Huh? Oh, sorry. Lost in thought."

"You in town for a while? You should stop by and check out my improved digs. I remodeled the folk's old place when they moved to a retirement village in Florida."

"I have to get back to Henlopen."

"One beer. Stop by for one beer? And for a swim?"

"I have no swimsuits with me," he lied.

"And when were you too shy to borrow a suit of mine?" He said with a little too big of a grin.

"That's true," Kyle admitted. Then leaning in close to his friend he whispered, "Are you coming on to me?"

"We're both single adults are we not? I put in an indoor lap pool."

Now it was Kyle's turn to smile.

"It's tempting, right? But business first," Mason explained and handed him a card. "Sign these."

Kyle checked out the cards observed, "Norman's not on the Signature card, only Dad?"

"Your Dad and you, once you sign below his name there."

As Kyle signed the card, he wondered if Mason still shaved his entire body. *One of the hairiest guys I know. He has five o'clock shadow and it's only noon. Sexy as hell.*

Mason led Kyle into the vault. He retrieved the three narrow safety deposit boxes and then led Kyle into a little room next to the vault.

"I will leave you to your mission," Mason told him, as he exited the little room and closed the door.

Alone in the privacy of the booth, Kyle quickly surveyed the contents of the boxes *Okay, we have here many stock certificates, several jewelry boxes – ah, one holds – Mom's charm bracelet. Whoa, how many Christmases and birthdays do those charms represent? And box number three, let me guess - her pearls? Yep, Mom's pearls. I am sure Norman will agree those all go to Trish. Mom would approve, I know she would. Trish will love and take good care of these things. But nothing in these boxes that looks like a will.*

He sorted through things more carefully. The envelope with the four names on it contained four five-thousand-dollar bearer bonds. All the coupons were intact.

*What are these worth now? No time for speculation.*

He replaced the bonds in the box. Then he tossed several jewelry gift boxes into his briefcase.

The second box brought more disappointment. No last will and testament. There was a stack of US Savings Bonds from the 1950's. A tidy sum. Under the Savings Bonds there were more stock certificates.

*Holy shit. More stocks. Texas Instruments? A couple thousand shares? No shit. Good call, Dad!*

There were others including blue chip industrials. Then an envelope marked "Last Will and Testament: Jonathan R. Wilson October 12, 1936." *Great grandpa's will? Damn.*

Under the stocks there was an antique coin purse. Inside? A $20.00 gold piece. He turned it over to read the date.

*1887? That's a collector's item, all right.*

Kyle tossed the coin purse back into the box. There was no other will in box number three.

Kyle put the stock certificates back into the oblong metal box and closed the lid.

*I will deal with all this next week. That's a plan at least. But what do I do now?*

Kyle opened the door and motioned to Mason to give him a hand.

Once the three boxes were in the vault, Kyle turned to leave, but Mason was blocking his exit.

"Here," Mason said as he held out a business card. "My address and phone number in case you forgot." Then he stepped closer and whispered, "It would be very cool to see you in a Speedo again. S'been a few years."

"That it has," Kyle replied looking into Mason's eyes. For an instant, he marveled at how similar his eyes were to Cyndy's. *What are the odds of having two lovers with heterochromia?* Then he smiled at his old friend and confessed, "some laps might be good to reduce some of the tension."

Mason returned the stare and stated, "take the card."

Kyle took the card and read the plain yet dignified lettering.

"Daniel Mason Museum Quality Rarities. Procurement and Discrete Brokering. For real?"

"I'm dabbling in antiquities. Pre-Columbian artifacts are hot right now."

"Interesting."

"Stop by. I get off at 4:00 today. It would be nice to catch up, share stories of good times we had with your Dad and with Johnny. It might help the transition."

Touched by his friend's sincerity, Kyle gave him a quick hug and whispered, "I'll call ya later. Promise."

He tossed his briefcase into the trunk of the car and then headed to the deli at the other end of the shopping center. There's a phone booth there, he remembered, and besides, he could do with a sandwich at about that time anyway.

The old delicatessen looked pretty much as he'd remembered it. There were the six little Formica tables with ancient kitchen chairs. The ancient Coca Cola sign still hung like a sentry behind the counter. It still held those funky letters listing the sandwich menu. Chicken salad was "chicken sal-d." They still hadn't replaced the "a." The expressions of sympathy from Mr. George behind the meat counter, gave Kyle a boost. His frustration was easing in the comfortable atmosphere of the deli he had known since he was a child.

He ordered a sandwich to go (egg salad, his usual.) Then he got change from Florence at the register and headed for the old phone booth in the back of the store.

*Some things never change. That's comforting. Mr. George is still making chicken salad and Ma Bell still has a wooden phone booth in the Woodmoor Deli. Damn few of them left nowadays.*

"Hello, Cookie, let me speak to your mother. Uncle Kyle, yes. Thank you, honey."

There was a pause and a crash. The handset must have fallen off the kitchen counter.

"Kyle. Hi."

"How are things on the home front?"

"I'm finishing up lunch with the kids. Mom and I are going over to Baker's Funeral Home. They're going to pick up Dad at the hospital about now. You make it to Silver Spring all right?"

"Wonderful drive. Found some interesting stuff in the three safety deposit boxes, but I couldn't find a will."

"Oh," and there was a pause on her end of the line.

"Well, Trish, any suggestions?"

"I don't know. There's Dad's strongbox. Dad kept a lot of papers in a strongbox under the counter below the bar in the rec room. That's what the fourth key on the ring I gave you is for. It's on the bottom shelf. There's a case of wine glasses in front of it."

"In the house in Woodmoor."

"Yes. In the basement. Go over there and pick it up, will you?"

"Yeah."

"Are you feeling okay?"

"Peachy. Everything's fine. Really."

"Okay. The will is very important. We need to go over it with Norman and Vicki."

"Norman there yet?"

"Martha called and told me to expect him on the 3:30 commuter flight."

"Okay. I'll see you in four hours or so. Good luck. And Trish? Hang in there."

"I will, thanks. Oh. Oh, oh yes. There's a message for you. Do you remember Cynthia Weaver?"

*Oh god.* "Yes. Why?"

"She called from Denver. She wants you to get in touch with her as soon as possible. "She was very insistent."

"Give me the number."

Kyle jotted down the number. (Fortunately, Mr. George always had a pencil tied with a length of string hanging in the phone booth.)

"Thanks, Trish. See you soon."

*Great. That's great. Memories are fun, but do I want to actually talk to her right now?*

Kyle stared at the wrinkled piece of paper in his hand.

*Oh, what the fuck, why not?*

He dropped another dime into the slot and dialed "0". He then read his credit card number to the operator.

*Denver. Bet she's living in a modern looking joint with big tall windows looking out on the Rockies.*

Cyndy picked it up on the third ring.

"Kyle!"

"Hey, Weaver. What's happening?"

"You tell me."

*I'm fucking freaking out, that's what's happening. But I better not go there.*

"Well, Cyndy, things are a little, I dunno, how's 'uptight' for a word?"

"I've been calling and calling all morning since seven; even your father's private line. Everything's busy. Are you all right?"

"I 'spose." Hearing her voice brought back a flood of emotions he'd not even touched on during the drive. Her voice served to remind him if he had never met her, he would never have talked to Johnny. He would be ignorant of his future.

"I got a premonition," Cyndy explained. "It was late last night. It must have been around 6:30 in the morning your time. Did something happen? It was a feeling you were in trouble."

*No shit, but I'm not about to tell you or anyone else in the world. Better tell her-* "Dad died."

"Trish told me. I'm so sorry, Kyle."

"Thank you."

There was a pause.

*You would like to be with her again, wouldn't you? No. Yes. No. It's hormones. Let it go at that. New topic.* "I finished law school couple days ago."

"You always were good at changing the subject. Congratulations on law school."

"You married? Engaged?" *Damn! Why did I ask?*

"No." *Why did he ask?* "Are you?"

"Nope."

"You're in trouble and I know it. Don't play games with me Kyle, please. Not this time."

*Don't start. Not now.* "Cyndy, things are confusing right now. I'll be okay. I appreciate your concern, you know I do."

"If you want company-"

"Are you still researching at the hospital there?"

"Stop it!"

"What?"

"You're doing it again!"

"I thought we finished on the subject of-"

"You haven't changed, have you?"

"I got a haircut."

"You know what Kyle? Someone ought to give you a spanking!"

"Hey, come on, Cyndy. It's not an easy time."

"You want me to come east or not?"

"I don't know if it would be a good idea right now," he lied. But it wasn't exactly a lie. He didn't want to handle two emotional powder kegs on the same weekend.

"You're still infuriating, you know that? But the offer stands. Don't be insensitive."

"I don't mean to be. I'll call you tonight, okay?" There was the old reconciliatory tone that he so often side-stepped.

"I'm sorry, Kyle, if I'm being a nuisance. It's I, well, you know I still get these feelings about you. I couldn't shake this one. I thought you needed my help."

It may have been too much to handle but the words slipped out. "I know, Cyndy. I still love you, too. God help both of us. I would love to have your help. But give me the afternoon to deal with all this stuff, okay? I'll call you tonight and let you know how things are going, okay?"

"Be careful, Kyle, please. There's danger coming at you. Be careful, okay? Please."

"Hey. Always. I'll call you tonight. Promise."

Cyndy wasn't pleased with the reception she was receiving from her former lover. She felt a bit of anger rising in her chest. He was avoiding telling her something again and it was starting to feel a little too much like three years ago. But her emotions, like Kyle's, got the best of her and she found herself saying, "I don't want to hang up. I want to know what's going on there. I want to talk to you. I want to see you."

He wasn't really ready for that. A flurry of feelings nearly overwhelmed him. He knew if he stayed on the telephone with her, he would start crying so he blurted out, "I gotta split, Cyndy. I appreciate all this. I do. I do. But I'll have to talk to you later." And he replaced the receiver.

\* \* \*

Cyndy hesitated then very slowly replaced the handset in its cradle. She was torn between wanting to hop the next plane East and tossing the telephone out of the window.

"I should have thrown him off the balcony the very first time he flashed that adorable grin at me," she told herself. Then she curled up on the day bed by the window.

It had been cloudy all morning in Denver. Suddenly there was an enormous clap of thunder and it started to pour outside. She shivered. *Something's up*, she thought. There was another clap of thunder. She felt very small and frightened. *Something is up*, she decided, and she had a strong feeling it was going to be a real doozy, whatever it was. She wanted to go to sleep, but instead, she got up, grabbed the phone and called the airline.

* * *

Kyle sat in the phone booth a full two minutes before he took his hand off the receiver. He was sweating. "What is going on?" he asked himself. *The three of them are coming out of the woodwork. Not now. Johnny, Mason and now Cyndy. I don't need this right now. I would be so easier if everyone left me alone!*

As he opened the door and rose to leave the phone booth, he heard a familiar voice calling him name.

"Kyle, come join us."

"Hello Mr. Henderson, how ya doing?" he asked, crossing over to the table.

"Sorry about your Dad. He was a great man."

"Thank you, sir."

"Sit. Please have a seat. I'll be at the funeral. Michael, too. Come on, sit."

"Well, I have to be getting-"

The old man turned toward the counter and called, "hey Michael, look who's here, huh? Get over here and say hello."

Kyle looked to the counter. There stood his old furry freak brother, Michael Henderson. He was holding a plate piled with two tuna sandwiches and lots of pickles. Michael – "Mr. P & C" himself.

"Excuse me, Kyle, I need cream for this thing." He took the little pitcher and headed over to the counter. "Hey George how about some cream for your best customer?"

Kyle looked across the table as his old friend was taking a seat.

"So, how's it hanging hippie?"

"Uptight. How about you, pig?"

"Hey, that's detective pig to you, boy."

"No shit?"

"Michael Henderson the detective."

"Congratulations."

"And well deserved," chimed in Mr. Henderson who was returning to his seat. "The boy's a regular Colombo now."

"Sorry about your Dad, Kyle."

"Yeah. Tough times, man."

"It's cool. I'm all right. The wake is most likely Saturday. When the clouds clear in Henlopen, I'm coming up here. You and I are going to get together and celebrate the new badge, all right? We'll raise so much hell they'll take it away from you the very next morning."

"Whoa, I like it!"

"I bet you would." Then turning to the deli counter, Kyle

asked, "Hey George you got my egg salad sandwich and a large coke?"

"Ready twenty minutes ago. Where you been?"

Kyle turned to his two friends. "Some things never change, know that?"

"Ain't it the truth." laughed Michael. "Take care of yourself, buddy."

Kyle paid for his sandwich and soda and left the deli. Walking back to his car he had a thought. *It would be nice if I could avoid going into the House of Usher.*

*What would I tell Trish? I couldn't find the strongbox? You gonna tell Norman you wouldn't go into the house because you were afraid of the bogeyman in the basement? Forget it. Go over there, cop the box and drive home.*

Kyle drove up the driveway and around to the back of the house and parked. He turned the air conditioning up high and, staring at the house, ate his sandwich.

Mr. George still makes a damn good egg salad, he thought.

As he munched away, he replayed his conversation with Cyndy. "Yeah, I'll call her tonight," Kyle decided, "and ask her to come on over to Delaware.

"Cyndy Weaver," he told the air around him and shook his head and settled back into the bucket seat of the car. A series of quick memories of their first weekend together flashed by as he continued his lunch in the car.

After their visit to Sandy Point State Park, they headed east.

* * *

"We're here," he announced as he gently shook Cyndy's shoulder.

She snapped awake, and pecking him on the cheek exclaimed, "you are so nice to let me nap! Now though, I am thirsty. Shouldn't we have stopped for some sort of provisions before we go in?"

"Nope. You'll see. Follow me."

The kitchen was fully stocked, as was the bar and this somehow impressed her. "Well," he explained, we do kinda of live here part time."

They grabbed a couple beers and he showed her where his room was on the second floor. She immediately disrobed. He reached out but she stopped him.

"Whoa, there, cowboy. I am going to shower first if that's okay."

He pointed her in the right direction then changed into his "beach uniform." Then he returned to the first floor and flopped onto the large pit couch and enjoyed his beer.

Next time he saw her she was up on the landing brushing her hair and calling down to him. "Found one of your t-shirts and a swim brief which I know is kinda kinky, but I liked the color of it. Very purple, don'tcha think?" She raised the t-shirt enough to reveal the dark purple Speedo with white panels. It fit her beautifully.

"Oh yeah, that's hot," he told her.

"You have quite a collection of swimwear."

*Yeah*, Kyle remembered as he swallowed the last bit of egg salad and took a sip of his soda. *That first weekend with Cyndy. It was pretty trippy.*

He drained his soda and marveled over the fact he couldn't remember eating food when in Henlopen with Cyndy that first time. *We must have done more than smoke and drink. We fucked a lot.*

He realized he was still smiling when something caught his eye. He thought he saw someone looking at him out of one of the upstairs windows. A little girl. *Could it have been? Ah no. Come on now Kye, you're getting freaked out over this whole thing. Clear your head and stop being so damn uptight. Next thing's gonna happen is you're gonna run into a bogeyman. Chill out, huh?*

But he couldn't shake the feeling that he had seen someone. He remembered the first tenants in the house lost their daughter one summer.

*Oh yeah. Mom wasn't in a hurry to move into the new house so they rented it out for a year. Something happened. Right. Their kid fell down the basement stairs and broke her neck. Could that have been her?*

*Cut it out Kyle. Enough of the ghosts and goblins. It's the middle of the day for cryin' out loud.*

*Well, let's get it over with.*

He retrieved the key to the alarm system from the dog house. (*Stupid place to hide a key,* he thought.) Then he went down the steps past the terraced garden to the back patio, and tried the sliding door. Trish was right. Unlocked.

The dining room looked different in summer light. (Few summers were spent in the city.) It was hot and the air seemed stale. *Dad never runs the air conditioning when he's up here weekdays in the summer.*

*How much time before the alarm goes off? I can never remember.* He inserted the key in the lock and gave it a turn. *Ah, safe from that horrible screeching noise. I'd make a hell of a spy.*

He crossed through the swinging door into the kitchen. He half expected to see his brother Johnny on the corner stool by the butcher's block. It was the kid's favorite place to visit with their mother evenings before dinner.

The door creaked.

*How appropriate. No one in the kitchen.* As he looked around the room his gaze came to rest on the intercom unit by the pantry door. He hated that thing when he was growing up. What schoolboy wouldn't? With a flip of a switch one parent or the other would call into their bedrooms and wake them on school mornings.

He smiled at the memory and ran his finger along the nine control levers: one for each other room with a squawk box in it. Seeing the three different settings for each knob - "off," "talk" and "monitor." His parents would leave the bedroom switches on "monitor." It would assure them everyone was getting ready for school.

*That was so long ago.*

Kyle cupped his hands and shouted, "Up and at 'em, kids!"

He chuckled and then told the empty room, "Dad, I am going to miss you." And a chill shot up his spine and he shivered. "Okay, that was creepy."

His gaze shifted. And there it was, to his right, the dreaded basement door. He wondered if he would run up the stairs once he had found the strongbox.

The basement of the house had always bothered Kyle. He had many nightmares where he was trapped in the basement by an evil bearded man. During waking hours, when he finished playing, he couldn't walk up the stairs. As soon as his foot would hit the bottom tread, he would get a chill at the base of his spine and charge up the stairs like there was no tomorrow. His family dismissed it as the energy of youth. Kyle wasn't about to reveal his fears of the basement. Boys aren't frightened. Boys aren't scared by empty basements. Besides, no one else was ever bothered by the basement. So, he never brought the subject up.

Kyle opened the basement door and down the stairs he went. Although after this morning's visitation, the basement was the last place he wanted to be.

Everything looked as he remembered. The trophy case displayed too many sports trophies and ribbons. The pool table was covered as usual. The area on the other side of the stairs was as neatly kept. There was the wet bar with its large blue tinted mirror behind it. The leather club chairs were in their places and the rifles and shotguns were in their wooden rack.

*Grizzly,* Kyle thought. *Especially that old double-barreled shotgun.*

He stood at the bar looking at his reflection. *Yes, there's a little of Dad in my looks.*

"I'm going to miss him," he told the empty room, then trembled with a chill. "Whew," he breathed and found himself asking, "Goose walk over your grave, Kye?"

He chuckled nervously, and walked behind the bar. Yes. There it was behind the box of wine glasses as Trish had described.

"Not very heavy, wonder what's in this here box?"

And he took a seat on the deacon's bench. It wasn't so bad being alone in the basement this time. "I made good time getting up here, may as well have a peek at this stuff before driving back to the Eastern Shore."

Seated on the bench, he balanced the box on his knees and unlocked it. *Trish was correct about the fourth key.*

Kyle flipped through and read the labels on the many envelopes inside the box. "Last Will and Testament" December 26, 1971" Great!

Some inner sense caused him to look up. What he saw startled him more than anything he'd ever seen in his years of paranormal research.

An apparition of a tall bearded man appeared to walk right out of the far basement wall and charge toward him. He was waving something above its head. His eyes were wide with rage as he mouthed silent threats and stalked closer and closer. The horrifying vision was about to brutally strike him when it vanished.

Kyle couldn't budge.

The basement was very quiet.

The entire house was very quiet.

The stillness was shattered as Kyle dropped the metal strongbox.

He leapt up the basement steps as he always did as a young boy. Only this climb didn't take him as far as the kitchen.

As he was about the make the last leap to the top step, he misjudged the distance and his foot fell in the wrong spot. He lost his balance and fell backward. He caromed off the stairway wall and into a somersault which ended on the cold tile floor. The fall – knocked him unconscious. It also slightly realigned his spine and gave him powers he had merely read about in his years of psi studies. Of course, he didn't realize it at the time. He couldn't realize anything at the moment.

Kyle Wilson was out cold.

# CHAPTER SIX

## *ORIGINS OF THE HAUNTING*

The specter Kyle Wilson encountered was his Great-grandfather's brother, Nelson Wilson. He was murdered on that spot more than eighty-four years prior.

\* \* \*

The Wilson family had farmed lands outside of Washington, D.C. for as long as anyone in the family could remember. Nelson Wilson and his two brothers carried on the family tradition.

Nelson knew when the Civil War ended, the family's government contracts would die. They would no longer be providing horses and grain in large quantities. Farming alone wouldn't cut it, in his opinion. He was looking for ways to make more money.

Nelson decided they would look for business opportunities in the South. All agreed and their sibling rivalry was stoked.

To Derrick's satisfaction, it was agreed he would stay home and manage their farmlands.

Middle brother Jonathan saw the opportunity to compete and surpass his oldest brother.

Nelson and Jonathan headed south as soon as the war was over. Though not fond of each other, they were good at doing business together. Nelson was showy and boastful whereas Jonathan was quiet and calculating. Both were ruthless when necessary.

They made money. Nelson and Jonathan Wilson bought themselves a run-down lumber mill in Savannah, Georgia. Soon they were making steady profits. After a while, they built and began operating a very prosperous dry-goods store.

With growing pride, Nelson lived what could then be called the "high life." He bought a big house and entertained lavishly. He particularly enjoyed the company of young southern war widows.

Jonathan watched his brother from the sidelines. He was hoping someday, Nelson's recklessness would send him home in defeat. Jonathan was determined to have the upper hand.

With that in mind, Jonathan lived frugally, sent most of his earnings home and had Derrick buy him land. Eventually, Jonathan owned hundreds of acres surrounding the original Wilson farmlands.

In 1873, Jonathan sold his share of the business to his brother, Nelson, and headed home. He wanted to settle down back in Maryland with his new wife, Amelia Campbell, the daughter of a wealthy Bermudan salt dealer he met in Savannah.

Stepping off the train in Washington, DC Jonathan Wilson felt very proud of himself. He had plenty of money in the bank and he had amassed more land than any relative before him. He was also returning with a beautiful wife. *No one,* he told himself, *could ever again say Nelson was better than me.*

As it would turn out, neither Jonathan nor his wife, Amelia, got what they wanted, especially not Amelia. She was not pleased to discover that her husband did not allow her what he called "extra frills." They lived far below their means and she knew it. They only had two servants- a Cajun woman who did the cooking and a young German immigrant for the cleaning. That wasn't enough in her opinion.

"There are more hands to tend to the livestock on this estate than to tend to our home," she complained one afternoon. "Who's more important around here? The people in this house or the horses and cattle?"

"That is enough!" Jonathan exclaimed. "We have everything we need!" Jonathan then turned away and went to tend to his chores.

Within a year, they celebrated the birth of a son. But, complications from the birth meant that Jonathan Junior would be an only child.

That was all right with Amelia. She left the child-rearing to Ann Marie Campbell who went from nurse maid to nanny to live-in tutor.

As time passed, life on the Wilson estate remained pleasant for all except Amelia. She grew bored with what she considered an uneventful life with the Wilson family. She quietly grew to hate her husband.

For Amelia, Nelson Wilson's arrival in the Spring of 1889 was a needed change. Nelson had sold the businesses in Savannah and was on his way to New York and "new opportunities." His stopping in on his old home for a visit was just what Amelia needed. She was smitten with the tall, muscular Nelson. She knew she would enjoy his more fashionable lifestyle.

Nelson insisted this reunion be special for all. He took his family into the city for a weekend of shopping and fine dining. He lavished gifts on his sister-in-law, his brothers and thirteen-year-old nephew.

They stayed and dined at the fashionable Willard's Hotel. Jonathan silently watched as Nelson paid attention to Amelia. He did not comment. He was getting pleasure watching his older brother dote on his beautiful wife. *I have something he admires,* Jonathan realized, *something Nelson cannot have.*

It gave Jonathan a good feeling. He was finally getting even.

The success of Jonathan's grand plan became more evident to him on the day before Nelson was to head north he asked his brothers to take a walk with him to discuss some business.

"I'm going to need more money for this new venture," Nelson explained as they strolled by the ice pond. "I want to sell you boys my third of the farm here."

"Sell? To us?" Derrick asked.

"It's your roots," Jonathan replied, "you should always have it to fall back on."

Nelson leaned against a large elm tree and folded his arms across his chest. "This opportunity is too big and too good to let pass," Nelson lied with studied casualness.

Derrick laughed.

"Derrick," Nelson cut in, "will you ever grow up?"

"What's so funny?" Jonathan asked.

"I've been waiting for this!" Derrick observed with a big grin. "I've been waiting. Just waiting!"

Jonathan finally got it. "What about the money you made in Savannah. Is there any left?"

"I'm going to need extra funds."

"Aw, come on, Nelson, tell him. Fess up."

"Shut up, Derrick!"

"Tell me what?"

"He's broke!"

"That's a lie!"

"Yeah? How come you been over to the bank three times these past three days? You sold those twelve acres of land of yours over by Adelphi Creek, didn't you? Even tried to mortgage your part of this place, didn't you?"

"I don't know what you're talking about."

"Aw, Nelson. Washington may be the capital of these United States, but it's still a small town. I've heard about what you've been doing. You blew it down there, brother, didn't you?"

"Derrick, my affairs are my business."

"Horse shit, Nelson. You're broke. You're busted!" And Derrick started laughing again.

Nelson started towards Derrick but Jonathan planted himself firmly between his two brothers. "We'll have none of that," Jonathan ordered.

"You still have a mouth on you, don't you Derrick?"

"Big bad Nelson," Derrick chided. "The one who is always on top of things, the heir, the oldest, the wisest, the smartest. You got screwed down south, didn't you?"

Jonathan quickly interjected, "Shut up Derrick!"

Nelson remained calm.

*He needs us now,* Jonathan realized.

"I had some debts. The sale covered them and left me with some money, but not enough to start anything of substance. What? Does it make you happy, you jackass?"

"Yes!" Derrick exclaimed, "Yes! And now you want us to bail you out. Piss on that."

"It's no use talking to you, is it?" Nelson turned away from Derrick and addressed Jonathan in a very even-handed way. "Jonathan, let's be honest here. My leadership in Savannah brought you opportunities you would never have initiated. If it hadn't been for me, all you'd have would be our original 98 acres and you know it."

Jonathan had no immediate reply. He considered helping Nelson. His silent calculations told him it was a good opportunity.

Derrick broke the silence. "I made this farm into something great, though, didn't I, Nelson?" he boasted.

"You did well for yourself, Derrick. Jonathan, you did exceptionally well."

"I don't have that kind of money on hand," Derrick confessed. "And I don't want to borrow any. Jon, you're the one with all the cash."

Nelson's comment, "Jonathan, you did exceptionally well" set Jonathan to thinking. *This is it. This is all he's ever going to admit. I've won the competition and it doesn't mean a damn thing. I'll buy him out, he'll squander the money and then he'll be totally broke. I'll then hire him as a field hand.*

Jonathan stepped up to Nelson. "I'll buy you out," he told his older brother. "And you," Jonathan said, turning to his other brother, "you, Derrick are not to tell a soul about this, understand?"

Derrick knew that look in Jonathan's hazel eyes. It was one Derrick understood, even feared. "Sure, Jon. Whatever you want."

"Thank you," Jonathan replied curtly. "Nelson, you own a third of the original 98 acres. That's all. The rest is ours. Am I clear?"

"One hundred percent."

"I'll have the papers drawn up and a cashier's check for you before dinner. You don't want to be traveling to New York with that much cash. Do we have a deal?" he asked presenting his hand to his brother.

"Yes," Nelson replied shaking his younger brother's hand, "we have a deal. I need to send a wire. I will see you at dinner."

As Nelson rode away, Jonathan thought, *so this is winning. It's not pleasurable at all.*

Amelia was quite sullen when Jonathan encountered her in the dooryard later that day. She mentioned to her husband how she'd miss Nelson once he headed north. Jonathan disagreed commenting, "If we lived such a lavish lifestyle we'd be broke within a year!

She knew that wasn't true, and, besides, it wasn't what she wanted to hear. For the first time in their many years of marriage, she spoke back to her husband, shouting, "a few 'extra frills' would help this dreary life."

Her outburst angered Jonathan. He raised his hand to strike her but checked himself. She stood her ground. He stared at her thinking, *I've given this woman and our son a damned decent life for close on to fifteen years. Now Nelson comes home. That lying failure turns her head and gets her thinking the life I give her is not good enough.*

Without a word, Jonathan turned, got on his horse and rode away. He wanted to hit her. He wanted to hit her hard, knock her to the ground and have her beg him for his forgiveness. He needed that sensation of power, that feeling of dominance. But he had never struck a woman in his life, and felt it was safer to remove himself from her presence.

* * *

Dinner that night was a festive affair. Amelia insisted they all wear their best clothes. It was, after all, their last night together as a family. The Wilson men complied. Each had their own reasons for making dinner a special occasion. Jonathan had, for the first time in his life, gained the upper hand over his brothers. Derrick enjoyed seeing his brother humbled. He was pleased they'd most likely never see Nelson again in their lives. Nelson felt that his departure marked a new beginning. In high spirits, he drank a little too much port after dinner and it loosened his tongue. He shared a variety of bawdy stories which his brothers and nephew found very amusing. Amelia feigned embarrassment over Nelson's tales, but she enjoyed them as well as the others.

As after dinner cigars and brandy were enjoyed, the men signed the necessary papers. Jonathan presented Nelson with a check. Jonathan then excused himself. He had to get over to the county seat where he needed to file the papers first thing in the morning. He said his goodbye to Nelson, changed his clothes and rode off.

Derrick excused himself. He then retired to his bedroom and a pre-arranged tryst with the young German house maid.

Amelia followed Nelson to the front porch. "I'll keep you company while you finish your brandy."

They took seats in the two rockers under the front window, and he asked her about her homeland. She described the island of Bermuda and told him of her childhood and how she met Jonathan. He seemed interested.

When she ran out of things to say, and he out of questions, they sat quietly and watched the rising full moon. Nelson smiled at Amelia and took another sip of his brandy. Amelia got up from her chair. She walked behind Nelson, reached over his shoulders and placed her hands on his chest. Even at 44, the man was very solid. She liked that.

"Take me with you."

"I can't guarantee I can afford to keep you in the lifestyle you deserve."

"We can work something out," she purred. And she ran her index finger across his chest, up his neck and let it come to rest on his lips.

\* \* \*

Just after ten o'clock, Derrick was woken from a deep sleep by loud knocking on his bedroom door.

"Mr. Derrick!" someone was hissing.

"Wha?"

"Mr. Derrick, come quick!"

*Damn*, he thought, pulling on his trousers and heading for the bedroom door. *I don't want to have to foal another breeched calf. Can't those hands down at the barn do anything themselves?*

He yanked the door open to reveal Dorothy standing there looking very concerned. The woman was dressed in her bed clothes and had thrown a shawl over her shoulders.

"I think you better hurry, sir. Miss Amelia, she's rode out of here with Mr. Nelson."

There was no sign of them as Derrick rode east on the Bladensburg road. But with the full moon high in the sky he could see the intersection up ahead.

*They've got to be on 29*, he thought. *It's been a couple decades since Nelson was living in these parts. It's the only route he's certain of. Hell, the woman probably asked him to take her with him and he's just stupid enough to do it.*

Lost in his thoughts of how he'd handle things when he caught them, Derrick almost missed the turn. He managed, however, to slow his horse at the crossroad, reign left once again, and head north on the old post road.

After about a hundred yards, the road began its long, gradual slope downward to the river. The woods sloped up to his left, and to the right was the low narrow marsh. Beyond that were Jonathan's timber lands. Up ahead, Derrick could see a couple lantern lights. A carriage was moving along the lodge's driveway. He slowed his horse to a trot.

*It's got to be them*, he thought. *They've been to the lodge. Oh hell. Jonathan's gonna kill me now.*

Derrick reigned his horse at the point where the two roads

108

intersected. And waited. He could hear their laughter as the carriage drew closer.

"New York," Nelson was boasting, "has become an incredible place. We will be able to enjoy-" But he stopped when he saw his younger brother atop his tall bay gelding in the middle of the moonlit roadway.

"Derrick go home." Amelia uttered as Nelson drew his team to a halt just feet from where her brother-in-law had stopped.

"Well, well, well, it's brother Derrick. Have some wine, brother Derrick?" Nelson asked, offering the bottle.

"Don't be foolish," Derrick told them. "If you've taken anything that's not yours, put it back. Come home now and I won't say anything to Jonathan."

"Get out of the road, Derrick," Nelson stated calmly, his speech slightly slurred from too much drink. "We're leaving."

"He will find you."

"He won't even bother. He's got his land and his money, well, some of his money." And he looked at Amelia and laughed at his own little joke. She was not amused.

"You're going to ruin a lot of things for a lot of people by doing this, you realize."

"Derrick," Nelson smiled, then addressed his brother with studied intensity. "You've got to learn someday that opportunities are for the takers. Now get down off your horse." And he deftly pulled his shotgun from under his feet, cocked it and pointed it at his brother.

"Nelson!"

"Remain calm, Amelia, and listen." Nelson spoke in a clipped manner. "There's a coil of rope there beside my trunk in the back. Get it."

"Nelson?"

"Get off your horse, Derrick."

What happened next, happened very fast. Jonathan Wilson stepped out of the shadows to Nelson's right. He cocked his rifle and stepped towards the carriage, his voice was steady, but he was furious.

"Nothing. He'll do nothing."

In his rage, Jonathan reached up, grabbed Nelson by the arm and yanked him out of the carriage. In the process, Nelson let go of the shotgun and it landed by the carriage as he tumbled to the ground.

"Derrick, you're my witness here."

"He was trying to take your money, Jonathan ..." Amelia tried to explain.

"Lying, crazy-" Nelson muttered into the dirt.

Jonathan ignored both of them and told Derrick to unhitch the team and send them down the road.

"But Jonathan ..."

"Down the road, damn it!"

After tethering his horse to the rig, Derrick did as told. Jonathan kept his rifle leveled at Nelson who was on his back at Jonathan's feet.

"Now, Derrick, get into the rig and sit with Amelia and keep her there."

Again, Derrick did as told.

"Nelson. Get up."

"Put the rifle aside, Jonathan and let's talk." He asked as he rose to his feet. Nelson was furious. At the same time, he knew full well that he was going to have to take things very slowly to gain the upper hand.

Jonathan kicked Nelson's shotgun under the carriage. Then he tossed his rifle up to his brother Derrick.

"Hold this," he ordered, "and if he kills me, kill him."

Jonathan turned and squared off to fight his older brother.

Nelson was normally the stronger of the two brothers. Jonathan however, was counting on the alcohol to have tipped the odds in his favor. He figured Nelson's drinking all evening pretty much made them an even match.

"Okay," Jonathan intoned. "Okay. You want my money? My wife?" Then take them from me."

Nelson drew himself up to his full height and laughed. "Jonathan, you're one prize horse's ass, aren't you?"

"You try and take them from me. Come on!" He yelled, connecting two quick jabs to his brother's right shoulder.

"It'll be a pleasure," Nelson replied, hooking a left to Jonathan's jaw.

The two brothers exchanged several punches, yet both stood their ground.

Amelia decided she'd had enough and wanted to get out of there. She hopped out of the carriage, crossed the road and headed up the hill and into the woods across the roadway. Derrick ran after her. He picked her up and carried her back to buckboard.

Jonathan and Nelson were still cussing and beating each other.

"That's enough, you two!" Derrick demanded, holding Amelia by the wrist to keep her from running off again.

"Stop this!" Amelia screamed.

But neither of the fighters would listen to their hollering.

"Give it up, Jonathan! You've found Amelia and your money. Don't kill each other!"

Neither heard them. Each was too hell-bent on killing the other.

With every blow, Nelson's hatred multiplied. *This self-righteous shit pile of a brother who always thinks he's superior. I'm the oldest, damn it,* and then blurted out, "I'm the one who was s'posed to get all Dad's land, not you!"

And with that, he charged at Jonathan, reaching for his throat. But he didn't quite make it. Derrick stuck out a foot and tripped Nelson, causing him to fall, and strike his head on a rock. Nelson was momentarily knocked unconscious.

Unknown to Jonathan, the awkward fall cracked three of Nelson's lower ribs. Jonathan took a couple of steps closer. He swiftly brought one of his boots up hard against the man's back, rupturing his kidney.

Jonathan then turned to Derrick and Amelia who were screaming at him. Blinded by his rage, Jonathan shoved Derrick aside and grabbed Amelia. He hauled her out of the carriage.

"Jonathan, stop," Derrick cried out.

"My business!" Jonathan growled.

She was crying as he flung her into the dirt.

"Don't, Jonathan!" she gasped as he towered over her, his chest heaving as he strained to catch his breath.

He swung a foot around and straddled her, gasping for breath and uttering, "My damn business!" And he started to remove the thick leather belt from around his waist.

"Jonathan, please! Jonathan, I'm sorry. I'm sorry, really. Please take me home, Jonathan!"

He just stared down at her, his mind racing. *My unfaithful wife*, he thought.

He saw she was terrified. He was in complete control and he knew it. He relished the feeling. He then raised the belt high above his head and brought it down as hard as he could across her chest. He screamed down at her and at the rest of the world, "Tease!"

She screamed.

He brought the belt high above his head again, and bringing it down once more, screamed "Damn- (Smack! The leather caught her right shoulder.) -whore!"

She screamed again. She was bleeding.

He would have continued the beating, but suddenly he was knocked away.

"Jonathan, no!"

It was Derrick. He had summoned the courage to knock his brother away from the crying Amelia.

It was an unfortunate decision on Derrick's part. About the time Derrick made up his mind to save Amelia, Nelson regained consciousness. He shook his head. He heard the screaming coming from a few yards away. The anger in him had not subsided. He was still furious. As he watched Derrick try to stop things, Nelson reached for the shotgun.

Nelson had heard the "Smack!" -sound of leather stinging flesh and Amelia's cry of anguish as he pulled himself up by the side of the carriage. The pains in his back were excruciating, but his anger gave him strength. He staggered forward, curling his finger around the trigger of the shotgun.

As Amelia screamed for her life, Derrick shouted and

headed for Jonathan. Nelson aimed as best he could in the direction of the three shouting figures and fired both barrels. The concussion sent him staggering backwards. He tripped and fell on his side; the pain was almost insurmountable.

The buckshot struck Derrick in the side and sent him sprawling to the ground and to endless sleep. Amelia mistakenly stood up at the moment Nelson pulled the trigger. She took a lot of the buckshot in the neck and face, blinding her, but not killing her instantly. She heard her husband scream, "Nelson!"

With difficulty, Nelson rose to his feet. He saw Jonathan stand. He had to finish it. He staggered up the rise toward his brother, wielding the shotgun like a bat. He wanted to crush the son of a bitch's head.

Jonathan took several steps backward, letting Nelson come at him- eight feet, four, two. Jonathan put his full weight behind his two fists and rammed them into Nelson's stomach.

Nelson doubled over. He dropped the shotgun, staggered a few steps forward, then fell face down into the dirt. Pain shot through his body. He died gasping for breath that never came.

Jonathan stood very still. He tried to make sense of what had just happened. Nothing fit. No logical thought processes were available to him. at the moment. One clear thought finally occurred to him. He had to get out of there.

He staggered to the carriage where he snatched up the canvas sack. He then untethered Derrick's horse and rode home.

Amelia lay there in terrible pain. She couldn't stand up, she could hardly move. The flesh on her face had been partially blown away and she was trying to cry out. But she could only make gurgling sounds. Her exposed jaw manically opened, closed, opened and closed again and again. She knew she was dying. She knew she was dying and all she could do was lay there and whimper, "Mama." She died half an hour later.

It was all over for Amelia and Derrick. The world tumbled onward in its orbit without them. Nelson on the other hand, would remain enraged and stuck to the plot of land for decades to come.

Not wanting to do time for a crime he'd felt was just, Jonathan Wilson concocted a robbery story. Thieves took his gold and took his wife hostage. During the fight that followed the three were killed, but the men got away with his savings. The loyal family cook and housekeeper both backed up his claims.

The ruse worked, but Jonathan had no recourse but to hide the cache of coins under the hearth in the hunting lodge.

As the years passed, Jonathan Wilson remarried and had a second family. Jonathan, Jr. headed west to Montana to get away from his tyrannical father. Jonathan's two boys by his second marriage headed to California. He was never sure if they ever made it or not until around 1919. That year, word reached him that both boys were killed in France during the first World War. It was the same year that his wife died from the influenza.

Several years later, he found out Jon, Jr. was doing all right for himself in Montana. This news came by way of a letter from his 12-year old granddaughter, Rebecca. She would write him often. He liked getting letters from her.

The farm was getting too big for him to manage and things started going wrong. The money wasn't coming in as it used to.

To hold on to his land, he had to mortgage it parcel by parcel to keep up on the taxes.

Then in 1932, a robust 18-year-old boy showed up on the farm and announced he was Jonathan Wilson's grandson. He was tired of life in Montana, he told his Grandfather, and wanted to settle in the east. Would the old man give him a job?

He did. And the boy worked hard and gained his grandfather's trust. The boy even helped the old man get out of debt. He contacted a paper company offering to sell them all the trees on the wooded acres for pulp. They agreed. A tidy sum was brought into the family accounts. The taxes were paid. Then, with the young man's help, Jonathan Wilson rebuilt his livestock herd. He made a few modest equipment purchases and revitalized his farmlands.

After the old man died, John Wilson took over everything and did well for himself. He began redeveloping the land by building single family homes at the end of world War II. One of the larger homes he built was not far from the old family hunting lodge. It stood right on the land where the Wilson brothers tragedy played out.

John Wilson's wife, Elizabeth, insisted she wasn't ready to move into the new home. So, he rented the new home to a woman whose husband was fighting in Korea. Poor woman, her daughter was running up the basement steps one day, tripped, fell and broke her neck.

The place remained empty for several months. John Wilson made some upgrades and moved his new family into it.

Some said the house was haunted, but he dismissed it. His family spent the school year in Woodmoor and summers in Henlopen, Delaware. Grandma Quinn, who moved in with the family in 1954 to spend her declining years. One morning, she came upon a little girl bouncing a beach ball in the living room. At first, Grandma Quinn thought it was little Patricia. She was about to reprimand the little girl for playing ball in the living room. *It couldn't be Patricia,* Grandma thought, *the hair's the wrong color. Isn't it?* As Grandma took a step toward the child, she turned, looked at Grandma, and then vanished.

John Wilson's son, Kyle, was, for some reason, always frightened by the basement. But the other kids never seemed to mind it.

But they should have. Because Nelson Wilson was still there. He was watching. Over the years, he would reappear, his clothes filthy, his hair disheveled. Nelson still wanted to kill his brothers.

# CHAPTER SEVEN

*NORMAN WILSON*
*Thursday in Woodmoor*

The offices from which John Wilson had run his construction company were modest. It didn't take a lot of people to run the operation. Father, son and five full-time employees worked together like a well-oiled machine. It was a tight, happy group working in the Wilson family's old two-story carriage house. For some reason, the old carriage house just never seemed comfortable to Norman. He was particularly uncomfortable on the morning his father passed away. He had to break the news to everyone at the office. He wanted to do it and then get the hell out of there. Besides, the call from Turlino required action. *Turlino needs ten grand. Now.*

The small staff waited on the first floor for what Norman

had called "a quick update meeting." Norman was on the second floor staring out the big oval window behind his father's desk. He was mentally kicking himself for having trusted a guy like Turlino. *If customs never releases them, what's it to Turlino? Shit. "Monday," Turlino tells me. "A man named Kent will visit you. You'll give him the $10,000 in cash and we'll get your stone carvings released." Why are all his "friends" named "Kent," anyway? Why did I agree? Just where the hell am I gonna get ten grand in four —*

Marge's voice on the intercom brought him back. "We're all here, Norman."

"Okay. Just a moment," he explained to the small plastic box on his Dad's desk.

Norman stepped away from the desk and headed for the stairs. At the top of the stairs he stopped. He turned as if to talk to his father as he had so many times in the past as they were called to a meeting on the first floor. Yet his time, there was no one there. There was no one to follow him down the stairs. No one to ask Norman some detail about crushed stone or faucets or window casings. Norman was on his own.

"Damn, Dad," he whispered. "We were eating lousy chicken and drinking really good bourbon twelve hours ago. I mean-" and the weight of loss started to build inside him. A sadness was forming and he knew it would overtake him if he didn't do something quick. He had to refocus and fast. But what to do, what to do what to fucking do? Then it hit him. There was something he could do. He went over to his father's desk and withdrew a bottle of bourbon from the bottom drawer. "Dad," he told himself, "is still at the country club and he's asked me to handle this meeting. Pin your brain on that, Norman, and deal with all the heavy shit later."

As he casually strode down the stairs he called out, "Marge could you please get us six cups?"

Taking a position next to the large drafting table, Norman looked at the assembled staff. *All these people are older than I am.*

There were three men and two women before him. They were casually dressed, as usual. Some were standing, some were seated on the high stools by the tables. They all were sipping their morning coffee.

*Every one of them*, Norman thought, *were pretty tight with Dad. Are they going to work as well for me, now?*

Marge lined up the cups. A drink with the staff was not an unusual occurrence in this office. Important occasions were always met with a toast with good bourbon. Norman figured it would be the appropriate way to honor his dad at this moment.

"Everyone grab a glass. Pour it into your coffee if you wish, but this morning we need to have a special toast."

As the cups were passed around, several exchanged inquisitive looks.

"Yes, I know," Norman explained. "but I need a bracer this morning and I don't like to drink alone. That didn't come out right. Let me get to the point. Early this morning I got some bad news from Henlopen. Dad-" He had to stop. He could feel the emotions starting to build and knew they would overwhelm him if he didn't pause for a moment. He took a deep breath and staring at the ceiling he exhaled slowly. *Control yourself – you're a leader now,* he reminded himself and then he continued. "Dad had a heart attack."

"Is he recovering?" Marge, his secretary, asked.

"Sadly, no." Norman explained.

The questions seemed to come from every direction at once. "I don't know a lot but I'll tell you what I've gotten so far. He was driving through Delaware late last night. He had pulled the car to the side of the road. He was only 25 minutes from our home when the heart attack happened." Pausing, he raised his cup and the others followed suit. "To Dad. To John Woodrow Wilson. God bless you and may you rest in peace. Amen."

"Amen," echoed the assembled staff. And they all drank.

Three of the staff stepped forward as if to console him, but Norman held up his hands. "Please," Norman explained, "I'm okay. Thank you. Now, Marge, please get me two seats on the next commuter flight to Rehoboth, will you?"

"Certainly."

Norman then continued: "There's going to be a wake on Saturday in Rehoboth Beach. We're a tight group. I certainly would like to have all you with the family for the wake and the funeral on Monday. We will make all the arrangements for your travel and lodging. Marge um, you know- I am sure you will take care of those things for us." The woman was an expert at logistics. For years, Marge could always step up when needed to handle things for the family as well as the business.

Norman looked from one stunned face to another, racking his brain for a way to break the somber mood. Nothing came to mind. He was never very good at dealing with emotional people. The tissues and handkerchiefs were out, "sorry" seemed to come from every direction. Norman remained polite and continued.

"We all know things are pretty slow right now. Yes, we were supposed to get the preliminaries on the Collingswood development under way today. It can wait until after the funeral. I think we'll take a long weekend. So, go home. Everyone take some time. Switch the phones to the answering service until Wednesday, no let's make that Thursday. We'll all get back together next Thursday morning and begin the new project."

There was general agreement to this proposal. Heads nodded, yet nobody moved.

"Come on, people, let's closed up shop," Ginny the receptionist directed. *Always the mother hen*, Norman observed silently.

Everyone turned to go as Beth the company comptroller announced, "I think I'm going to drink an early lunch."

"Um," Norman interjected, "Beth, I need to have a private word with you, first."

The others turned. Norman could detect their alarm at his meeting with the company comptroller privately.

"Hey," Norman spoke up. "Everything's okay. It's no big deal. We've got a well-oiled machine here and our next project is going to proceed as planned."

The others didn't seem certain, so he quickly added: "I need a small advance on my allowance, okay?"

Without intending it, his little quip lightened everyone's mood. They'd heard Norman use the expression before. It was a running joke among this very tight group.

"Wrap up whatever needs to be wrapped up today and take a long weekend." He repeated over his shoulder as he headed up the stairs with Beth following him.

Once upstairs, he turned to Beth. "Everything's fine," he began. "I've checked out all the paper work. I'm written in on the deal, so everything's going to go as planned now I'm in charge."

"I'll make sure the others understand. This is all so sudden-"

"Right," Norman interrupted. "It's horrible, but a small problem needs immediate attention."

"How much?"

"An investment of mine has gone sour and I need to cover my margin. I need cash until I can move a few things around in my own holdings."

"Don't bullshit me, Norman. How much are you talking about?"

"Ten thousand."

Beth didn't say anything. She just gave him one of her motherly looks.

"Yeah, I know," Norman chimed in after a pause. "Dad would be pissed. I know. Well, I'm pissed enough for both of us so he doesn't have to be here. Can you help me out?"

"I can't help you today, Norman. The new lines of credit don't begin until next Friday. The first part of the Collingswood money is not in place until the twenty-fifth of the month."

"Yeah, I know." Norman added with a sigh. "Shit."

"Can your broker carry you until next Friday?"

"I hope so," Norman mumbled, turning away and glancing out the window.

"I beg your pardon?"

"I'm sure he will," Norman lied. *Damn, where- shit. How risky is it to leave pre-Columbian artifacts in the customs shed at JFK.? Things disappear. Ten grand by Monday. Where? Maybe that freak at the bank? I do not want to ask Turlino to call things off until next Friday. And worry for eight days that those artifacts are safe in the fucking customs shed.*

"Excuse me, Norman." Beth's voice brought him back to the moment. "Is there anything else?"

"No. You can go. Have a drink for me, will ya?"

At that point the intercom buzzer went off, followed by Marge's instructions. "Norman, you're on the 11:30 flight out of National. I've called a cab to get you in twenty minutes."

"Thank you," he replied into the machine. Then looking up, he noticed Beth was still standing there. "Yes?"

"I'll stick around. I mean, if you, if you want, I mean, I'll continue for you- doing the work I've always done for your Dad."

"That is good to know, Beth, because I am going to need you."

Biting her lip, the elderly accountant turned and left the office.

Norman was unmoved at the sight of this woman's pain. But her words did remind him of one important thing. He was in charge. He was getting the company. Not Kyle. Not Trish. Him. A small consolation, if Turlino can't get those artifacts out of customs.

Deciding to jump right into the fray, Norman tried to reach Turlino at his office, but he was "out."

Hanging up the phone, he reminded himself there was a bit of good news. *Since Dad's gone, I'll be able to finagle the whole amount from the business and get my ass out of hot water. Even if they do wind up with a part of the business, Trish and Kyle will be too stupid to find out about it.*

* * *

As the plane was taxiing down the runway, Norman's thoughts shifted. The reality of the situation was becoming clearer. He was only 28 years old and he was returning home to bury his father. He wondered to himself, *does it mean I'm getting old?* But the thought shifted. He wondered about funerals, and remembered the last funeral in the Wilson family. Johnny's.

He hadn't thought a lot about the twins for some time. When he was younger it was different. He thought about them a lot. He was alternately fascinated and annoyed by his younger brothers. They were so close. He marveled how Kyle and Johnny looked so much alike. It mystified him. It also made him very competitive with them. He always needed to win, always needed to dominate.

Norman's mind wandered through memories of life with the twins. He recalled a night years ago when he was ten and the twins were eight years old.

His gaze turned to the window of the plane and he watched the Virginia suburbs recede behind them. *Even then they were strange. Dad and Mom had gone out for their anniversary, leaving us with Venus, the housekeeper. Yeah, it was at the dinner table. Kyle started to get a very strange look on his face, like he was going to throw up his dinner all over the place. Johnny got off his chair, stood next to Kyle, placed his hand on Kyle's chest and said, "don't be sick, now." Kyle looked at Johnny and the two of them stared at each other silently for the longest time. No words. Just stared. Right. Trish shouted something dumb like, "they're being weird again!" Venus came back into the room and was standing behind the boys asking if everything was all right. Kyle tilted his head to the side, swallowed once, then once more and said, "Okay."*

*Johnny then said the strangest damn thing I will never forget. "See, it works," he told Kyle. Then he returned to his chair and both the twins finished up their dinner like nothing had happened. What is it they had between them?*

The evening Norman was remembering was a milestone in the lives of his twin brothers. Of course, Norman was unaware of it.

"What works?" Norman asked impatiently. "What are you talking about Johnny?"

"They're being dumb- as usual," Trish chimed in.

Johnny finished chewing a mouthful of food. He looked at Norman, shrugged and said, "I don't know." With great concentration, he took his spoon and began moving peas from one side of his plate to the other.

Norman became insistent, but Johnny wouldn't answer.

"Johnny! Tell me what you're talking about!"

Finally, Kyle spoke up. "He thinks we can help each other. Since we're twins, we can do things like that. He knows all my spelling words without me telling him and I know all his math answers- ya know- stuff like that."

Norman was mystified. Trish thought it was pretend because Kyle was always trying for attention. Venus chalked it up to kids being kids.

The old feelings of annoyance crept back and tightened Norman's jaw. *Damn*, he thought. *The twins*. He stared out the window, looking for a distraction. The plane was flying over the

Chesapeake Bay. He looked for boats, even saw a few, but they weren't enough to distract him. The other memory came back– the one he wouldn't recall too often. The memory of the night he'd stolen his mother's car at two a.m. for a joy ride with a couple of buddies. It was two months before he was to get his driver's license. He considered it good practice, and it definitely impressed the guys.

But one joy-riding night did not end well.

# CHAPTER EIGHT

## *A TWIN IS MURDERED*

In 1962, Norman Wilson was 15 years old, and he loved cars. The most important thing to him that year, even more than coping a feel off Lisa Carlton, was getting his license. And the new Pontiac GTO his Dad had promised.

He was also impatient. He couldn't wait until he was 16 when he would be able to get his driver's permit and legally drive an automobile. So, he would sneak out of the house at two in the morning and take his stepmom's sedan for a drive.

Part of it dealt with his never-ending desire to be tough, cool and grown-up. His good looks and athletic achievements had gained him some notoriety. But he was certain he could turn more heads driving his new GTO around the local hamburger drive-in.

The last time he would ever sneak out with the family car, he drove around Woodmoor with a couple friends. Norman was feeling like a real hot shot.

They had never kept the car out that long. Minnie became very paranoid and thought every car behind them was the police. After several such "sightings," Norman and Paul got very irritated with their friend. They threatened to de-pants Minnie, kick his ass out of the car by the high school, and make him walk home. At that, Minnie clamed up.

Shortly thereafter, they dropped him off a couple of doors from his home.

Paul and Norman cruised around for another ten minutes. Then Norman drove his buddy home, and headed for his own.

A block from his house, Norman came to a stop before pulling out on Route 29. He was about to enter the intersection when a kid stepped out in front of the car. It was his brother Johnny. Norman broke quickly. Then he hit one of the buttons to his left which lowered the passenger's side window.

"Jesus, Johnny, what the hell are you doing out this late at night? Get in!"

Johnny crossed around the car to Norman's window, and answered: "No. You shouldn't be out. I saw you leave and been waiting."

"Get in the damn car!" Norman cut him off.

Johnny refused.

Norman quickly opened the door of the car, causing Johnny to jump back, and he hopped out of the car. Norman was still a little annoyed at his brother from earlier in the day. Johnny was teasing him about his inability to handle the day's "new math" homework.

"Get in the-"

"Be realistic, Norman. Dad's seriously going to punish you if you get caught, you know. I wanted to-"

Norman cut him off. "And how's he gonna find out, huh? You gonna tell him?"

"He's gonna find out some time. You're gonna get caught."

Norman couldn't quite comprehend why his brother gave two shits if he got caught or not. He couldn't comprehend that the kid cared for him.

He was about to comment on it, *why does he even give a shit?'* he was thinking, when he noticed the lights of another car coming over the rise. A touch of Minnie's paranoia crept over him. No time for questions. He grabbed his protesting brother with one hand and shoved him into the vehicle. Norman hopped in, threw the car into gear then headed away from their block.

"Let's take the car back."

"Why?"

"Take me home," Johnny demanded.

"Maybe."

"Take me home, Norman!"

"Shut up and stop being such a twerp."

"You stop being such a show-off, Norman. You're so hot you have to sneak out of the house in the middle of the night and drive around with your friends? Who are you trying to impress? You could ruin a lot of things if you get caught, you know?"

This made Norman particularly angry because Norman knew Johnny was right. Nothing made Norman angrier.

"Shut up Johnny and behave a little more mature, huh?"

"Oh yeah, sure, Norman Wilson, the mature male. You're so full of yourself. Kyle's right."

"What's Kyle saying now?" Norman asked, bringing the car to a stop by the dead end on far side of Woodmoor. Ahead of them was a wooden barrier that blocked cars from driving down the steep wooded hill. Beyond that were woods and the path leading down to the Northwest Branch of the Patuxent River. "Kyle's got a lot of opinions, doesn't he?" Norman added.

He switched off the car's headlights. They reflected too intensely off the wooden barrier's black and yellow stripes.

"All you think of is right now. What Norm wants when Norm wants it. There is a future, you know."

*The last thing in the world I want right now is to have a snotty, fourteen-year-old feeding me that kind of shit.* "Get out of the car," Norman demanded.

"No."

"Get out!"

What are you going to do, huh?"

"Something I've wanted to do for a long time, you little shit."

Norman flung open his door. Then he slammed the gearshift into park, grabbed his brother by his left arm and hauled him out of the car after him.

At the onset, Norman pretended he was angrier than he was. He figured he's punch the kid around a little, put a little fear into him and get the twerp to stay out of his business.

Norman pulled a little too hard. Johnny landed on the

gravel beside the car, scraping the palms of his hands and tearing the knee of his chinos.

"Get out!"

"Ow! That hurt, Norman!"

"You're a little shit, you know that?"

"You know I'm not gonna tell!"

"How do I know for certain?"

"I won't!"

"What about telling me how to run my life? Who the hell are you giving me advice, huh?"

The anger swelled up in Norman. He wasn't acting any more. He couldn't contain it. He punched out at his brother, catching him on the shoulder.

"You gonna talk to Dad?"

"No," Johnny replied.

Norman punched a little harder against Johnny's shoulder. Then he faked a punch to Johnny's face, pulling the punch short of the boy's nose. Johnny reached up to cover his face.

"You're lying!" Norman shouted.

"No, I'm not!"

Johnny brought his hands away from his face. The blood from his scrapped palms left markings on his forehead and left cheek.

The sight of blood on his little brother's face made Norman feel powerful and mean. He liked the feeling and punched out again. This time, Johnny successfully dodged the punch. That really pissed Norman off.

"You're a liar most of the time, aren't you, John-John?"

"Not true! Come on, Norman, let's-"

"You are, Johnny! A liar!" The anger overpowered Norman's reason. He swung out, striking his brother square on the mouth. Norman was overwhelmed by an irrevocable desire to hurt his brother as much as he could.

Johnny moaned and blood dribbled out his mouth.

Norman landed another punch in the boy's face which made him stumble backwards.

"Come on, fight back, you twerp!"

"Let's go home, plea-"

But the "please" turned into a yelp as Johnny fell against the wooden barrier with some force. With a look of panic on his face, Johnny flipped over the barrier and out of sight. There was a crash and a rustling of branches and leaves as Johnny tumbled down the hill into the dark woods.

Norman began laughing, but his laughter caught in his throat. There was suddenly a very sick, very hollow, feeling in his stomach. His legs felt like dried hollow reeds.

It wasn't Johnny's continued cries of anguish. It was the sickening thud that silenced them.

"Johnny?" he called tentatively.

Silence.

"Johnny, cut it out now!" Norman yelled, hopping the barrier and staring out down the hill. "Johnny!" he hissed. "Stop this!" A tree branch poked him in the eye causing Norman to flinch and lose his balance. His shirt snagged on the underbrush as Norman fell over on his side and hit his head against a stone.

The pain rekindled his anger.

"Johnny, you shit! Answer me!" He hissed, snatching his shirt away from the annoying underbrush.

Nothing.

No response; merely the sounds of the woods at night.

Norman heard the sound of a big truck barreling down route 29 in the distance. Then it was quiet, and there was the cold stinging pain on the side of his head.

Norman stood up. He took a few steps. His eyes were now used to the darkness and he found his way back onto the path leading down to the river. There was something by the side of the path a few feet away. He hurried to it. With a little moonlight coming through the trees, Norman could see his brother was very still. He could also see Johnny's head was lying in an unnatural position.

Instantly, Norman knew something he didn't want to know.

He hurried over, knelt next to his brother. The boy's lifeless eyes were open, staring at nothing. Norman couldn't move. He looked down at his dead brother for what seemed like the rest of his life. Then he took Johnny into his arms and began crying unlike he had ever cried in his short lifetime. He held his brother tight, as if trying to force some of what was his life into the warm, but unmoving boy in his arms. He continued to rock back and forth. He cried the remorseful cry of a young man who, at the moment, wished he'd never ever been alive.

He held Johnny tight in his arms for quite a while.

It took two people to separate them: a county cop and the man who lived up the hill who had earlier heard the sounds of a scuffle, a scream and then the sobbing of a young man.

The police, the ambulance, the emergency room, Norman could recall very little. He was in shock and remained in the hospital the next three days for observation. Then he was fine.

He never could recall exactly what happened, or so he said.

* * *

As the plane landed in Delaware, Norman realized he hadn't thought about Johnny's death in a long time. *But then again, I've had more important things to occupy my mind. Money for one. Money is a lot more interesting than remembering a clumsy kid falling and busting his head.*

Before they unbuckled their seatbelts, Susan put her hand on her husband's thigh. She leaned over and kissed him on the cheek.

"So deep in thought. I'll bet you have big plans now."

"You bet I do."

"And you'll be more successful than ever. Remember, I'm here for you, lover. Whatever you need."

They snapped their seatbelts open, leaned into each other and kissed passionately. She then whispered in his ear, "later, how about an 'afternoon delight?'"

"You got it," he whispered.

*Damn, sometimes she knows exactly the right thing to say. She is a keeper. Certainly, a keeper.*

Susan snuggled closed to him as he drove the rental car from the airport to Henlopen.

*Maybe, just maybe,* Norman thought, *"everything is going to work out fine."*

* * *

John Wilson, Jr. was dead at age fourteen leaving Kyle feeling very much alone. He stayed at the funeral home all day long, seated on a couch near the open casket. He stared at his brother in a box of polished wood surrounded by floral tributes from family and friends. He would not eat. He was not sleeping and he would only talk to his Aunt Rebecca. He didn't cry, not at the wake, not at the church and not at the graveside ceremony. Big boys weren't supposed to cry. Many remarked how "strong" Kyle was.

The evening after the burial, he and his Aunt Rebecca snuck away from the family and she drove Kyle to the cemetery.

Aside a wilting mound of floral arrangements, Kyle tried to comprehend his loss. It was too massive. He found himself telling the flowers, "it hurts so much!"

That was it. Saying those words out loud cracked his forced composure. Massive waves of grief overcame him. He dropped to his knees sobbing uncontrollably and it seemed nothing would stop him. In his delirium he could feel someone holding and rocking him. A hand was holding his. Kyle imagined it was his twin brother.

*Don't leave me again! Don't leave again!* Kyle suddenly remembered the first time he knew fear. It was before they had entered this world.

*It was dark and warm and I could feel you next to me- then you left and I was alone in that dark world. I was scared I would never be with you ever. I was so frightened.*

He started chanting "don't let me go, Johnny, don't let me

go, don't let me go," over and over and over. Tears continued to flow until he was cried out and he was so hoarse he could only produce guttural sounds. Every breath he exhaled became a pitiful moan.

Rebecca rocked her grieving nephew as long as her back held out. It became too much for her.

"Kye, honey. Kye, it's getting dark. We should get you home. Come on, time to get up and-"

"No."

"Sorry honey, I gotta-"

"I wanna die," he uttered. "I wanna die."

"Well, you will someday, but it seems the good Lord has other things in mind."

With some effort, the boy repeated slowly, "I want to die."

"You maybe, not me, honey, but I just might if I remain on this damp ground."

With some effort, the boy moaned hoarsely, "I am not leaving him."

His Aunt Rebecca then held him tightly and began weaving a tale for him. She conjured images of guardian angels. She explained how good souls like Johnny don't lay around heaven with their feet up. They join forces and watch out for others all over the world. "He's a spirit now," she concluded, "free to be anywhere he wants. If you were him would you want to stick around this gloomy place?" She reached down and placed her hand over the boy's heart as she explained, "And a part of him will always be right here. Here inside you."

Kyle experienced a moment of loving warmth beneath his

solar plexus. It reminded him of a moment at the dinner table when Johnny put his hand on his chest and the pain disappeared.

It all made perfect sense to Kyle. *He still loves me.* He got up, held his hand out to his aunt, and helped her get to her feet. He hugged her tightly, then took her by the hand and led her to the car.

Standing next to it was his father. Kyle ran and enjoyed his warm embrace.

"We'll get through this together, son." The elder Wilson intoned, "together. I promise."

*  *  *

Norman was never prosecuted for Johnny's murder. The death was ruled "accidental."

He and his father agreed Norman would go away to a military academy for the remainder of his high school years. And the boy would not get his driver's license until he finished high school with good grades.

Norman did both.

# CHAPTER NINE

## *THINGS GET TRIPPY*
### *Thursday Evening in Woodmoor*

When Kyle awoke on the cold basement floor, there was a moment where he could not remember how he'd gotten there. He stood up. He felt very light.

"Hello, Kyle," came a familiar voice.

*Huh?* Kyle turned. On the bar nearby sat his twin brother.

"What the fuck? Oh shit. I'm dead. Son of a bitch!"

"No not dead," his brother explained. "Easiest way to explain is to think of a cosmic hold button."

Kyle turned and looked back to where he fell and saw his unconscious body on the floor. "Johnny, how the fuck —"

"You did it once before. Way back. We were twelve years

old. It was your first out of body experience and it scared the crap out of you."

"I'm not dead?" Kyle asked, turning to his brother.

"No," Johnny said punctuated by one of his familiar 'I know something you don't know yet' grins.

Kyle looked back at himself on the floor. "I look dead." He looked down at the floor and exclaimed, "I am not standing on my feet! What the fuck?"

"It's kind of like floating. Cool, huh?"

When Kyle studied the ghost of his twin brother he experienced the warmest embrace ever. Affection and joy washed over him.

*How is this happening?* he wondered.

"Kyle!" Johnny's voice broke Kyle's reverie. "Stop mind-fucking with it. Enjoy it."

"Is this what it is like to be dead?" Kyle asked.

"Don't go there. Too complex."

"I don't know what to —"

"Of course, you don't."

"I —"

"I love you, too. It's time you leave." He declared and pointed to the body on the floor.

Kyle looked down at his unconscious self. Two shades; two dark evil feeling shadows were approaching his body.

"They will steal you. You have to go back!"

"But I need to know so much!"

"Know I love you and I am helping."

"Is Dad okay?"

"He's fine. Go!"

"How-"

"Dive!"

"Huh?

"Drop and roll! Now!" Johnny commanded.

Kyle did. He rolled toward his body and within less than a second the weight of his flesh and the pain from the fall all returned.

He opened his eyes on a quiet, empty playroom; so familiar to him, so still. He looked toward the bar though he wasn't sure why.

He sat up. It didn't make him feel dizzy, so he started to rise.

"Well, a little woozy," he told himself, and he grabbed the arm and pulled himself up on the deacon's bench.

"What time is it?" he wondered out loud.

The sunlight was coming through the basement windows at a different angle. His watch said four o'clock. Three hours?

He sat.

Still.

Very still.

Then, one at a time, he reconstructed the events of the afternoon like a child assembling tinker toys.

*Mason at the bank, the safety deposit box, okay.*

*Mason invited me for a swim, I went to the deli and Henderson was there. He is now a detective.*

*Then I came here to the house, ate lunch in the car and I fell down the stairs. Oh- whoa - that angry old man came out of the wall, charged at me and disappeared.*

"Time to get the hell out of here," he told the empty room and started to stand but stopped.

"Better sit a moment." He looked toward the stairs. *Are you sure you could navigate without taking another tumble? Tumble? I'm an ex-fucking gymnast. How the hell was I not able to control that fall?*

He looked down at his hand. It was resting on the side table next to a little metal toy car. He picked it up. It was something to do while his head cleared.

In his haze, he turned the toy over and over in his hands, then examined its underside. "Sears Roebuck & Co." it read. He remembered how he and Trish had found it at a flea market in Pennsylvania years ago. They gave it to their stepmother who collected antique toys.

At this point, Kyle discovered the fall on his head brought him more than a bruise.

The fall had ignited his hidden ability- an expanded intuition.

*Whoa. It's like she is here with me. Not like, standing here, but her, what's the word? -presence? What's that scent? Vicki's perfume. Damn! Vicki is happy and giving, isn't she?*

"Where the hell is all this coming from?" he asked himself.

*What the hell? A kid. A boy. He's wearing knickers and scuffed brown shoes, a newsboy's cap and white shirt. He's playing with this car on the* stoop *of a brownstone in the middle of a big city. Cleveland, Ohio. It's 1911 and the boy is missing a finger because of a snake bite two summers prior.*

Kyle shook his head. *I know all that from holding this toy? Un-fucking-believable!*

That startled him. He was well-schooled in that particular psychic power. Years ago, he had studied it. He ran tests on those who had the "gift". *Some gift.*

"Yeah, well," he told the empty basement, "I don't want it!"

He replaced the toy on the end table. Glancing down he saw the files and papers on the floor, and remembered he had to get somewhere. Where was that? For a full minute he tried to put it all together and remember where it was he was supposed to be going. But his search was interrupted when he heard a voice upstairs. It was faint, but discernible. It was a little girl's voice.

"Daddy?" she was whimpering. "Where's Daddy. When are you coming home, Daddy?"

*That is what she is saying, isn't it?*

He was certain.

The haze was beginning to clear and he remembered his father. *Dad. Is Dad here?* he wondered? *No. He's died,* Kyle reminded himself. The recollection made him very sad. *The girl is sad, too,* he found himself thinking, *and I'm alone. I'm never going to see my father again, either. Dad. Dad had a heart attack and died.*

He looked down at the floor and at the scattered papers. He was feeling very sorry and very alone and a little frightened and he started to cry. It was as if he were a little boy again; a little boy left alone, and he wanted to be with his father very, very much.

*But Dad's gone now. Gone.*

The words echoed in his head as he leaned against the back of the bench. As he often did when he was little, he drew his knees up and held them tight to his chest. He couldn't stop crying. He wanted to be held and comforted and rocked and taken care of. But he was alone.

As the emotions ebbed, he was sobered by another thought: *I need to go home.*

*But I am home, aren't I? No, Kyle,* he corrected himself, *home to Henlopen. The Henlopen home near the ocean. Take those papers and go home to the family.*

"Okay," he said aloud.

In a little boy fashion, he wiped his tears away with the back of his hands. He then knelt down, gathered the papers and put them back into the strongbox.

He had nearly completed the task when he heard voices upstairs. They were the muffled voices he had heard so often as a child; when he was much younger and was alone in the basement. Then, as in the past, he remembered he was alone in the house. The fear began to rise, starting as it used to do, at the base of his spine. A warm sensation crept down each of his arms and turned into gooseflesh. He remembered the face. He remembered the man in the hunting jacket, the cut above his eye, the distorted, evil face so consumed with hate.

Kyle's hair stood up on the back of his neck.

He gripped the strongbox and started for the stairs, all the while knowing he didn't want to run. He wanted to be more cautious this time. He had to be. He had to get home. He carefully took each step up to the first floor. All along he knew something was behind him. He knew it. And whatever it was, it wanted to grab him and drag him back into the basement. But it didn't. It lingered back there, laughing at him. It was laughing and staring and it knew he would be back.

*Be back?* Kyle asked himself. *No way. No way I will ever step foot into this house again.*

"Yeah," he admonished himself, "said those words before, haven't I?"

He closed the sliding door behind him and headed across the wide patio toward his car. As he pulled his car keys from the pocket of his jeans there was something snagged to it.

*Hmmm. Business card. Mason's business card.*

He studied it for a moment. *The address- his folk's place up the road.*

"Well, I could use some human company right about now," he told himself aloud trying to lighten his mood.

He tossed the strong box into the trunk of the car and headed north to the old gentrified Burnt Mills community. The old oak trees, winding roads and rolling lawns read "old money." He recognized the stone wall and turned up the driveway towards a Tudor style home. You wouldn't call it a mansion, but it was bigger than your average suburban home.

He pulled up beside a corvette stingray parked outside the double car garage.

Kyle pressed the doorbell and could hear the chime echo inside the house. *This place is sure big for one guy.* There was a light on in the living room and a couple widows on the second floor had a soft light glow of lamplight.

He waited. No sound of footsteps. *Aw shit, maybe he is occupied. I don't want to barge in on him. Maybe this wasn't such a good idea. Probably swimming and doesn't hear the bell.* He was torn. *Run for the car? Pound on the door demanding sanctuary?* Instead, he turned toward the lawn expecting to see some horrible specter.

147

Behind him the door opened with a very loud screech.

"Holy shit!" Kyle screamed.

"Yeah, gotta remember to oil those hinges one of these days."

Standing in the doorway backlit by the hallway light was Daniel Mason in a white bathrobe.

"Mason! I am very happy to see you!"

"What a nice thing to say. Come in! Come in! You're in time for a swim!"

"First I need a drink." And with that, Kyle walked past his friend and into the house. "Yes, right where I remember it," Kyle said as he spotted the liquor cart next to the large stone fireplace.

"Sure. Make yourself at home."

"Thank you," Kyle responded heading for the bar. But something on the massive glass coffee table stopped him. "A water pipe? Mace? A water pipe?"

"And this surprises you? A lot has changed in five years, Kye."

"But you were so straight!" Kyle marveled.

"Kyle, you say the damnedest things. I thought you- well, I guess after Key West we didn't see much of each other, did we? "Would you like a toke or two?"

"You are my savior in more ways than one," Kyle responded taking a seat on the couch near the pipe. Mason started to sit in a chair opposite.

"No, Mace, please, sit here. Right next to me. Please."

Mason complied and as he settled on the couch he reached over to touch Kyle's face asking, "have you been in a fight? I mean your eyes are so red- oh shit, I didn't mean- sorry. That was insensitive, I mean in light of your Dad passing and-"

"You got it, Mace." Kyle figured, why lie? "A real honest to god crying jag. I am kind of a mess."

Mason reached out and hugged his friend, "Kye, I am so sorry." Kyle was happy to lean his head on Mason's shoulder and Mason began stroking the back of his friend's head.

"Ow! Gentle there Mace, gentle."

"That's a lump! You were in a fight!"

"No. Nothing so exciting. I fell down the basement stairs and landed on my head. I sure would love it if we could fire up your little friend here. Do that and I will tell you the saga of Kyle and the ghost in the basement."

"You want some ice for your head?" Kyle shook his head, no. "Okay then," Mason continued as he reached for a small silver box on the table. Lifting its lid, he took out a pair of tweezers. He used them to put several little brown squares into the bowl of the water pipe. "You're gonna enjoy this," he said with a grin and handed one of the pipe's tubes to Kyle.

They each took several tokes, lounged back on the couch and then Kyle began.

"Remember how we used to joke our house was haunted? Well, it's true."

"You saw Johnny?"

"No. That would have been pleasant. Whoever it was, he was one ugly, angry son of a bitch who I could swear was out to fucking beat the shit out of me. He had these wild eyes and a big woolly beard and he came charging at me. He was right in my face and he vanished."

"In the basement of your home down the road there?"

"Believe me I have seen all kinds of shit in the past, but it was the scariest thing I have ever seen."

Kyle reached over, hugged his friend's arm. "You have no idea how glad I am to find you at home. Yes, I know I am sort of stoned, but I fucking mean it, Mace. I need human contact right now and of all my old friends I could turn to I am so glad it is you."

"You are welcome. Any time."

The two young men stared at one another for a moment. Mason went to kiss his friend, but Kyle stopped him by asking, "Why did you leave me, Mace?"

"Oh," was all he could reply then he took a deep breath. "Not one of my better moves, was it?" He tried to sit up, but Kyle wouldn't let go of his arm.

Pulling his friend close to him, but not looking at him, Kyle found himself asking, "Was Mr. Key West better than me?"

"Geez, Kye, no. No. Definitely not better. Not better in so many ways. It seemed like such a good idea at the time. But when I finally realized I was being a total idiot, you had latched on to Cyndy so I figured we were done."

"You came to the apartment when I was out, cleaned out your things, took all your clothes, and some of mine."

"Hey, we bought those Speedo's together. I only took half."

"That's fair. Oh, and thanks for doing the dishes by the way." With that they looked at each other and both started laughing.

"Oh god, I did, didn't I?" Mason shouted between laughs. "I washed the fucking dishes for you! I can be such a faggot."

"We were each other's faggots, weren't we?" Kyle asked, again squeezing his friend's arm.

"That we were," Mason agreed.

"And then- then you went off to Stamford-"

"Then Columbia."

"And not even a Christmas card."

"I didn't want to be 'the other woman'."

Kyle laughed at that.

"What is so funny?"

"Funny? The most butch of homos I have ever met cannot refer to himself as 'the other woman.' That is so not you!" Kyle paused, looked at his friend for a moment and then observed, "you still have such a grounded presence. And I don't say it because I am stoned and have experienced the fright of my fucking life. And not because my need to be with someone strong and steady right now for fear of losing my fucking mind."

"You are safe here. I grant you sanctuary! And I will protect you from the boogieman, promise."

Kyle didn't reply. He laid his head on Mason's shoulder and snuggled closer to his old friend.

With his head leaning against Kyles, Mason was contentedly thinking. *After all these years, the man I still love very much is seated right here. If this moment never comes again, that's okay. I have this one. For now, life is good.*

Kyle broke the silence. "I am sorry I hurt you, Mace. I mean that sincerely.

"Thank you, Kye. I'm sorry I hurt you. You chose to be with Cyndy. We both moved on."

"Does it have to be straight or gay, Mace? Does it have to be one or the other? Don't answer now, my friend- some other time. For now, a swim would help wash the bad parts of the day off of me."

"Then come on, let me show you my favorite part of the old homestead. I did the upgrade last summer."

He led his friend toward the back of the house and down a couple steps and stopped. Mason hit a light switch. There, laid out before them was a two-lane lap pool. The underwater lighting created shimmery reflections on the ceiling and the windows.

"My very own natatorium! Such a great word, huh? -'natatorium.' So fucking nineteenth century. Two lanes and it's heated!"

"That is far fucking out, Mace!"

"Thank you." And over here-" he led Kyle along the flagstone pool deck for several yards. Then another room opened up on their right. "-a cabana with wet bar. And through that doorway a bathroom and a private shower.

"All right! Let me get my bag from the car!"

"No need," Mason explains as he opened one of the doors on a tall wardrobe. "Plenty of towels and in those drawers there- go ahead, open them. Check it out. Plenty to choose from."

Kyle opened the drawer. It was almost overflowing with colorful nylon swim suits for both men and women. Kyle ran his hand across the pile of silky nylon speedo swim briefs.

"That's quite a collection."

"There are more upstairs. Kind of excessive, I guess, but I have every suit I ever bought since we started swimming. You still keep all yours?"

"Mine and Johnny's believe it or not."

"I kept those three of Johnny's you gave me. It's a harmless fetish, don'tcha think?"

"Yeah," Kyle agreed, taking a green speedo from the drawer. Then turning to Mason, he began, "I like to wear them as often as-" but he stopped. Mason had dropped his robe. He stood there clad only in a red speedo that had white side panels framing its rather over-stuffed front. "Well, you stayed in good shape."

"Thank you. I swim every day when home."

Kyle made no move to change.

"What? You've gotten shy since our days together? S'not like I haven't seen every-"

"Oh, no, I'm admiring the scenery." And with that, Kyle slipped off his shoes, removed his shirt and dropped his Levi's. "Take the compliment."

"Hmmm, thanks. Still wearing skimpy briefs, I see."

He was. But not for long. He removed his briefs and stood there a moment, allowing Mason to see what he was sure Mason was waiting to see.

"Stuff all that into the Speedo and meet me in the water," Mason remarked then turned and walked over to the pool.

Kyle slid the Speedo on as he watched his friend's very sculpted butt cheeks slightly rise and fall as he walked. Apollo came to mind. Not Rodin's or Michelangelo's. Not that beefy. Mason was muscular but lithe, more like Bernini's Apollo.

*Oh yes. What was once a very sexy boy, he thought, had become a very sexy man.*

As he admired his friend's physique, Kyle realized his hand was on the bulge of the Speedo. It was doing what it always did when he put on another guy's swim brief.

153

Then Quickly shifting his focus away from Mason's butt to his back, Kyle noticed- "Wow! The scar!" Kyle commented a little too loudly.

Mace turned and grinned.

"Sorry, buddy, Kyle added. "A little too loud, huh? It's the crazy smoke."

"Um hum," Mason commented as he slid into the water. It wasn't deep. The water line was not as high as Mason's well-defined pecs.

"I remember where you got it: Dickerson's quarry. We skipped school to spend the day swimming. You insisted you had to swim down to look for the school bus, didn't you?"

"Found the legendary crane on the steam shovel down there, didn't I?"

"You left some of your flesh on it, too. Damn good thing Montgomery General wasn't too far a drive, huh? How many stiches was that? Eighteen or twenty?"

"Twenty-three, but who's counting. Get into the water, Kye."

As Kyle slipped into the water, Mason explained. "I am going to do a mile, but you do as many laps as you want. If you finish before me, there are robes in the wardrobe there. Grab one and relax on one of the chaise lounges there."

"Good plan."

"Here," Mason said, handing Kyle a pair of swim goggles. "You are going to need these."

"Yes. Yes of course. Whew, almost forgot. Thanks."

"I take good care of you." And with that, Mason slipped his goggles off his forehead and over his eyes and took off swimming.

Kyle found the goggles fit him perfectly. Then realized why. There were once a pair of his.

Kyle kicked off and began his swim. He did not even try to keep pace with Mason. He simply enjoyed the water flowing over him along with memories of the handsome man in the next lane who he had known for most of his life. There was regret that he and Mason had been out of touch for so long.

# CHAPTER TEN

## *IN, OUT AND AROUND THE POOL*
### *Later Thursday Evening*

After swimming a little more than half a mile, Kyle wrapped up in a robe. He took a seat on the chaise lounge and enjoyed watching Mason's steady progress in the lap pool, wondering at their dedication to fitness. Neither of them was a "body queen." They liked to stay in shape.

"Ya feel better and it gets ya laid!" Henderson would often say whenever physical fitness was debated.

Kyle laid back on the chaise and stared at the light reflecting on the natatorium ceiling. Like the rippling reflections on the ceiling, a variety of thoughts flowed in Kyle's memory.

*Henderson. Nice seeing him this afternoon. Great thing about Mike Henderson is he never made a big deal of our being gay. If*

*Johnny had lived would he be bisexual like me? Nah, he would have probably chosen to be a breeder he was pretty tight with weird Alice. Henderson's not married, but I heard he was living with some chick. Not exactly a question I could have asked him in front of his Dad this afternoon though.*

Kyle watched Mason's smooth flip turn and debated whether or not to return to the pool for a better work out. *Mom always encouraged us to stay active, Trish as well. Both parents discouraged them from watching television even on rainy days. There was always table tennis, bowling or the massive roller rinks in the area.*

*It was always important we stay "in the pink" as Dad called it.*

*Ah yes. Dad. Funny thing is he was never too demanding or a bully about it. Getting exercise and staying fit was part of our lives. Since Mason was practically the "fifth Wilson kid," he picked up on all our sport obsessions. Dad had us all swimming at a very early age. Most of my earliest memories are near water. Like sitting with Mom at the club and watching Dad swim laps in that enormous pool.*

The steady sounds of Mason cutting through the water helped lull Kyle into a more relaxed state of mind. That made it easier to shove aside thoughts of what happened back in Woodmoor.

*Positive memories. Keep focused on positive memories. Growing up with Johnny was positive. I'm positive I'm enjoying wearing Mason's Speedo right now or is it Johnny's?*

Kyle closed his fingers on the waistband of the swim brief and concentrated. "Reading" the Speedo was not an easy task. The thoughts were fuzzy.

*Must be the THC. Hmm. Being stoned hinders my power. Pot is my kryptonite? There's a concept.*

He concentrated on the swim brief again. The knowledge it was Mason's caused him to slowly bone up.

*Speedos and boning up. Classic memories. How often did that happen? Just about every time I read my comic books. Wasn't it one of Batman and Robin's adventures I was reading when it first happened? Yes. I was on my stomach on the floor reading when Johnny came bursting into the room – "I got my first stiff dick! Want to see it?" -and I rolled over and Johnny pointed down at my Speedo. "Kye! Kye! You, too! That is fantastic!" He wanted to run off and show Norman but I stopped him. Why did I do that? Johnny was always so more open about things sexual. He was much more comfortable about those things than I was. Was. Yeah, he kind of changed that in me, didn't he?*

*Oh shit, the first time Johnny and I got our gymnastics clothing. No way could either of us put on a leotard without popping one. Yeah, jacking off became a necessity. Then we learned wearing a snug dive Speedo under the 'tard held things down. At least until there was an appropriate time to "please yourself" as Dad once put it.*

*But the second season of gymnastics- I have never again been that horny. And Mason, holy shit, what a machine. And it made him so aggressive that even Alice complained. Then there was the time during gymnastics practice. We were vaulting. Pushing off the vaulting box, Mason would let out a guttural wail. It was so weird Coach Cooper commented, "you attack the vault box like an animal in heat! Be gentler, Mason! There's a grace to gymnastics. Imagine you're a feather on the wind, not a moose in heat."*

*How could we not? For the rest of high school, he was "the moose" or just"moose." And he seemed to enjoy it because it had such manly connotations. Yeah, he did more and more to maintain the image of heterosexuality. In the privacy of our bedrooms, however, it was different. And he missed Johnny so much after "the incident."*

*Happy memories. Come on, Kyle,* he reminded himself, *happy memories. Good memories of Dad?*

Kyle felt a warm feeling in his chest. *Teaching me to jump off the side of the pool without my swim ring —he was so patient. Did I thank him enough?* He had a feeling that would return many times for the next year or so: to reach for a phone and call his father. *Telephone call to Dad?*

The silent conversation with himself continued. *That's never stopped you from talking to Johnny, has it? Oh fuck. No way am I going to trance out and have a chat with Dad. I am done with that shit.* "I don't do that anymore!" he muttered as he came out of his reverie.

"Huh?" Kyle opened his eyes to a wonderfully homoerotic sight- Daniel Mason in a tight red Speedo.

"You just said, 'I don't do that anymore.' Are you having an argument with someone I should know about?" asked Mason who was standing there toweling off. "I know you've communed with spirits —"

"That's consumed spirits, my friend."

"Uh huh. You forget one of my friends followed your exploits. She kept me informed of your chasing haunts in four states and the District of Columbia. I, my friend, have kept tabs on you."

"Weird Alice?"

"Please, she's 'Lady Alice' now and a respectable authoress and seer. Did you know she's done work with your old inspiration,

Mr. Holzer? Did you know she is currently shacking up with one of the county's boldest and newest police detectives?"

"Henderson? Oh my god. Alice is living with Henderson? Our Alice? No fucking way. You have to be kidding me. Weird Alice and Mr. PC himself?

"Their P and C seem to be getting along quite nicely. And careful what you say about Alice. We were all once virgins together."

"You, me and Johnny. The big difference was with Johnny it was love, for me it was doing me a favor. She was so in love with Johnny."

Mason didn't respond immediately. Then, almost choking on the words, he uttered, "Weren't we all?"

"Whoa, Mason, buddy," Kyle had to ask, "are you uncomfortable talking about Johnny?"

"Ready to shower?" was his response.

"You just dried off."

"Oh. I guess I did."

Kyle realized Mason was nervous. A change of subject was mandatory. He stood up next to Mason as he explained, "a long time ago you asked us to stop calling you 'Moose,' but you know what? You're bigger now, you're taller and you're more solid than ever- like a big bull moose and I think the name is appropriate."

"You're making fun of me."

"No, I am lusting for you." Kyle replied with a grin. He reached over and started massaging Mason.

Kyle stared into Mason eyes. The blue seemed bluer; the green eye brighter than ever.

Kyle wanted to dive into Mason's eyes and stay there where he would be safe from all the challenges ahead.

*How amazing is this, My love for Cyndy and Mason both heating up on the same day? How the hell will this end?*

# CHAPTER ELEVEN

## REBECCA WILSON THOMPSON
### *A Rightful Inheritance*

Rebecca had a window seat on the plane from Chicago to Baltimore's Friendship Airport. It was a clear morning and she enjoyed watching the landscape pass below.

*Why do they insist on calling those things the Appalachian "mountains?" "Foothills" is more like it.*

It was a reaction of someone who grew up in the American Northwest. Compared to the Saw Tooth Mountains and the Rockies, the Appalachians were bumps.

*Then again, a few million years ago the Appalachians were taller than the Himalayas.*

She'd been in an argumentative mood since getting the news that her brother had passed away. Yes, she was sorry her brother had died. She was also angry because there was business between them that has never been resolved.

*Maybe between me and that jackass of a nephew of mine, Norman Wilson.*

For about the seventy-fifth time since yesterday she found herself thinking: *John dies and has the gall to show up at my bedside and tell me to take care of his kids? They're adults now. Why the hell are they my responsibility? Right now, John, I need the help you could give me but you bailed.*

"Excuse me, Ma'am," she heard someone whisper. "Would you like another drink?"

Rebecca forced a smile and told the stewardess, "Yes please. Another Bloody Mary." She watched as the pleasant young lady poured the ingredients into a tumbler. Then she reached over her sleeping husband and exchanged her three dollars for the drink.

"Thank you."

Sipping her drink, she assessed the situation yet another time.

*Goal one: find out who is executor. Is Kyle still cut off? He would be an ally. Goal two and most important: what became of Grandpa's gold coins? He promised me half of it long ago. It will get us out of this mess we're in and I'll actually be able to retire at sixty-five.*

At one point, years ago, Nick had put their savings into real estate investments. The building boom in Chicago proved to be a good thing for them and their friends. Then they got ambitious and overconfident.

Those two Rabbi's had talked them into buying into a proposed chain of nursing homes in New York and New Jersey. The due diligence looked good. The number crunching showed it to be a great investment, but at the time they had no cash. No problem. Mortgages on their real estate holdings were easy to get.

Unfortunately, they ignored the number one rule of investing: "if it looks too good to be true, it probably is."

They saw almost a hundred thousand dollars disappear overnight. There were no real Rabbis, there were no new nursing homes. There was only the one prototype. Unfortunately, it was fake. In reality it was a sleazy rest home where old people were ignored and were dying painful and lonely deaths.

Rebecca paid a visit to her brother on the east coast. She wasn't ready to confess their mistake. She simply told her brother she and Nick needed cash and John had put her off long enough. Where is the inheritance Grandfather promised me?

John patiently explained he had promised the old man he would not touch the money. "You can have it after I am gone."

"Where is it?"

"Rebecca, please let it go. It is safe."

"So, it does exist! He said there were over a thousand twenty-dollar gold pieces. True?"

"One thousand and twenty-three. You have one, I have one and there's one in the safety deposit box. He said it was bad money, Rebecca, and we should leave it alone."

"John, I am in a jam and I need it!"

"I will lend you the money."

"I don't want any more loans! We have loans up to our asses. I need cash, damn it!"

"No!"

No matter what she said, he wouldn't budge.

"It's because I defended Kyle, isn't it? You're still pissed I criticized you for cutting him off when he wanted to try something different other than working with you!"

John Wilson held his tongue.

"Do you know he is still grieving for Johnny? Do you think working with you will fill that hole in his heart? It won't. His work in paranormal research was his way of crying out for help, but you didn't get it, did you? Now he's in Harvard, I hope you've changed your will. If you leave Norman in charge after you die the whole family is gonna be in deep shit, John- the deepest. And you won't be around to bail him out like you always do!"

She had crossed a line. She could see in his eyes that he was about to retaliate, but he took a deep breath and he changed the subject. He invited her to bring Nick and the boys to Henlopen as soon as the weather changed.

Then she lost it. She said things she later regretted and John Wilson never forgot.

She returned to Chicago empty handed.

*And now, he's come to me and asked me to look after Kyle and Norman and make sure they do okay.*

*I am going to have to suck up to Norman. Fine. I got through med school, I birthed three big boys. I have had children die in my arms and held parents in their grief. None of that was as hard as it is going to be for me to be nice to that asshole. But he holds all the trump cards.*

*Maybe there is a new will. Maybe Kyle is in charge.*

Truth is, she truly loved Kyle. She also understood and admired his interest in paranormal activities.

Yesterday's encounter with her brother was not her first

"other worldly experience." Her interest in the paranormal began years prior in the pediatric ward of St. Luke's hospital in Chicago.

She got along very well with the staff at that hospital. They all put effort in caring for the youngsters even though it meant heartache more times than not. They would, after all, lose more young patients than they could cure.

She had heard several legends about the ward. Supposedly, there were several mischievous ghosts. A cart would occasionally travel on its own from one side of the hallway to another. Supplies would go missing from a cart and reappear later at the nurse's station. On rare occasions, they would hear someone whistling "How Much Is That Doggie in The Window?" when there couldn't possibly be anyone there to do it.

One year they had one eight-year-old orphaned Black kid everyone called "little Eddie." The nickname was given to distinguish him from one of the orderlies named Eddie Miller. Little Eddie was favored by the staff because he refused to let the leukemia break his spirit.

Miller would organize the kids for simple games. On some days he had them tossing a playground ball in the wide intersection of the two main corridors of the floor. The tiled floor had a big star in the middle of the intersection, and it would always be used as "the winner's circle." Miller would insist Little Eddie wheel himself into the winner's circle every day because it provided "good mojo" and would energize the boy. In turn, he would tease Miller and call him "witch doctor Ed." He would also take Miller's Newport cigarettes and hide them from him.

It was around Easter time and the staff and some of the children dyed a big batch of Easter eggs. One of the nurses showed them how they could blow the egg out of the shells and keep it intact. The result was several painted eggshells and a colorful mobile hanging near the nurse's station. It hung about six feet from the star.

At the same time, Little Eddie took a turn for the worse and the day they hung the mobile, he died. Everyone did their best to avoid breakdowns in public and to comfort the other children. But there were several of the staff who had an extra drink or three after work to help them cope.

That night, Rebecca was finishing up her paperwork at the nurse's station when she heard a distinct" crack!"

A chill ran up her spine causing an involuntary shiver. Her shoulders shook.

She stood up.

The hallway lights were at their nighttime level. Even still, she could see a broken eggshell in the middle of the tile star. She could also see that one of the eggshells was missing from the mobile- the mobile hanging six feet away.

Rebecca walked over to the star. She looked up and down both corridors. There was no breeze that could cause an eggshell to get loose from the mobile and sail over to the star on the floor.

She then saw Miller was coming out of the lounge. "Hey, Doctor T," he asked as he grew closer. "You seen my Newports? I had the box with me in the lounge. I was reading the paper and when I reached for another smoke the box was gone."

Rebecca didn't answer. She simply pointed to the floor and the broken eggshell.

"Holy Mary, Mother of God," he breathed.

"We were his only family. I think he doesn't want to leave," Rebecca observed.

And for the first time since losing his little friend, Miller broke down and cried. He cried like a baby. Rebecca held him tight.

Miller just sobbed. There seemed to be no bottom to his grief; no way he could stop himself.

When he was able to pull himself together, he took the eggshell pieces, wrapped them in some gauze. He placed the little bundle into his locker.

Then it happened again the next night. Rebecca and Miller were at the nursing station when —"crack!"

Another eggshell dropped.

In the middle of the star.

Again, Miller gathered up the pieces and wrapped them in gauze.

Next morning, they went to the chapel. The nuns had little Eddie dressed in a suit and tie and laid out in a white casket. As his "goodbye," Miller put the two little gauze bundles into the casket with the boy. Then he and Rebecca stood next to the opened casket holding each other. They stared at their little friend for the longest time. There were no tears, only wonder.

After the short funeral service, they accompanied Mother Elizabeth to the cemetery. More prayers were said. Miller helped the attendant shovel dirt over the casket. (Later he would explain it helped him reach a resolution of sorts with his anger.)

It wasn't long before Dr. Rebecca Thompson stopped working at St. Mary's and moved to the new Women's Hospital.

But gossip from St. Mary's would find her. It seemed that every year around Easter, some item from the nurse's station would disappear. Then it would be found on the floor in the middle of the star.

Miller's flip top box of Newport cigarettes would grow legs. He would find them somewhere other than where he had last put them. Eventually he gave up smoking.

Rebecca started reading up on paranormal activities and psychic abilities. At family gatherings, she was fascinated to hear Kyle and Cyndy's stories of their research. Kyle told her of Grandma seeing the little girl bouncing the ball in the living room. And how, when Grandma started to say something, the girl vanished. Rebecca loved the story and had hoped for a sighting when she was in the living room alone. But no luck.

Back in Chicago, Rebecca toyed with the idea of hiring a trance medium to go to the hospital with her. It would be nice, she thought, if they could speak with Little Eddie and help him move on. But on second thought, she felt no one would believe her nor allow such a ritual in the pediatric ward.

She took a swig of her bloody Mary and looked out the plane's window at the pasture lands of Pennsylvania below.

*Farmland. It was a long time ago. Yep, a good life, but I am sure as hell glad I left it; left it to become a veterinarian but became a pediatrician instead. Things don't always work out the way we expect them to.*

The wedding check from Jonathan Wilson helped the young couple decide on their next step. In the Spring of 1937, they left Montana and headed east. They planned to move to

Baltimore, Maryland and study at Johns Hopkins University. First stop, however was to spend time with their benefactor, Jonathan Wilson.

She enjoyed life on the Wilson farm. Nick got along well with the old man and with Rebecca's brother John. Grandpa Wilson was particularly taken with Nick because he was a good listener.

One day, Rebecca and the three men were on the side porch sipping iced teas. Jonathan Wilson was going on about Gettysburg.

Only half listening, Rebecca was watching one of the hands lead a new horse from the trailer to the paddock. Something happened. Something spooked the horse and it started acting wild. It got away from the farmhand and was charging towards the porch.

Rebecca jumped down and grabbed a coil of rope off the fence. The stallion charged straight towards her. Remaining calm, she created a lasso, swung it over and over above her head and at the precise moment let it fly. She got the rope around the horse's neck. She started running to her right as the horse reared up and looked as if it was going to strike her. But Rebecca held on to the rope and she kept moving.

"Get out of there, woman!" Grandpa yelled.

"Rebecca, let him go!" John screamed.

Rebecca ignored them.

"Easy, gentlemen," Nick reassured the men. "She grew up on a horse farm."

Rebecca held up her hand calling for silence and she continued to move and to pull on the rope. She would move, stop and pull on the rope again while talking to the big animal in a flat calm voice.

The horse stopped bucking. It stayed on all fours and snorted at her. It didn't move. She didn't move.

They simply stared at each other for about a full minute.

Rebecca then held up the rope, as if making sure the horse could see what she was about to do. She held out the rope and then dropped it to the ground.

The horse, still looking at her, tilted his head. He snorted, pawed the ground with his right front hoof, but stayed in the same spot.

Slowly, Rebecca walked up to the horse.

He snorted, nodded his head once, then again, never taking his eyes off of her, nor she off of him.

She reached out and took the rope off of his neck and dropped it to the ground. She was talking to him all the while though no one could hear what she was saying.

Then, to everyone's surprise, she grabbed a handful of mane, jumped up on the back of the horse and rode him to the porch.

"Well, Grandpa," she said, "I don't think he liked the travel accommodations." She took a carrot from her jeans pocket, leaned over his neck and gave him a treat. "-and I think he's thirsty."

Grandpa clapped and laughed. He was so impressed he did something he had never done before. He called for a bottle of bourbon and drank with a female member of the family.

After dinner he and Rebecca sat on the porch and talked. He wanted to know her plans.

"I want to go to school, Grandpa. I want to learn all I can

about medicine and caring for animals. Nick plans on studying engineering."

The old man took a few minutes to consider what she's told him, then spoke. "I don't have much time, Rebecca. I know all I've put together here will be well cared for by your brother John. He's worked very hard to make the place profitable. I'm leaving everything to him in my will because he earned it. I would like to do something for you and Nick."

"You've already been so generous, Grandpa."

"Those colleges cost a pretty penny, don't they?"

"Yes, sir."

"I tell you what. I'm going to give your brother and my lawyer strict instructions to take care of that for the two of you. Maybe you'll even come back here someday and give your brother a hand."

"Thank you, Grandpa, I appreciate it very much." She wanted to jump up and give him a hug, but she knew he wasn't comfortable with public displays of affection.

"All I ask in return is you make something of yourselves. I think you have the brain and the guts to do it. Am I right?"

"Absolutely, grandpa. Absolutely!"

"Good. Now, one other thing. You know the coin I had John send you with a check for your wedding?"

"You mean this one?" she said, showing him the coin she had on the chain around her neck.

"Yes, ma'am. You need to know something. There's a whole sack more. You and your brother are the only ones I have told about it. But leave it alone. It's cursed. Maybe someday you two will have a need for it. But for now, leave it be.

"Whatever you say, Grandpa."

"You're gonna get a considerable amount from me so you should never have need to touch that gold. But I guess you should know it's there."

"Can I ask how much it is?

"There are one thousand and twenty-three twenty-dollar gold pieces. Someone was stealing it from me. People died over that money. There's blood on it. You should leave it be, but after I'm gone, well, it's up to you and your brother, understand?"

"Yes, grandpa."

"Good girl. Now, one more drink? A toast to your future in the medical profession."

The old man nodded off in his chair. Rebecca woke her husband and the two of them picked the old man up and put him into his bed.

Before leaving for Baltimore, the old man, John and Rebecca made an agreement. John would keep the gold safe and if it ever became necessary, they were each entitled to half of the gold coins. When the old man died, John continued to pay for both she and Nick through their university years. He also paid Rebecca's way through medical school. Both Nick and Rebecca were making plenty of money. The gold was never a concern until they were swindled. Now that they are over extended and on the verge of losing it all, Rebecca was determined to get her share.

Rebecca looked out the plane window and saw the plane's shadow on the surface of the Chesapeake Bay. She played with a gold coin she wore on a chain around her neck and remembered how a medium had once "read" the coin.

"This is one of many. Very many and it is dormant and

buried. There is blood on this money. The dispute over this money," the medium continued, "has to do with generations. There will be trouble in your family until the dispute is settled."

*Damn right. The gold is there somewhere, and I'm going to make trouble until I get a share. The woman said 'dormant and buried.' But where? Is it in the "lodge"? Is it in the house? In Henlopen? Does it even exist? Kyle must have met someone in his research days who can help us further.*

# CHAPTER TWELVE

## *A LOVE REKINDLED*
### *Just Like Old Times*

Wearing one of Mason's polo shirts and a pair of his jogging shorts, Kyle perched on a kitchen stool. He watched Mason prepare a salad for them. He had called his sister in Henlopen who told him Norman was calm but insisting he get the legal papers.

"Keep filling his glass with Chivas Regal when he's not paying attention," he told his sister. It'll take him out of the game for the night. And tell him-"

Kyle could hear Norman in the background, "Is that Kyle? Gimme the phone, Trish."

"How you doing, Kyle, you okay, buddy?" Norman asked a little too energetically.

*Oh great, Kyle thought, Norman is in his "team captain" mode.*

"I'm fine Norman, I-"

"It's a tough time for you and me, I know. I'm having the duce of a time keeping the emotions under control. But we have to handle things for Trish and Vicki and not let the emotions get away with us, right? One of the most important things is handling the legal details and-"

"Norman, slow down. I have all the papers. It's going to be hours of fascinating reading for you come lunchtime tomorrow."

"Actually, it would be best for you to come home now," Norman commanded as if it were the next play for the team.

"Tomorrow," Kyle insisted.

Mason could hear only one side of the conversation. But knowing Norman as he did, Mason was amused at the brothers' bickering. On the other end of the line, Trish became annoyed. She picked up the extension phone and stated, "Norman calm down and let Kyle handle this."

"Norman," Kyle continued, "like you said, we're both dealing with big emotions. We each need to do it in our own way. Did you and Trish get things set with the funeral home and the florist?

"Yes, we did," Norman shot back.

"Good. Your way is to keep busy, my way is to spend time with some friends over here on the western shore. See you tomorrow."

"First thing, Kyle, understand?" his brother shot back.

"As soon as possible without breaking any land speed records, okay, Norman?"

"Fine." Click. Norman hang up.

"Kye? You okay?" Trish asked ever so gently.

"Doing ok, Trish. Doing okay. You?"

"Peachy."

"And Mom?"

"She and Mr. Beefeaters are keeping close company."

"Watch out for her, okay?"

"Will do, Kye, will do. You drive safe. Love you."

"I love you, too, Trish."

"Thanks. Goodnight."

Mason placed plates of lasagna and salad on the kitchen bar where Kyle was seated. As he poured them both a glass of red wine, he explained, "It's leftovers. Next time give me more notice and I'll make us a nice meal."

Kyle looked from the plate to his friend and then back and chuckled.

"Well," Mason remarked, "it's nice to hear you laugh after an encounter with the mighty Norman Wilson."

Pointing at his plate, Kyle simple quoted. "Lasagna. It's spaghetti that's been in the steam room.'"

Mason smiled. "The Boys in The Band," he said, "interesting you remembered."

"Our one trip together to New York. We were on our way to the Worlds' Fair in Montreal after graduation and we saw the play together."

"A great trip. Did you know Mart Crowley was nearby at Catholic University when we were in high school? His new play opens off-Broadway this fall."

"You keep up on all that stuff, don't you? This is very tasty lasagna, thanks."

"You're welcome. The theatre's good for me. My escape. I try to get to New York every few months; catch a couple shows. Some say characters in his play were based on CU theatre department staff. Only rumors. You know how fags can be. They want everyone to be as miserable as they are."

"Are we miserable?" Kyle asked trying to sound neutral.

"Living with *our secret*? It can be depressing except for clowns like you who swing both ways, I suppose."

"Oh? So, since I am bisexual I am never depressed?"

"Truth?" Mason asked to which Kyle nodded. "I want to think it was so. I admire you for that, um, ability."

"Come on, there are several women who claim to have bedded the 'moose' and bragged you were quite the lover. Were they lying?"

"No. No, I just prefer the company of men. And you, you wanton male with the enormous libido?"

"It's been on my mind a lot since leaving Boston. And let me tell you I don't buy it. Almost every story of a homosexual man ends in misery. I don't believe it has to be that way."

"How long do you think I would keep my job if corporate headquarters knew I was more than a "confirmed bachelor'?"

"The butch jock image suits you fine. I'll bet it's a magnet when you go to the bars- whether straight or gay."

"The bars?" Mason asked, "I go as seldom as possible; straight or gay. You want more lasagna?"

"I'm fine. Thanks."

"There's this manager of another branch of the bank. I saw him at the bar one night dressed in leather. I think, 'oh shit, this can't be good.' But ya know what? He doesn't even acknowledge he knows me- walks right by. I am invisible. At the next area managers meeting? -not even a sideways glance from the leather queen."

"So, there's no trouble for you."

"No trouble. True. But how long do I want to be invisible?" he asked as he took their dishes to the sink and began washing them. "I don't want to become one of those guys who begins to hate themselves for living a lie. So, um, you were telling Trish you wanted to spend time up here tonight. Who you planning on seeing?"

"You don't know?"

"Grab a dish towel and dry, will ya"?

Kyle grabbed a towel and moved next to his friend and began drying dishes. "Just like old times."

"We were pretty good at sharing the housekeeping, weren't we? I mean, you said 'spend time with friends on the western shore,' so I figured-"

"Oh shit! Oh. Damn. You thought it was one and done and I am out of here? Mace, no! You gave me sanctuary. And unless you want to kick me out of here, I intended to invite myself to stay the night. That is, um, unless you had plans."

"No. No plans," Mason told him as he put the last item in the dish drainer and turned to Kyle with a grin.

"It's your poker night?"

"No."

"Let's go to my room and play."

"After you, buddy, after you."

Upstairs they disrobed and then, as if years had never passed, they hopped on the bed with the excitement of teenage boys wanting to be naughty.

Mason winked: "Want to get high again?"

"Always." Kyle replied with a grin. "But before we do, I need to tell you ... well, I haven't told you everything. Hand me your watch."

Mason leaned over and reached for the watch. "Is there something about this watch you need to know?"

Kyle took the wristwatch from his friend, held it a moment, then spoke. "It's from a jewelry store in Ann Arbor Michigan. A woman bought this who was not your mother. She bought this on her way to a big event. Um, a relative, Aunt Betty, no Bessie."

He looked at Mason and simply asked, "Well?"

Mason stared at his friend eye to eye then averted his gaze. "Whoa. That is out there, Kye."

"And the speedo I was wearing earlier?" Kyle continued in a very clinical tone, "the swimsuit wasn't yours originally. It belonged to a guy named Albert. Must be local because he bought it at the five and dime store in Woodmoor. You liked it. He left it for you. You've stained it a few times enjoying your favorite contact sport."

"Kyle, are you trying to scare me?"

Kyle raised himself up on his elbows and looked into Mason's eyes. "I am scared enough for both of us, Mace. The last several hours I have done everything I could to distract myself from this new, what? -talent? I fell on my head, okay? I fell on my head and got knocked out. When I woke up, I discovered it. Jesus, Mace, if I think twice about anything I touch I get its history!"

Mason quickly cupped his privates with both hands.

Seeing this, Kyle erupted in laughter. "Oh, my god. Oh my god!"

He reached forward, wrapped his hands around Mason's head, pulled Mason down on top of him and kissed him deeply. Then holding Mason's head just inches from his, Kyle explained, "I needed that. Thank you. I think I almost cracked a rib, but once again, Mace you have done something perfectly. And you promised me weed."

"Fine, but you have to answer a question first. What about Johnny?"

"Please. Later?" Kyle asked.

"Goddamit, Kye, I haven't talked to you for years because you were running around chasing ghosts. No one in your family would tell me where you were because they'd disowned you." He paused. "You did. I can tell you talked to Johnny. Something in your eyes, Kye."

"It's not a subject I —"

"I want to know he's okay." Mason insisted.

The room was silent for a moment.

Then Mason heard a meek, "Johnny was fine."

"It's difficult to talk about Johnny, okay? Can you be patient, please because there's something more important right now and it's called my sanity. I need your help, Mace. I was correct about your watch, wasn't I? And the Speedo?"

"Yes, but how?"

"Fuck if I know!" he interrupted Mason a little too loudly. "I fell on my head a couple hours ago in my parents' home and woke up on the tile floor with this talent! This is psychometry."

"Holy crap," Mason almost whispered.

"Let's get high and take the edge off. What do you have for us this time?"

"I have some Thai stick and we'll do it in a toker. Lay back while I prep things." With that, Mason went back into the bathroom. He added water and a small amount of mint flavored mouthwash into the bulb of the toker.

As Mason added pot leaves to the bowl, Kyle observed, "You, my old friend, have become quite the freak."

"I will take that as a complement," Mason responded coming back to the bed. "This very clever devise cools the smoke. The mouthwash gives it a cool and minty flavor like the Salem cigarettes we used to steal from your mom."

The instant Kyle's fingertips made contact with the bulb, images flashed in his mind. He gasped and insisted, "you first! Take it. Please, Moose, you first."

"What?"

"Nothing. Being polite."

"You did the touching thing! What did you see? Damn it, Kye, tell me what!"

"You were smoking weed with Norman with this," Kyle blurted out.

"Kyle?"

"Norman has used this thing," he exclaimed as he took the glass toker back with both hands. "Norman and you have both-" Kyle closed his eyes and concentrated on the object in his hands.

He was quiet for a long moment, them with his eyes still shut he began to utter, "and you- oh- and- you and-"

Suddenly, as if rising out of deep water, Kyle opened his eyes and gasped for breath. "Take it!" he shouted holding the toker out to Mason.

Kyle continued to draw one deep breath after another as Mason took the toker from him and put it aside. Then, afraid his buddy was hyperventilating and might pass out, Mason gently stroked the top his head and Mason purred, "Easy boy, easy now. Take even breaths. Slow, even breaths."

Kyle followed Mason's coaching and got his breathing back to normal.

"Now," Kyle said quietly, "I *want* to kill him."

"What? Kyle, what are you talking about? Who do you want to kill?"

"Oh fuck. I didn't mean to say that out loud but damn it, damn it all, sonofabitch, shit, fuck, piss! What has Norman done to you?"

Mason didn't answer.

Kyle studied his buddy's face. He hadn't seen Mason look so pained since the two of them were standing next to Johnny's open casket so many years ago. "What is going on, Mace? Why was Norman threatening you? What is he making you do?"

"Stop, Kye, stop. I can explain. Let me — Fuck. Fuck! Mason backed away from the bed, retrieved his white bathrobe and put it on slowly.

"Okay. Okay. About two years ago, I hired your family's company to put in the natatorium," he explained. "It was the day they broke ground. The workers had called it a day and Norman showed up with this very cute young guy who was supposedly a summer intern. Norman wanted the kid to 'walk the site' and prepare a progress report. Well, we're back inside and I offer them beers thinking the kid is of age. He sees the toker and asks to use it. I figure what the hell. He fires up the toker and we get to smoking and drinking. Norman gets a phone call and has to leave. Yeah, hah! The kid puts some moves on me. I- well, I was pretty hammered and the kid and I got very creative. Next morning, I woke up alone in my bed hardly remembering anything. Then Norman shows up a couple evenings later. He shows me ten Polaroid snapshots of me and the guy being rather adventurous. Norman tells me the guy is only 17 years old and I'm in a great big pile of shit. So, Norman-

Kyle interrupted, commenting "the fuck face threatens to 'out' you."

"Not if I do him a favor. I simply had to help him out laundering money for his illicit smuggling of goods."

"The Pre-Columbian artifacts you mentioned this morning."

"I came up with the artifact idea- long story- but I had a few contacts with very rich collectors. Norman had the mechanism, so we worked several deals. I maintained a proper cover, moved the money here, then there and then around the corner and it all looked legit."

Mason wrapped the robe around himself, tied the sash and curled up in the easy chair next to the walk-in closet.

"He called me this morning," he continued. "A recent delivery of artifacts has been seized at the border. He needs money to straighten up the mess and he tried to get me to 'appropriate' some funds for him. I refused. Now he's threatening to show the pictures to all the wrong people."

"How much is he pressing you for?"

"Ten thousand dollars," Mason whispered.

"Shit we have that in the-" but he stopped. Mason wasn't listening. Kyle didn't know what to say. He felt he'd never seen anything more pathetic than his handsome friend in that chair. He looked humiliated and frightened and as if he wanted to sink into the cushion.

Kyle went over and put his hand on his friend's shoulder. Mason pushed it away.

"You should leave, Kyle. Go and leave me alone," he commanded with some vehemence. Then he whispered, "Please, please leave me alone." He then he pulled his knees to his chest and slumped even further into the chair.

Kyle moved to the opposite side of the room and snatched up the telephone off the bedside table. He dialed the number to his home in Delaware.

When the phone was picked up at the other end, Kyle put on his most casual voice and began, "Trish? Kye. Something has come up and I have a question for Norman. Need to talk privately."

"You okay?"

"I am fine, Trish, put Norman on and promise you will not listen in. It's something very personal between Norman and me."

"Sure, Kye, sure." Then there was a pause of half a minute or so. Kyle was about to say something reassuring to his debilitated friend, but Norman came on the line.

"Brother Kyle! How's it hanging ole buddy?" Norman had obviously been hitting the Chivas.

With a calm voice, but clear intention, Kyle let his thoughts be known. "Norman, I understand you have some pictures you are using to make a friend of mine's life miserable."

"What are you talking about?"

"Norman, no games. I want the pictures."

"I don't know what you're-"

"Cut the crap, Norman! I know you need money right now and I can make it happen for you real fast but only if you —"

"I don't know what you're —"

"Shut up, Norman. Let me make this simple. You will give me those pictures tomorrow. I will put fifteen thousand dollars in bearer bonds in your smarmy hands. That should take care of your little problem."

"Have you been talking to, Mason?"

"Never the fuck mind who I have been talking to, Norman. You do anything more to hurt my friend and I will hurt you so bad you will wish you and Dad could change places. Do you understand me? Do you have the pictures?"

"Yes."

"Give me the details and no fucking beating around any fucking bush, understand?"

"Office safe —sealed envelope with 'old deeds' hand-written on it. Inside is another envelope the Moose's name on it."

"Good. Then here's what you are going to do, Norman. You are going to call Martha and have her meet me at the office at 9:15 tomorrow morning. Tell her she is going to give me that envelope once I show her that I have the bearer bonds, understand?"

"Kyle, I don't —"

"We are doing this my way, Norman, understand?"

"Yes."

"You will call Martha and have her give me the envelope tomorrow at 9:15 am at the office."

"Yes. Martha. 9:15 am with the envelope."

"Thank you. I will bring you the bonds by one o'clock. Sleep well, Norman. Goodnight." And each then hung up their phones.

Over in Delaware Norman poured himself a double of the Chivas Regal.

"Everything okay?" Trish asked.

"A minor detail," Norman told his sister, "Kyle's got it under control. No big deal."

"Oh good. Goodnight."

"Good night, sis." Settling into an easy chair, Norman assessed his situation. *Well this,* he told himself, *could be more trouble, but then again, I can take care of the problem with customs. What the fuck. I can find another banker. I'm safe. Neither of those guys is going to make any noise about my little scheme without expos-ing Moose. Damn! I just won that round.*

Standing next to the bedside table, Kyle wanted to take up the phone handset and slam it down. But it was more important to quell his anger and to help Mason. The man was now curled up in a fetal position in the easy chair looking defenseless and beaten. Kyle's anger towards Norman was immediately replaced by compassion and caring for Mason. His heart went out to his old and dear friend.

189

Kyle reached out and took Mason by both hands. He pulled him up off the chair only to turn around, sit down and draw Mason to his lap.

He held his friend and rocked him. He held him tightly. He was determined the physical contact would feed healing energy to his buddy's soul. Both men enjoyed feeling the warmth their bodies generated by being so close. Without either knowing it at the time, they both reveled in the fact it was not about orgasms. It was about caring deeply for another.

Kyle held on to Mason for a long time before saying a word. When he did speak it was no lovey-dovey cooing, but flat out man to man honesty. "I love you Mason, I care about you. I care deeply what happens to you. And it's not because I am all you have left of Johnny who cared for you so much, but because I care for you as well. I used to imagine since Johnny was gone it was my role to love you for the both of us."

"Imagine that," Mason responded.

"Yeah, imagine that," Kyle echoed.

Kyle then picked up his friend and carried him over to the bed where he put him down and then laid beside him.

They stayed quiet for a while. Kyle was waiting for Mason to make the first move. He never did. He fell asleep and so did Kyle.

# CHAPTER THIRTEEN

*TAKING CARE OF BUSINESS*
*Friday Morning in Woodmoor & Henlopen*

They each swam a mile before breakfast, ate, showered and arrived at the bank a little before nine. Kyle retrieved all the bearer bonds from the safety deposit boxes as well as the US Savings Bonds.

Standing inside the bank vault, Mason and Kyle sorted through the certificates. They spoke in hushed tones.

"This is twenty thousand dollars in bearer bonds, Kyle."

"Yep. Gonna give Norman fifteen and five to Trish. I'm going to take her all her Savings Bonds, too." Then grabbing a pen and began signing all his bonds.

"Please cash all my Savings Bonds and put all the cash into a checking account for me? List Trish as co-signer. You can bring all the paperwork to Henlopen when you come down for the funeral, okay?"

"Funeral?" Mason asked.

"Oh shit. Norman'll be there. Sorry, that's kind of insensitive of me."

"No. Realistic. I'm gonna have to deal with him eventually. If this money does get those artifacts freed up, I will have to meet with him soon enough.

"Is this a big deal?"

"If this bribe Norman has arranged fails, we are each out fifty thousand dollars."

"No shit?"

"I put up everything I had earned from a couple smaller importing deals. It had nothing to do with the pictures. It's a good investment. Norman got his in a loan from the company. He told your Dad he was investing in a land deal in Atlantic City. If you give Norman these bearer bonds, he'll give them to his buddy in New York. If he's right, it'll grease the skids and get the artifacts to Norman. I have a buyer ready to take them off our hands for very big bucks.

"I'm a little shaky on the "if" thing. What do you mean, 'if'?"

Mason took a deep breath and then answered. "We have to be prepared to see all our money go down a rat hole. If the deal goes south, it's history."

Mason read the astonishment on his friend's face. "Then again, there's a good chance a quarter of a million will be in each of our pockets when the deal is complete. Fuck it. I will be in Delaware. Thanks again for doing this for me."

In case any of the staff happened to be watching them, Kyle gave his friend a big manly hug and slapped him on the back. "Butch enough for the staff?" Kyle quietly asked with a big smile.

Mason laughed. "Thank you again, Sir Kyle."

"Fuck off. I will call you this afternoon."

* * *

Kyle met with Martha at the company office and showed her the bonds. She gave him the envelope he had come for and got out of the office as quick as possible. He was uncomfortable being there without his father. Or to be more precise, afraid he might be watching.

About a quarter of a mile away from the office, Kyle pulled into a strip mall and parked. First thing, he tore into the envelope and looked over the pictures. Mason was right. Norman had snapped pictures of Mason and the young man. *Undoubtedly, a professional male whore, Kyle figured. Hmm, nothing I've not done before, but pictures like these could ruin Mason.*

Kyle shoved the photos back into their envelope. He got out of the car, popped the trunk and buried the envelope under the spare tire.

"Mason and I," he said as he slammed the trunk of the car shut, "will burn them as soon as we get a chance to be alone again."

He got back into the driver's seat and sorted through the other papers. He looked over the contents of the envelope with the will.

*Oh. Two wills. Interesting.*

He quickly read through both documents catching the

basics. The will from 1969 was signed, but the will from December '71 was not. The old will only mentioned Kyle by name by stating he was cut out of all but a relatively small amount of money.

*Yeah Dad, I know you hated me chasing ghosts.*

The second will, stamped "draft," was equally generous to all three of the Wilson children. It also reiterated the very nice but very clear terms of his prenuptial agreement with Vicki.

*Well, I am, after all, a lawyer now. I can deal with all this. Let's first see what Norman plans to do with it.*

This stopped him. It occurred to him- he could be black-mailed like Mason.

*How can I ever come out and be a K Street lawyer? Can't happen even in this age of "free love." Homophobia. Fuck. Can I close the closet door? Can I abandon my friend Mace? Mace. Right.* Kyle found a pay phone and called Mason to assure him the photos were safe then hit the road to Delaware.

* * *

As he drove up the driveway, he saw no unfamiliar cars.

*Good. The relatives haven't descended yet. But there he is. Huh. Big surprise.*

Norman reached the car before Kyle could even put it in "park."

"Let's go," Norman commanded as he opened the door and hoped in.

"Where?"

"Liquor store, I need to talk to you, and we need to do some restocking. I want us to talk before the ladies descend on you with their cares and worries. 'How is Kyle handling all of this' they whisper to each other. Jesus H Christ! Are those women ever going to let you grow up? So? Go!"

Kyle stared at him. "Good morning, Norman," Kyle gushed with a forced smile.

"Not funny! Make tracks, before they come out of the house!"

"Ten-four good buddy," Kyle shouted with a southern twang.

He executed a perfect three-point turn and headed down the driveway and into town.

"Thank you. Now, what did you bring me?"

"In the briefcase at your feet."

Norman placed the case on his lap and opened it.

"There are the bearer bonds," Kyle explained as he drove into downtown Rehoboth Beach. "Yes - large brown envelope. The bunch of US Savings Bonds under it are Trish's. The Will —"

"Yeah, I see, the will. But first things first," Norman responded as he drew the bonds from their envelope. "This is outstanding. Four bonds, five thousand each, total of twenty thousand dollars. Bless You Dad!"

Kyle pulled into a parking spot in front of the liquor store, shut off the car and turned to his brother. "I figure you take yours, mine and Johnny's and the fourth bearer bond goes to Trish. That takes care of your ten-thousand-dollar problem. It also leaves you with a pile of walking around money. Do we have a deal?"

"Three to me, one to Trish. Deal!" Norman took Kyle's

extended hand and shook it. "Now, you hold onto this, I have to make a phone call."

Norman closed up all the papers in the briefcase, left the car and headed for the phone booth on the corner.

Kyle locked the case in the trunk of the car and caught up with his brother at the phone booth.

"Good afternoon, Mr. Turlino, I have the payment we talked about last night. I have ten large in bearer bonds. Can your man 'Kent' meet me tonight at 6:30 at my folk's home in Woodmoor? Good, good."

There was a pause. Norman had a look of amazement on his face.

"Thank you for doing- Indeed, sir, yes indeed that is good news. Thank you. I am sure we will talk a-"

Norman looked at the handset, hung it up and exited the booth.

"That was quick," Kyle observed.

"He's a man of few words but I have to say the guy delivers. Oh man! He's already greased the deal with his own cash. I get the artwork tonight at 6:30 in Woodmoor. The man trusted me to the tune of ten g's and he is very happy with bearer bonds. They are better than cash because they are easy to pass. So, to him? It's like honey to a bear. Brilliant Kyle! Brilliant!"

"You're welcome."

"Do me a favor now. Call your friend. Tell "the moose" the artwork will arrive tonight.

"Norman? You should call him yourself."

"Are you fucking kidding me? Do you listen to yourself? Mason is not going to take a call from me and I don't want to leave a message with that snide bitch who screens his calls. I'll go in there and pay for our beverage order and meet you back at the car." And with that, Norman turned and walked off.

Kyle quickly telephoned Mason.

"Mason, Norman asked I give you a call and let you know the artwork you're brokering will arrive at our home at 6:30. Tonight."

"Well, Kye, you have managed to deliver good news twice in one day. It is much appreciated."

"Now I need you to do something for me. Remember your Hardy Boys games? -you and Johnny spying on us using the house intercom? Can you do it tonight starting around five?"

"Anything for you, buddy, anything."

Kyle gave Mason detailed instructions, finishing up as Norman exited the liquor store.

"Gotta go, talk to ya soon! Thanks!"

* * *

The siblings, Norman, Kyle, Trish and Norman's wife Susan assembled in John Wilson's study. The mahogany desk and the red leather chairs glowed in the sunlight streaming into the room. Norman took a seat behind the desk, Kyle stood to his right and the ladies all took seats in the leather chairs. No one would even consider sitting in the wooden rocker. Leaving the chair empty now seemed the right thing to do.

Vicki spoke first.

"Kyle, dear, you're the lawyer here, tell us what we need to do."

"He hasn't exactly started practicing-"

"Norman, I've got this," Kyle butt in.

"Okay," Norman sighed and settled back into the leather chair behind the desk.

"Top priority – we get through the next few days and properly honor Dad and his memory. We need to take the time to adjust. As for estates and wills, I'm sure Norman and I are executers for the estate. For now, we should let Norman go over everything and we can meet with the company's lawyer after the funeral. That is, if we can all agree to let Norman carry the ball for now."

"Thank you, Kyle," Norman responded with a hint of surprise.

"Girls, I don't know about you," Vicki began, "but I agree with Kyle."

"Me too." Trish added. "Dad's estate is considerable. Relatives are going to be all over us asking for details. If only Norman has the facts, we can all avoid-"

Kyle cut her off by declaring in his little boy voice, "We can sic them all on Normie! How cool is that?"

Everyone chuckled at Kyle's cartoon voice.

"That's what I mean- if it's okay with Norman. For me right now, ignorance is bliss," Kyle concluded.

"Excellent," Vicki concurred. "It is too soon to get into legal details. I would prefer to have time to adjust.

"I'm sorry, kids. But I-" Vicki then took a deep breath. She was trying to maintain control but her body betrayed her. Tears began to fall as she continued. "He's not coming, back is he? I'm not ready for that. I'm not ready for him never to sit there or in his rocker reading the Sunday newspapers."

Trish grabbed the box of Kleenex on the desk, pulled a few tissues and offered them to her stepmother.

"Thank you, Patricia."

"Absolutely," Trish assured her.

Vicki wiped her eyes, then blew her nose.

*How is it that woman can be so dainty and cool when doing that?* Kyle wondered.

"Then we are all agreed," Vicki announced with finality. "Norman will be our guide through all the estate details and we defer all questions to him."

"Agreed," Kyle replied.

"Me too," added Trish.

"Thank you," Norman replied.

Susan winked at her husband and continued to stay quiet.

"Well then," Vicki said as she rose from her chair," It is time for a drink" And out she went.

"Be there shortly," Susan chimed in. She went over to Norman, wrapped her arms around him and seemed to be whispering in her ear.

Norman smiled and said, "deal!" as she nibbled on his earlobe.

"I know I could use a drink after that shameless display of devotion," declared Trish.

"I will join you, Patricia, and we need to talk about finding you a man."

The women laughed and left the room.

Norman followed as far as the door. He shut and locked it behind them.

"Whoa, that was hot!" Kyle observed. "Someone is gonna get some tonight. Holy shit, Norman, you are blushing! Money is a real turn on for Susan, isn't it?"

"Kyle, you know I am not comfortable talking about my personal life. As for personal things- the photographs- strictly business. Let's not bring up the subject ever again, understand?"

Kyle started to speak but caught himself.

*Okay, he's gone from friendly big brother to dickhead business-man. What a scumbag. Breathe, Kyle, breathe.*

Kyle took a deep breath.

Norman continued to look at Kyle and repeated. "Is that understood?"

"Yes. And now, what I'm gonna do is catch a nap while you go through all those papers. I'm with Trish on this, ignorance is bliss. I'm going to rely on your honesty."

"A wise choice."

Norman followed Kyle to the door, and he sounded like the caring brother again. "Get some rest, Kyle. I didn't want to say anything in from of the ladies, but you look like you need sleep."

Kyle could hear the click as Norman locked the den door behind him. But at that point he didn't care. He could guess what Norman was going to do.

*"Rely on your honesty." I actually said that. I don't trust him for a minute. That's okay. I have more arrows in my quiver now.*

Kyle hurried up the stairs and went into the guest room where he flopped down on one of the twin beds. Putting every-thing out of his mind, he went to sleep.

In his father's study, Norman removed the contents from Kyle's briefcase. Opening the envelope marked "Last Will and Testament" he found two documents. He immediately noticed one had "draft" stamped on it. Noting the dates on each document, Norman compared the two. He then phoned the lawyer on the western shore and arranged for them to meet in Woodmoor at 7:00 that evening.

Realizing he had plenty of time before he had to hit the road, Norman changed his clothes and went for a run. He went three miles down the Coastal Highway and back. It felt good. It worked out a lot of the tension. By the time he reached the house and dove into the swimming pool, he felt great. He was abso-fucking-lutely sure he would get everything he wanted from this situation. He felt on top of the world. At least until he climbed out of the pool and was immediately confronted by his least favorite Aunt.

"Hello, Aunt Rebecca!" he declared with a big smile and walked toward her with his dripping wet arms extended.

She put her hand on his chest to stop his embrace. "While I appreciate the gesture, Norman, don't you dare hug me when you're just out of the pool."

"Aw, you're no fun," he cracked and kissed her on the cheek.

"Norman, you and I have to talk. Victoria says you're the one who knows all the details of the estate. I want to know about my grandfather's gold coins. It amounts to a considerable amount of money and both grandfather and your father promised me half of it."

"That's a family myth. Listen, I have to get cleaned up and

over to the western shore to take care of some business for Dad. We can talk later."

"Fine, Norman," she assured him a smirk. "I'm not going anywhere. Nick and I are here for the duration."

"Good to see you too, auntie," Norman shouted so all could hear, and went into the house.

\* \* \*

Once he had showered and changed into his "business casual clothes" he headed for Kyle's room. He needed to flat out ask if Kyle had read the will.

Finding it empty, he looked further, and he found his brother asleep in the guest room.

*Oh.*

Then checking his wristwatch, he realized, *hmm, still have time before I have to hit the road. Why not cop a twenty-minute nap and then wake up Kyle?* After closing the guest room door, Norman took off his blazer and laid it over the tea chair in the corner of the room. Then he stretched out on the empty double bed.

*This is good,* he thought, some *time to sort through a few things. Bottom line, Norman old man, is work things out so I get the business NFP- no fucking partners. But if the second will is signed? Everyone has their price. Wills are not filed in Montgomery County Maryland until you have a death certificate to go with it. The lawyer can be bought, I am sure. I will get all copies of the draft will and kick Kyle out of the picture. Mason is going to move those artifacts next week. I'm going to have so much cash Susan will be sucking my cock any fucking time I ask for it.*

Norman Wilson was one of those fortunate people who could nap at the drop of a hat. All he did was set a mental timer and he went to sleep and woke up refreshed after the chosen amount of time.

He drifted off remembering Susan's hot breath in his ear as she whispered, "you are so hot, lover, when you're in control." And then she promised him the best blow job in the history of the world before she nibbled on his ear.

# CHAPTER FOURTEEN

## *ANOTHER EERIE VISITATION*
### *Friday Afternoon in Henlopen*

Kyle drifted back into consciousness at around two o'clock Friday afternoon. Lying on his stomach, he opened his eyes and his gaze settled upon the oval braided rug on the polished wooden floor. He drowsily reached down and touched it, aware of its many colors.

*This isn't my room. How in the world did I get in here?* Then he remembered.

*Of course. Real brilliant. Avoiding another visitation by napping in a different room? Sure. That is so lame. When Johnny wants to find me again, he will. Whenever any of them want to find me, they will. Wait a minute. Who the hell is 'any of them.'? What made me think that?*

Running his fingers lazily along the braids of the rug he recalled the day's events. Then he got the feeling he was not alone. Fear began to chill the pit of his stomach.

*I'm not going to look away from this rug. No. No way. Oh, come on, Kyle. No. I'm going to crawl out of bed. I'll slither across this rug and out the doorway over there.*

He giggled at the image and turned over to see who was in the next bed.

*Norman. Good. Only Norman. Norman? Curious he'd be napping in here and he's into his "business meeting clothes."*

Kyle settled back against the pillow, lazily stared at the blue ceiling. Childhood memories of sharing a bedroom with Johnny came to him. It was a comforting feeling he'd not had in years; knowing his brother was in the next bed.

He bunched up his pillow, propping himself up so he could stare out the window at the lake through the pines.

*So calm and comforting.*

But his reverie was shattered as his thoughts moved to immediate concerns.

*Did yesterday happen? Did I dream about Johnny? -about the man in the basement? I dreamed that, didn't I? No way Kyle. It was real. Who wants it? Yesterday. Damn. Forgot to call Cyndy again. I promised. Fuck it. I don't need more complications. Not right now.*

He returned his gaze out the window, then back to Norman in the next bed. The flannel stadium blanket was pulled halfway up his chest and smoothed out.

Kyle propped himself up with his chin in his left hand and marveled anyone could sleep so neatly. Norman always was fastidious about his physical condition and his clothing. But this was the first time he realized it carried over to his napping habits as well.

His gaze remained on his brother; his breathing was light though audible. His muscular torso was slightly rising and falling. And Kyle wondered at his brother's having such a classical athlete's body.

*How do you develop a chest like that, anyway? My pecs are pretty good, but his are like picture perfect. He's got to be lifting weights. I'm only swimming. And his jaw line. Firm. Determined. Just like those pictures of Great-grandfather Wilson.*

*I should do more lifting.*

Suddenly Norman's jaw tensed noticeably.

*Interesting,* thought Kyle. *Maybe he's having a bad dream. Should I wake him? Nah, best not. Norman looks more like a man than the boy who came to mind when I think of him. We're getting older, Norman. It was nicer when we weren't faced with things like adult responsibilities, wasn't it? Adult relationships? Whew.*

Kyle suddenly got a chill. He pulled the comforter up to his chin. The steady breathing from the next bed was different. A dry rasping sound had replaced his brother's soft rhythmic breathing.

He wanted to say, "Too many of those illegal Cuban cigars giving you a touch of the wheezes?" But he was silenced by a sense of angry energy that made his skin crawl. A chill shot from the back of his neck to the tip of his toes. There was something terribly different about the man in the bed next to him.

Slowly Kyle turned his head to his left. His veins ran ice water and every muscle in his body went tight.

In the bed next to his was the partially decomposed body of a man, half-rotted flesh clinging to his skull. He was wearing partially disintegrated clothing from another time; another century, perhaps. His skull shone ghostly white where patches of the man's long black hair and scalp had fallen away. His parchment-like eyelids rose. He turned towards Kyle and his piercing hazel eyes bore a hole to the very bottom of Kyle's soul.

Kyle tried to find his voice, but his throat had turned to sandpaper.

"Nor-, Nor-, Nor-", was all Kyle managed to utter.

It sat up effortlessly still staring at Kyle. It uttered words on breath as foul as any rotting thing could smell. "Don't cross me, boy. Don't cross me, ever!"

He reached towards Kyle.

Kyle screamed. The thing laughed and reached out for Kyle with both rotting hands.

Kyle screamed even louder because it was getting out of the bed and coming at him as if to kill him.

Kyle turned to run, but a hand gripped his shoulder. A human hand. Kyle let out a yell. He could feel two hands, one on each shoulder.

"Kyle? Kyle wake up! You okay?"

Kyle screamed again. Someone was holding him back with very strong hands. He yelled and then turned, realizing it was his brother Norman.

He froze.

*Norman. Yes, Norman —no decay, no skeletal arm and hands. The face —Norman —clean shaved, tan face, blue eyes.*

"Jesus, Kyle, bad dream?"

"Oh god," he sobbed and embraced his brother tightly.

Norman was unsure of what to do exactly. He was

uncomfortable, but at the same time knew he had to calm his panicked brother. Sitting beside him, with Kyle sobbing and clinging to him, Norman began to rock back and forth.

"Hey, man, it's okay. It's okay. Tough times, man, tough times for all of us."

"You don't know, Norman, you have no idea."

The bedroom door slowly opened. Trish and several of the kids appeared in the doorway. Norman motioned them away with a fierce wave of his free hand.

They quickly left and closed the door.

"It was horrible," Kyle uttered and continued sobbing.

"It's okay now. A good old-fashioned nightmare, right? Hey. Only a movie, right? We've all got some shit to kick around, Kyle. Everyone has."

Kyle nodded his head not being able to find more words, just wanting everything to go away.

They stayed together for several moments. Norman was growing more and more uneasy in the role of comforter. He was wondering how to break away from his clinging brother without insulting the poor kid. But Kyle slowly pulled away from him.

*Damn*, Norman thought, *the kid looks panicked.*

Kyle found great comfort in being rocked by his brother. It brought back a sense of security from times long gone by. It was exactly what he needed. And if it was Norman doing the consoling, what did it matter? It felt good for the time being.

As he pulled back from his brother, Kyle looked him straight in the face. He looked deep into those blue eyes and suddenly felt frightened. It had nothing to do with the moment, but a notion of things yet to come. A sense of impending trouble washed over him. Even amidst his own upsets, the senses could continue their cruel power over Kyle.

*There was a gun. A pistol. And a shotgun. Death. Whose?*

*Not clear.*

"Norman. Be careful. You're in trouble." He hadn't meant it to come out exactly that way. Never before had he ever told a member of the family when he'd had such impressions or feelings.

"What are you talking about?"

Kyle turned away from Norman and started to get out of the bed.

"No, wait. Please. What"s this all about?"

"Just a sense. Sorry. Thanks for just now."

"What are saying about me being in trouble, huh? What do you know about it?"

"Norm, you know. I get these senses sometimes. I was looking at you and I saw a pistol. Sometimes these things come to me."

"Calm down. It's all right. I promise I'll stay away from guns. What did Mason tell you? Did he tell you about Turlino?"

"He only told me you needed ten thousand dollars really bad. I am sorry I called you all those names, but Norm, did you have to do that to him?"

"Kyle, I was in a desperate situation and I made a bad decision. I needed a quick fix. Honestly, I have felt bad about it ever since." Norman looked down. His hands were tapping his knees. He was waiting to see how his explanation set with his brother, but he got no reply. "We all do stupid things at one time or another," he continued sounding a little desperate. "That was one of mine. Bad form. Really bad form."

Kyle studied his brother's face. Norman could never fake sincerity. He was flat out lying and Kyle knew it which made it difficult for Kyle to respond.

"How about this, little brother: I will apologize to Mason when he comes to the funeral. And I will think of some way to make it up to him. How's that?"

Keeping his best poker face Kyle finally spoke up. "I always knew you were a gentleman at heart, Norm."

*Two can play your game you liar.*

"Did you destroy the Polaroid pictures?"

"They're history."

That's a good thing. I should never have- but the bonds. I guess I should go. You good?"

"Yeah, good." Kyle responded, "Yeah."

"Okay then- I gotta run up to town and meet Turlino's man in Woodmoor."

"I could come with you."

"Nope. Unnecessary. What's more important is you get some rest. We have to host the funeral home thing tomorrow evening, and we have to be the noble courageous family. Oh. By the way. You go through any of those papers in the strong box before you fell on your head yesterday?"

"Saw an envelope with 'will' written on it. Didn't take time to read anything before I gave it to you," Kyle lied.

At that, Kyle thought he detected a smile starting on his brother's face, but then he became more serious.

"Any surprises in there?" he asked his brother.

"Don't worry about it, Kyle. There's plenty to go around. You get some rest now."

"You sure you don't want company on the drive?"

"I think you should stay, get some rest and definitely get something to eat. You look like you could use it." And with that, Norman rose to leave the room. "Better dreams this time round." And then he left, closing the door behind him.

*Yeah. Better dreams while you hatch bitter schemes, you shit. I didn't read the two wills before I fell on my head. But I sure as shit had a look at them this morning before I turned them over to you, dear bother. Who the hell knows what's gonna happened next? And what was that I saw? Was it another dream? A hallucination? Oh god. Who knows?*

Kyle sat up causing the comforter to fall off the bed to the floor between the two twin beds.

"To hell with it," he declared. "It's suppertime."

He stood up between the beds and gathered up the comforter in his arms. Looking down, he noticed the oval rug and wood floor he had studied earlier looked different. There were muddy smudges on the rug.

*Boot prints? Yes. Wet dirt and a bit of wet moss.*

Kyle froze. He wanted to scream.

He dropped the comforter onto the bed and bolted out of that room as fast as he could.

# CHAPTER FIFTEEN

## *NORMAN WILSON, NFP*
### *Friday Late Afternoon in Woodmoor*

Norman Wilson was feeling good as he drove to the western shore.

*In a short time, I will be number one and stay number one; with the family, with the company and in any new moves I want to make. Alone. NFP. No fucking partners. Yes!*

For the first time in his life, Norman had the opportunity to be his own boss.

*Number two. I was second in command. With Kyle getting through Harvard, there was even the possibility of me falling down a peg. Third in the family pecking order would suck. Well, Dad's dead, so fuck it.*

*Two wills. Work the problem, Norman, work the problem.*

*There's one of three solutions. If the new will is unsigned, I am golden. If the new will is signed and the lawyer agrees to destroy it, I am golden. If the new will is signed and the lawyer won't destroy it, Kyle can be eliminated.*

He flipped on the radio. It seemed just about everybody was talking about the Watergate hearings.

*Watergate, Watergate, fucking Watergate. What a mess.*

"It's what happens when you don't control your people!" he told the empty car.

*If you want it done right, do it yourself or get the best in the world to do it for you. Those guys working for Tricky Dick, should never have gotten caught. Incompetents. The leader of the most power-ful nation in the world is going to be brought down by incompetents. Amazing. That is not going to happen to me.*

He switched off the radio confident a major change was going to occur in his professional life. There will be no more getting shot down whenever he has a plan for growing the business.

*Well, rest in peace, Dad. I am not your monkey anymore. Nuh uh! No way. Now I make the decisions. I make my opportunities. As long as Kyle is not around to fuck things up, I will be on top of world.*

Being a Friday afternoon, the traffic wasn't too heavy in the west bound lanes. Norman made it to the house in Woodmoor in plenty of time. He headed straight down to the basement where he unlocked the basement door to give Kent easy access to deliver the crates.

He then went to his favorite spot in the house, the rec room bar and nabbed himself a nice cold Heineken from the bar frig.

*Funny. I've only had coffee today. Damn. Better get this done before Kent gets here.*

He glanced to his left at the three shotguns on the wall. In the rack were a Browning twelve gauge; a Remington four-ten and a Winchester. The last was double-barreled and supposedly from his great-grandfather Jonathan Wilson. All were looking pretty dusty. He polished off the beer and then went about the chore of setting the stage for a future confrontation.

It wasn't difficult for Norman to find what he needed. Everything was where it always has been: the cleaning kit; the boxes of shells. He took one box of 12-gauge shells for the Browning, picked out the box of three-inch shells for the four-ten, and a couple of loads for the Winchester.

Norman was very comfortable around firearms, much more than his younger brothers. The twins would shoot the twenty-two rifles on the firing range but only went trap shooting once. Norman enjoyed those shooting trips to the Izaak Walton League with his Dad. The old man was always a patient teacher when it came to firearms. On the range, he wasn't the judgmental, dictator he became when Norman joined him at the company.

Standard procedure was to clean all guns when returning from the range. Since they hadn't been used in several years, Norman decided it wouldn't hurt to give them the once-over. So, he cleaned all three inside and out, and made an adjustment to the old Winchester. He then loaded each of them, being careful to engage the safety. Then he returned the supplies to their proper storage places.

He got himself another beer and it wasn't long before he heard a knock at the back door. Kent.

Norman opened the door to a young man in casual clothes with short cropped hair and a tattoo on his neck. It clearly indicated ex-Marine.

"Good evening sir, my name is Kent. Are you Norman Wilson?"

"Yes. Could you bring the boxes in and place them on the pool table through there," Norman asked, pointing the way. You need a hand?"

"Not necessary, sir," he replied, turned and walked away.

*Definitely ex-military. I wouldn't want to go hand-to-hand with him. He must spend half of every day in the gym. Then again, in his line of work, it probably doesn't hurt to have that zero percent body fat look.*

When Kent had deposited the second wooden crate on the pool table and headed back out for the final load, Norman decided to inspect the goods.

A crowbar from the workshop was the perfect tool. He pried off the top of the crate, rummaged through the excelsior and found the first stone object. It was about the size of can of shaving cream.

*How could a primitive carving this small be worth almost six figures? Mason must know what he's doing. It's kind of an ugly little fucker. Amazing.*

"On the pool table with the others, Mr. Wilson?" Kent asked as he came into the rec room carrying the third of the three wooden crates.

"Yes, thank you."

Norman fished out a second primitive artifact as Kent placed the third crate on the pool table and turned to Norman. "Now, the boss says you have something for me?"

Norman set the small stone figure on the third crate and handed a manila envelope to Kent. "These bearer bonds are like cash. Anyone can cash them so-"

"Due respect sir, I know what bearer bonds are."

"Sorry. I get very cautious when it comes to getting Turlino his money."

"Relax," Kent explained as he removed his work gloves and tossed them on the table. "A present. Keep the gloves."

"Thank you."

"Use them. The oil from your skin isn't good for sandstone."

Kent opened the envelope and withdrew the bonds. "Hmmm. Very nice artwork," Kent said as he examined the two sheets of colorful paper. Kinda wild to think these two pieces of paper are ten large."

"Indeed."

"And the c-note in here?"

"Is 'Kent' your first or last name?"

"Does it matter?"

"Well, Kent, when there's money to be made it never hurts to give everyone a taste."

Kent replaced the bonds in the envelope and the hundred-dollar bill in his pocket. "Too bad the customs agent got greedy."

"Cost of doing business sometimes," Norman added with a shrug.

"That's a very level-headed way to look at it. I can see why

Mr. Turlino trusts and respects you," Kent responded. "Thanks for the Ben Franklin, Mr. Wilson."

He turned to go, but Norman asked, "Um. Tell me, Kent. You do a variety of work for Mr. Turlino?"

"You could say I'm his go to guy when it comes to critical aspects of our operations."

"Do you handle sensitive matters for Mr. T?"

"Sometimes."

"What if there's someone causing trouble and getting in the way of a critical operation. Do you ensure they no longer are in the way?"

Kent looked at Norman a moment then removed a billfold from his sports coat pocket. He withdrew a business card and handed it to Norman.

"Mr. Wilson, I can tell you we are definitely not in that business. S'not the way we operate," Kent explained pointing toward the business card. "Strong-arming stuff is not the way we do business."

Norman looked at the card. It was Turlino's home improvement company's business card.

Kent wind-milled his hands and pointed to the card.

"Ah yes." Norman responded and he flipped over the card.

Hand-written on the back was a note: "Norm- call me if you need anything. Anything. Private line 237-555-6292."

"Mr. Wilson, we're willing to help our friends find solutions in business or home improvements. We can offer very good prices on demolition and hauling discards. Call me. I'll give you a terrific price on new aluminum siding on this house here," Kent concluded with a wink.

Norman nodded his understanding.

"Hello?" someone called from upstairs. "Norman? Anybody home?"

"Down here!" Norman shouted up the stairs. "Come on down!"

"Expecting company?" Kent asked.

"Another business matter. Yeah. Family lawyer."

The old man came down the stairs and immediately took a seat in one of the leather chairs by the pool tale. "Farkakteh air conditioning in the car is broken again and that heat out there is too much me. Could I get a little seltzer?"

"No problem," Norman responded and headed to the bar. "Arnold Rosenberg, Tim Johnson, a business associate."

The two men shook hands as Norman went behind the bar and found a small bottle of Perrier.

"Nice to meet you, young man," Rosenberg said as he mopped his face with his handkerchief. "And what business might you be in?

"Home improvements."

"Ah, thank you!" Rosenberg remarked as he took the green glass bottle of from Norman and then drank greedily.

"Yeah, well I gotta-" Kent began.

"No problem. I will be in touch."

"Young man," Rosenberg piped up, "if you need kitchen appliances, I have a cousin. He'll give you the best wholesale-everything you need."

"S'not my department, sir, but I will keep it in mind. Good afternoon, gentlemen." And Kent left the rec room.

Norman casually walked over to the laundry room doorway and waited until Kent was out the door.

"Be right back, Mr. R."

"No hurry, I'm happy to sit. I can't get cooled off for some reason."

Norman checked the basement door was locked and latched then returned to the rec room.

"Since you are not feeling well, Mr. Rosenberg, I will make this quick."

"First put the stone things away. I shouldn't see them," he said waving his handkerchief at the artifacts on top of the wooden crates.

"Why?"

"There are some of your business dealings I should never know about." Again, he wiped his face with his handkerchief.

"But as my lawyer there is confidentiality, right?"

"Yes, there is, but, there's always a 'but,'" Rosenberg explained as he rose from the chair and removed his jacket. "So hot —"

"You want more to drink? Maybe a whiskey?'

"No thank you. Confidentiality only goes so far, Norman. Say you are brought up on Federal charges for illegal dealing in antiquities. If they could prove I knew something about it, both you and I would be in Lewisville. So, you keep such business to yourself. I never saw it and you never saw me see it understood?"

"Yeah, you saw nothing. So, let's talk wills," Norman tells him.

"Yes, your father signed the new will. I have it here." The old man asked as he reached into his old leather satchel and produced a business envelope.

"Is there another copy?"

"No. You can make copies if you want."

"What you have there is a signed copy of what I read in draft- or were there changes?"

"No changes." He removed the document from the envelope. "What I have here is your father's one and only legitimate last will and testament."

"Okay, Mr. Rosenberg, here's what's going to happen. I never heard you say that and you are going to make those pages disappear."

"Norman?"

"Play it my way and you'll get a serious bonus for helping our family through this difficult time. A very serious bonus no one will ever have to know about."

Norman showed the lawyer the third of the five-thousand-dollar bearer bonds.

The old man leaned in for a closer look. "A five-thousand-dollar bearer bond?"

"My way of saying 'thank you' Mr. Rosenberg."

"Interesting. A very attractive document. But I am sorry, Norman, I do not work that way."

"Of course, you don't. No one will know and your integrity will be intact."

Holding the envelope in one hand and the will in the other, the lawyer shook the papers and shouted, "I will know!"

Norman paused. He let the words hang in the air as if dodging them and then he calmly responded. "This one time you are going to look the other direction. You will let things unfold the way I need them to unfold because it is the best thing for the Wilson family."

"Norman, I am telling you no."

"Listen old man, Dad is gone. You work for me now."

"You have that correct. The man who protected you is gone, God rest his soul. Take this," he commanded, waving the folded pages at Norman.

Norman instinctively knew he should not touch the papers.

"No. You never gave it to me because it doesn't exist."

"You think you are the center of the goddamn universe, don't you? You father cleaned up one mess after another that you created. He protected you too much. Kept you safe! I won't do it."

"Destroy those pages. I know what's best for this family."

"You stupid putz. Are you kidding me? You think you can have it whatever way you want it? I will not be a part of it."

"Listen to me old man! This is what Dad wanted. That nutso brother of mine can run around the country chasing ghosts from now until doomsday. He's not getting half of the company!"

The men were now face to face, but Norman was too into himself to notice how pale the old man was turning.

"This is my turn! I am finished being told what to do. My turn. Mine. Kyle has no right."

"And you do?"

"I earned the right! I-" Norman stopped. Rosenberg's face was contorting, and he was staring at something over Norman's shoulder.

"Norman!" he screamed.

Norman turned in time to see the specter of Nelson Wilson charging at them. His arms were raised high above his head as if wielding a weapon. His face twisted with rage.

Norman stepped aside and watched as the vicious specter was almost on top of them.

Rosenberg covered his head with his arms screaming "God help us!" As the specter passed through him and into the wall.

Neither man moved.

Norman could only stare into the empty space before them with wonder, but not for long. His attention was quickly drawn to Rosenberg who was gasping for breath. He was reaching out to grab something, anything, to steady himself. The will and the empty envelope fell from his hands.

Rosenberg felt as if someone had slammed a cinderblock into his chest. Sharp burning pains spread down his arms. He tried to speak, but could only gasp, "Nor —" as he dropped to his knees and then tumbled over on the tile floor.

Norman knelt down and rolled the old man onto his back. He untied Rosenberg's tie and loosened his shirt collar.

The old man was trying to say something, but all Norman could hear were guttural sounds.

*Fuck! If you help the old guy, you could be screwed, Norman. This is opportunity knocking.*

Norman headed to the bar. He snatched up the telephone handset with one hand. He then blocked the call by holding down the plunger with the index finger of his other hand. He punched the buttons dialing 9-1-1 being careful to block Rosenberg's line of sight to the phone. *Should he come to, there's no need for him to spot what I'm doing.*

Trying to sound near panic he shouted into the phone handset.

"Yes, please send help. I have an elderly gentleman here who seems to have had a heart attack, please send help!" He gave the address then hung up the phone.

Norman look around, but couldn't see the will nor the envelope. Damn old man must have fallen on them. Shit.

"Mr. Rosenberg! Mr. Rosenberg! Are you still with me? Help is coming! Mr. Rosenberg?"

He held his hand on Rosenberg's neck. No pulse.

Unsure how long he should wait, Norman walked behind the bar and found the scotch. He flipped open the ice maker, took a tumbler and filled it with ice then poured a very generous helping of Chivas.

Norman had stood here many time serving up drinks to family and friends on many occasions. But this was a new one, he figured. *I mean what the fuck were we seeing just now? What the hell was that? It literally scared Rosenberg to death. What the fuck? You mean there are such things as ghosts?*

He sipped the scotch until it was half gone then went over to Rosenberg again. No pulse.

*It's been ten minutes at least. It'll be another ten before the ambulance gets here. Twenty minutes without oxygen to the brain, even if they do revive him he is going to be a vegetable. Okay. Make the call.*

Norman returned to the bar, downed the rest of the scotch and called 9-1-1 for real. He gave them all the information they needed - particularly to come by the rear driveway to the back of the house.

Hanging up the phone, he looked over at the pool table. Oh shit! He repacked the stone carvings and hammered the lids shut. He took a comforter off the lounge chair and spread it over Rosenberg's body.

*The will. The fucking will. Damn.*

Norman knelt down next to the body on the floor. He reached over and pulled the body towards him so Rosenberg was on his side. As Norman did so, he leaned over the body to look for the documents and froze. As he rolled the body and leaned over it, the body heat trapped beneath Rosenberg rose up past Norman's face. It was as if he felt the old man's soul leaving his body. His first inclination was flight, but he spotted the papers. He shook his head.

*"Freak out later Norman, Get the papers! Get the damn fucking pages!*

His hand was shaking as he grabbed the pages, but he held them tightly. He quickly covered Rosenberg again with the comforter.

As he stood up, he glanced around the room as if expecting to see another ghost.

*Get a grip. A grip, asshole, or you're going to start seeing things again. Just focus on the papers. The will and the bearer bond. Put them in your briefcase. It is on the pool table. One foot in front of the other. Move it, Norman. The briefcase. Good. Open it. Will, check. Bearer bond, check. Safely inside briefcase. Close it. Tight. Leave it on the pool table- and get another drink.*

He returned to the bar and poured himself another scotch, but didn't stick around. He went out through the laundry room and waited for the ambulance guys outside the basement door.

He heard the siren coming down the street.

*Well, who is in charge now, Dad? I'm number one. Norman Wilson, NFP.*

# CHAPTER SIXTEEN

## *A READING AT THE BEACH*
### *Saturday Morning in Henlopen*

The Delmarva peninsula is a long stretch of beach. It runs from Lewes, Delaware to Assateague, Virginia and the mouth of the Chesapeake Bay. Near the northeastern end sits Henlopen State Park, a protected "wilderness area." In 1973, the beach had no boardwalk or games like nearby Rehobeth Beach. It was sand dunes and reeds and a large cinder-covered parking lot. During summer months there would be a little trailer where you could buy drinks and snack food.

Dotting the beaches in Delaware are several concrete "fire control towers." Those tall, weathered, cylindrical sentries were erected during WWII. They still stood watch decades after the German submarine threat had ended. The slits running parallel to their flat tops give them a very serious, expression.

There are two such towers in the park not far from the Wilson's home. The sloping sand near one of them was Kyle's favorite spot on the beach.

* * *

"What you said yesterday about the little toy car? What was that all about?" she asked.

It all poured out of him. He was finally given an opportunity to explain to someone what happened in the basement. He told the story from leaving the bank to the point he just threw everything back into the strongbox and left.

Kyle and his Aunt Rebecca were seated on the weathered tree trunk at the base of the watch tower.

"Would you mind if I tried a few tests with you?"

"As long as you don't tell Norman. He'll raise all kinds of hell."

She took a simple gold ring with a shiny red stone from a velvet pouch and handed it to him.

"Have you ever seen this before?"

"No."

Kyle took the ring. He turned it over and over in his hand.

"Now. Clear your mind. Tell me what comes to you when you meditate on this ring."

He noticed there was something stamped inside in miniscule letters. *14 carats? Something. Are those initials in there? Never mind.*

"It's hard to get anything. The sound of the ocean and everything out here."

"Don't worry about it," she explained patiently, "Make it all part of your experience and settle into that."

"Yeah."

"All right. Relax and tell me what you get."

"A young woman in her bedroom. Hmmm. She's just had a baby. A man has just given her a present. This ring. It's Norfolk, Virginia and the stone is the baby boy's birthstone which is garnet. That makes it January. Something is foreign here. Greek. There is very strong love in this ring."

He felt a cold chill on the nap of his neck, and then his mind went blank.

"Anything else?"

"Nope."

"Very nice. Very nice. Relax and give me the ring."

Kyle opened his eyes and placed the ring in his Aunt's outstretched hand. "How'd I do?"

"The ring belonged to Nick's maternal grandmother, a Greek woman. Her husband brought her this ring the day after she gave birth to Nick's mother in Norfolk, Virginia in 1902. You couldn't have known any of it.

Kyle got a chill that trembled his entire torso. He reached for a cigarette, then realized he forgot to bring them.

He giggled and was nearly as amazed as she.

"Got something else?" Kyle asked. "Like an unfiltered camel cigarette and a lighter?"

"Forget it. Nicotine and caffeine are the last things you should put in your body when doing any kind of reading."

"Aw shucks."

"All right. Try these."

"These are your sewing scissors. I've seen them a million times."

"Yes, but tell me what you get."

"I get you. Busy. You think a lot when you sew. Sewing is equal to worry beads for you, isn't it? Busy hands. Snip those threads. Cross-stitch-o-rama." He started to return the scissors to her, but she held up her hand.

"Hold on to them. Get all you can about me and see if there's something else. Anything." She paused, then added, "anything beyond me."

He shrugged and held on to the scissors, staring at them and then past them down to his sand and his sandals. He opened and closed the sheers as he continued to study his big toe.

Nothing was said for a minute or two. There was only the sound of the ocean and an occasional shout from the vacationers on the beach. A breeze rustled the reeds behind them near the tower.

"Kyle?"

"Huh?"

"Not your feet, the scissors."

"They're my great grandmother's. And I can't tell if the sadness is mine, her's or yours." And he began to feel very tired. It was as if he was about to weep.

Rebecca waited a moment, then asked, "Anything else?"

"Something British. A young girl on a porch looking at an ocean. It is very blue. It's Bermuda. Lots of fruit- banana trees. The sadness though- the sadness wasn't there. There's a farm.

Whoa. She's not a happy camper. There's like some heavy shit around that farm."

She took the scissors from him. "Your Great-Grandmother, Amelia Wilson, brought these with her from Bermuda. The sadness is accurate. She was happy to get off the island, but not happy living on Jonathan Wilson's farm. It was a pretty austere place. I visited the farm years after she had passed away. I think she expected something else when coming to America. A farm hand I spoke with told me she and her husband didn't get along very well, as it turned out. There is plenty of family lore about the three Wilson brothers. The old man gave these scissors to me when I visited.

"I got the origin, the owner and the sadness. Not bad. I'm getting pretty good at this stuff. Why did you smile when I mentioned the bananas?"

"You surprised me."

"How? What did I say?"

"They raised bananas on the farm in Bermuda."

"Banana farmers?" Kyle started to laugh.

"Now what's so funny?"

"I'm the one who's bananas!"

He gave her the scissors and she replaced them in her purse.

"Bananas!" He started to get frightened. He wasn't sure, but for some reason there was the feeling of fear somewhere inside him. It wasn't a great fear, but a little nagging pang he couldn't laugh away. He took a breath then asked his aunt, "Can we take a break? My head is kinda' tired. Let's watch the waves for a bit, okay?"

"Sure," she told her nephew, but she desperately wanted him to "read" a final item, but she knew better than to push.

So, they sat quietly and watched the ocean.

Kyle looked up the beach. It wasn't very crowded yet. He marveled at how colorful beaches can be- umbrellas and towels and tans and swimsuits. *How many bodies of lily white vacationers will be burned red on the beach today?* he wondered as his eyes wandered up and down the beach from his perch atop the tree trunk in front of the watch tower. *Those damn things usually spook me,* he remembered, *but today they're no big deal. All relative, I guess.*

Four young women, sleek and scantily clad were sunning themselves. *The brunette in the brown bikini is very promising,* he thought. *They've caught the eyes of those three young men, college boys, there tossing a Frisbee. Why do such well-developed young men insist on wearing those damn baggie broad shorts? At least one of them was sensible- a green Speedo, not skimpy, but sporty nonetheless. Nice package.*

A mother and father had their young daughter between them walking into the gentle surf. Several grandmothers, daughters and grandkid groups he noticed. And he caught occasional glances between the frisbee boys and the girls on the blanket. *What a ritual that is. Seek and conquer. Those girls have no intention of dropping their bikini bottoms tonight or any other. Do they even know what they want?*

"Do I?" Kyle quietly asked himself.

"Beg your pardon?" Rebecca. asked

"Nothing. Admiring this picture-perfect day at the beach."

He enjoyed watching the girls watching the boys– especially

green Speedo guy. Kyle marveled at his admiration for both the male and female form. Once again, he wondered if he would make a choice and settle down with one or the other. *Or do I stay single?* Memories of his night with Mason flashed through his mind.

Then his gaze shifted from the beach, past the dune and down towards the parking lot. There, next to the refreshment trailer, he saw a young boy and what looked like his grandmother. *What was he? Six years old?*

The cinders must be hot on his bare feet. He kept stepping up and down impatiently waiting for their order to be complete. The refreshment man passed a cardboard tray across the counter to the grandmother. Drinks. The family forgot the thermos, no doubt.

The little boy reached up and Grandma took a soda cup from the tray and handed it to him. She was smiling as she inserted a straw through the plastic lid. The moment the straw was in place, he slurped up the soda. The old woman said something to the boy. He stopped drinking, and with a smile nodded energetically. And they started their trek back to the beach.

A shriek from the ocean distracted Kyle. One of the pink blanket girls was being dragged into the surf by a companion and one of the sophomores. *Contact. Who will conquer? Maybe he'll get to first base. Maybe he won't.*

Nearby, Grandma and her charge were walking along the sand towards their umbrella. The boy was walking cautiously so not to drop the drink. He would stop, take a sip of the drink he so carefully gripped in his two little hands, then proceed further.

"Come on, Nanna," Kyle heard him cry, "all the ice is going to melt."

Then turning back towards the ocean, he had only enough time to shout "hey!" before green Speedo guy, not seeing the boy, leapt to make a stellar frisbee catch. He knocked the boy over and that spilled his precious soda.

The old woman set down her tray of drinks and reprimanded the student as she picked up the crying child.

They were too far away for Kyle to hear what they were saying exactly, so the scene continued in pantomime. The student seemed very apologetic, the boy inconsolable, and the grandmother indignant.

The girl in the brown bikini got into the act and this seemed to calm grandmother and the little boy. The girl ran to her blanket then returned to the little group with her handbag. A moment later brown bikini girl and green Speedo guy led the boy to the refreshment trailer. Nice. They were going to buy the child a new cup of soda.

The little boy turned and waved back to his grandmother as they reached the snow fencing. She smiled and returned his wave and then headed towards her umbrella.

Why, Kyle asked himself, can't everything be that simple? And then he had to laugh. What if every life problem could be made right by a beautiful brunette in a chocolate brown bikini? -or a boy in a shiny green Speedo swim brief?

Kyle smiled at the thought then turn his attention to the Frisbee tossing boys. He was grateful for the distraction.

Rebecca Wilson Thompson watched him staring and waited to continue their conversation. She was fingering a double eagle - a twenty-dollar gold piece from the 1800's. She switched it from one hand to another. Finally, she spoke.

"Kyle?"

"Huh?"

"Feeling better? Ready for one more?"

"Sure."

"So far, your readings have been accurate," she told him. She then held out the gold coin as she instructed, "take a deep breath, clear your mind. Hold out your hand and tell me what this tells you."

He held out his hand.

She placed the shiny small gold coin in his palm. "Tell me …"

But Kyle couldn't hear her. The pain and anguish were overwhelming. He heard screams and he saw blood. He pushed the coin off his palm and covered his ears with both hands.

The gold coin fell into the sand.

"Kyle?" His Aunt Rebecca asked. "Kyle, are you all right?"

He dropped his hands to the driftwood log to steady himself. "Headache," he lied. "A powerful headache. Whoa. Maybe we better try this again later." He stared at the breaking ocean waves for a moment, stood up, kicked off his sandals and removed his t-shirt. Without a word to his Aunt, he ran to the shoreline and he dove into the surf.

He wished something could undo everything that happened since Thursday two days prior.

# CHAPTER SEVENTEEN

## *A REUNION WITH CYNDY WEAVER*
### *Saturday Morning in Henlopen*

It was the routine for guests at the Wilson's place in Henlopen to park on the grass beside the driveway. So, out of habit, Cyndy Weaver parked her rental car in the grass behind a couple others. Then, grabbing her suitcase, she headed up the walk. She was more nervous than she would have liked.

"Okay," she whispered aloud, "let's see if you made the right or wrong diagnosis here, Dr. Weaver." She pressed the doorbell button.

Her uncertainty was immediately erased when Trish answered the door.

"Cyndy? Cyndy Weaver?"

"Yep. It's me. I hope I'm- "she began to say but was cut off.

"I am so glad to see you!" Trish shouted and gave her a warm welcoming hug crying, "This is perfect! Vicki! Vicki! Come here!" she shouted over her shoulder. "Cyndy, come in, come in."

"I am very sorry about your Dad," Cyndy began, "I talked with Kyle a couple days ago, and he-"

Once more she was interrupted, this time by Vicki hurrying over and giving her a hug and kisses on her cheek. "Cyndy, Cyndy, Cyndy, thank you for coming!"

"I am so sorry."

"Thank you. It's an adjustment. But," she continued, "it is easier to handle when we have friends around us." She took Cyndy's hand and led her into the house.

Both women offered to prepare breakfast or least some coffee for Cyndy.

"Thank you, but no. I want —"

"Kyle!" Trish exclaimed, "Of course. Of course! He's at the beach. Let's get you settled and then you can go on over there. Follow me."

"Have her put her things in Kyle's room for now" Vicki instructed.

Cyndy turned and shot Vicki an inquisitive look.

"Well," Vicki responded, "we're all adults here, aren't we? We will let you and the boy work it out. There's always the guest room if you would prefer."

"Thanks." Cyndy responded.

"Go on. Go on. Get changed and find Kyle. He needs you. Trust me."

"Okay," Cyndy uttered then turned and followed Trish up the stairs.

"I think you will find Kyle in his favorite place on the beach," Trish explained. "He's taking all this pretty hard. He had some horrible nightmares yesterday. Aunt Becca took him for a walk to the ocean first thing this morning."

"Near the old observation tower. They'll be easy to spot."

Trish reached out and touched Cyndy's shoulder. "Vicki is right, Cyndy. It's great you are here and," she paused as if for emphasis, "he's not had a steady girl since you left for med school. I thought you should know."

"Thanks."

"Okay. Norman and I need to handle details and do some shopping for the wake. It helps me to keep busy. I'll talk to you later. And I love your hair that way." With that, Trish was out the door and headed downstairs.

Cyndy stood in Kyle's room and marveled at the good memories it inspired. Then catching her reflection in the mirror, she uttered, "let's get a move on." She changed for the beach, threw a couple items into her beach bag and headed downstairs.

Norman Wilson was at the bottom of the stairs.

"Well, the lovely Miss Weaver. Welcome!" and he embraced her and purred into her ear, "as scrumptious as ever." He let his hand fall down her back and rest a moment on her behind.

She pushed him away. "And I believe you are as married as ever?"

"Details."

"Excuse me, Norman, I am off to find Kyle."

"Yes, Kyle. By the way, I think you should know Kyle has reunited with his old friend Mason. He spent last night at Mason's place up in town."

Cyndy, looked at him blankly. "And this should have special meaning to me, Norman?" she asked with no emotion whatsoever.

"I thought you should know," he told her with seeming confidentiality.

She gave him her most flirtatious smile saying "And now we both know, don't we?" With that she turned and went out the front door. As she closed it behind her, she loudly told the front lawn, "once a sleaze always a sleaze."

She hopped into the car and drove to the beach.

"Well, hello, Cyndy!" Aunt Rebecca called from her perch on the tree trunk as Cyndy approached. "What a pleasant surprise. How have you been?"

"Fine, thank you. Three years of extra effort and I got through it all."

"You are Doctor Weaver now! Isn't that wonderful!"

"Thanks. If you know of any hospitals looking for an internist with a background in general medicine let me know."

"I will keep that in mind. Kyle's out there somewhere. I am happy you showed up for one very selfish reason. Since you're here I won't be leaving Kyle alone if I return to the house for some lunch. If I weren't so hungry, I would stay and chat," she said as she got off the log and shouldered her large wicker beach bag. "We will make time to speak later. I want to hear about your studies."

"It's a date."

"Good. Oh. And here's a towel for Kyle," she added leaving a beach towel on the log. The old woman paused, looked Cyndy in the eyes and asked, "help him, dear. He is very troubled about something."

"I'll do what I can," Cyndy assured her.

"Please do." She then kissed Cyndy on the cheek, turned and walked up the beach to the break in the snow fence and home.

Sitting on the log, Cyndy reviewed the situation. *Okay. He's "very troubled." What am I supposed to do? –fuck his brains out to take his mind off the "current situation." I can only imagine Daniel Mason already helped him out in that department. Stop. Remember how much you once loved him. Still love him. And the truth is, neither of us have been celibate these past few years. Period. Oh, screw it,* she told herself. *Don't go trying to guess anything. Wait and talk when he finishes with his swim.*

She spread her towel out on the sand and had a seat.

Leaning against the big old tree trunk, she stared at the ocean trying to guess which one of the bathers was Kyle. *Why are you obsessing on this situation with Mason?* And then she spotted Kyle as he walked out of the surf. *And how about that?* She could only smile.

"Oh my god," she whispered. *He looks better than ever. This would be so much easier if he'd gotten pudgy or something. And he's wearing that suit? Both of us in purple with the white panels? We're going to look like some Speedo advertisement.*

He spotted her and waved. She waved back wondering about his "hello." *That wasn't very enthusiastic.*

As he walked up the beach, Kyle was filled with mixed feelings. *She looks great. Her hair. It's the bangs and cut like, who? Yep,*

*Jane Fonda in Klute.* He walked to where she was seated and grabbed his towel off the log.

"Nice suit," he said with a grin. One of my favorites" he added as he took a seat next to her on the towel and gave her a quick kiss on the cheek.

She stared at him for a moment, and he fell into her gaze. *Her green eye is brighter than Mason's and, oh wow, Mason.*

Cyndy was unsure how to read his more serious expression. When he looked away, she asked, "Are you not happy I have arrived on your doorstep?"

"You still look so hot in that suit," he blurted out.

"Oh please, now you sound like your brother Norman. That sleaze was coming on to me earlier. Can you believe it?"

"Yeah."

"You have not answered my question, Wilson."

"Well, Miss Weaver, I am not handling the events of the last two days very well, so you are going to have to be patient with me. And yes, I am happy you have arrived on my doorstep. Very happy."

"Sorry about your Dad, Kyle. He was a good man. Have you spoken to him since —?"

"Don't go there, please. We will get to all that. Whew. Huh. There is so much I need to tell you. You are the only one in the whole fucking world I can tell this stuff to, and I don't even know where to start. Actually, I am very, very happy you are here. I don't know if I am ready to share all the gory details."

"Start with the juicy stuff. Trish told me you weren't seeing anyone regularly, but Norman told me you were back with Mason. What's up?"

"Really? You want to start with that?"

"Why not?" she said defensively then added, "oh come on, the relationship details are on both our minds so let's get it out of the way." Kyle looked at her in wonder so Cyndy continued. "I guess you want me to start, fine. Three years is a long time, Wilson. I had a couple short term relationships and a handful of one-night stands, but nothing that could last. You?"

"I haven't seen many people since you moved away-" and with that, Kyle stopped. It dawned on him he hadn't kept count so he couldn't be precise. He stared at the ocean until she spoke up.

"Come on, let's get to the good stuff here! Did you come out?"

"Was I ever in?"

"Goddam it, Wilson, did the door start swinging one way?"

"No. You think Mace and I?" Kyle asked and she nodded. "Things are kind of complicated on so many fronts right now!"

She pulled a slender joint from under her hair behind her ear which made Kyle smile broadly.

"What?" she asked feigning ignorance.

"What do you mean, 'what?' On the beach that first night..."

"Yeah, I picked up several bad habits from you, Wilson. But they were all endearing. What do you say we toke up and talk about the gory details, huh? Bring me up to date."

Kyle took the joint and leaned forward to her cupped hands to light it.

"All the way from the Rocky Mountains, Wilson. A present for you."

"Thanks," he uttered as he inhaled deeply.

"So," she began and toked on the joint. Then, as she exhaled asked, "how you doing really, I mean since your Dad? The doctor is in. Lay down and tell your old pal all about it."

Kyle stretched out perpendicular to Cyndy and laid his head in her lap. It was something he had done on this beach so many times in the past.

"This is familiar," she said taking the joint from him and taking a hit. *Whew. Gotta admire how the guy fills out a Speedo.* "Very familiar," she added.

"And very comfortable."

They continued to smoke the joint in silence until there wasn't much left.

"Got any more back there?" he asked reaching up and slipping his finger into her hair and stroking the side of her head."

"I have one in my bag-"

"No. No, I'm good. Actually, I wanted to touch your hair. Very soft. Very pretty."

"That's very nice of you to say, Wilson, but the question is still on the table: what do you mean by 'not too fucking good'?"

"You didn't roll that joint by the way. A girl named Teresa, a candy striper at the hospital gave you a few j's for your trip when she dropped you at the airport."

He had never seen her look more surprised.

"Yeah," Kyle answered her unasked question. It's weird, huh? And it gets weirder by the day. Give me something from your bag.

She handed him a pack of matches. He took it and held it between his thumb and forefinger. After staring at it for a moment he spoke. "Nothing. Good. Just as I suspected," he said returning the matches to her, "the THC kills the ability."

"You, you- Jesus, Wilson! I'd call that psychoscopy and retrocognition."

"Yeah, well I call it a pain in the ass."

"But you never-"

"Wait Dr. Weaver. Let me give you the whole picture. You see, I got home from Boston Wednesday night and moved into my old room here. I was planning on a nice three-week vacation with the family. Then Thursday morning about dawn I had a startling wake-up call from The long-deceased Johnny Wilson. Yep, my brother Johnny was standing at the foot of my bed. 'It's time,' he says. That's it. 'It's time.' I tried to say something, but he dropped that morsel and vanished. Less than twenty minutes later we got the call from a state trooper. They'd found Dad dead of a heart attack in his car by the side of the road."

"That had to be hard."

"And how are these two things connected? Years ago, when I spoke to Johnny, he told me when Dad died, Norman's business dealings would destroy the family. Johnny also told me, 'you're going to have to stop him, Kyle, even if you have to kill him because if you don't, he will kill you.'"

"Oh my god! That April when I was in Ellicott City! That's what you wouldn't tell me."

"I am so sorry, Cyndy. I wasn't honest with you. You deserved better. It's taken me over three years but ... I am very sorry."

Cyndy was stunned. She looked down and began stroking

his hair. She wanted to hug him but wasn't sure if he was ready to be hugged.

"Up to that point, you and I had seen or heard some pretty far out shit in our research, but that - what Johnny told me? It was too much."

"Why didn't you tell me?"

I couldn't talk to you about Johnny's prediction because I was too busy denying it."

"And I was a total shrew about it, wasn't I?"

"Stop. You were rightfully pissed. I broke the fundamental agreement of our relationship: always tell the truth. I betrayed you and I am sorry, Cyndy, very sorry." He took a deep breath and continued, "but Johnny showing up the other morning was only the start. Remember how I used to tell you I felt we had a boogieman in our basement? Well, we ran into each other on Thursday."

He went on to tell her about his trip to Woodmoor, the specter in the basement, and falling on his head.

"That," he explained, "is what triggered the psychometry and retrocognition."

"Who else knows about this?"

"Mason. It's freaked him out, but not her. Aunt Becca was always interested in our PSI work, so she's delighted. There is a heavy aspect. Aunt Becca gave me a gold coin to read. Somehow-somehow the coin is connected to incredible anger and a tragedy in our family. Retrocognition can be horrifying."

"What did you see?"

He tried to be clinical about it. "I heard a lot of arguing and screaming and gun fire. I saw a beautiful woman getting half her face blown off by a blast from a shotgun. It was my great-grandmother."

Kyle stopped. Being clinical and detached didn't work. He rolled over, reached his arms around Cyndy and hugged her very tightly. It seemed as if all the fear he'd been suppressing had caught up with him.

"Kyle?" she asked and she tenderly stroked the back of his head. "Kyle? Oh my god, you're shaking." She reached over and spread the beach towel over him. "Easy, Kye."

But he continued to shake.

Kyle's surrendering to fear ignited years of suppressed emotions. He had lost his brother to a freak accident, his mother to cancer. Now his father had been taken from him and he had gained a frightening new power of perception. In that moment, it all combined and totally overwhelmed him. He alternately sobbed and gasped for breath. Wave after overwhelming wave of grief burned through him. He would not loosen his grip on Cyndy. She was his anchor.

He wept until his head hurt and he had cried himself out.

It took some time, but he finally eased his grip on her.

"I'm a mess, he said hoarsely. "And I have made a mess of your swimsuit."

"It's not the first time."

He looked up. She was smiling. "Clever, Dr. Weaver." He realized she had been crying, too.

"Share my towel?" he asked, sitting up and handing her one end of his beach towel. "No, allow me." And he reached over and dried her cheeks with the towel then turned and leaned against the log.

She sat up straight and extended her arm around his shoulders reassuring him, "I'm here for you."

"Cyndy, you haven't seen me in three years and here you are, come all this way to coddle a pitiful wreck."

"Well, I can't flee. My legs are asleep," she replied trying to lighten the mood.

"Damn good thing."

"And," she assured him, "I love you too much to allow you to face all this alone."

"Thank you," he told her sounding quite humble. "Is this the part where we make love right here in the sand while the sun sets and music swells in the background?"

Not possible. My entire lower half is asleep. For now," she reached over with both hands and, drawing his face to hers, she kissed him. It was a long slow kiss; their tongues caressed lovingly over and under and around each other.

Then she released him and they both leaned back against the tree trunk.

"Wow," he said, "thank you. What do we do now?"

With her hand on his face, she turned his head towards her. "We go back to your bedroom and have the most incredible make up sex in the history of the world."

"What?" Kyle asked and sat up.

"What?" she asked.

"Stop! There's more I have to tell you! I need your help and now is not exactly the time for you —"

"I know," she said, overlapping.

"I would love to share makeup sex with you. But you have to help me gain some perspective on this crazy situation, okay?"

"Okay. Now lie down again and tell the doctor the rest of what's going on."

"You know everything. Now, here's what's happened." Kyle related the details of his time with Mason including that Norman was blackmailing Mason. The result, he explained, was the scheme with the bearer bonds.

"That was a very generous thing for you to do."

"And," Kyle added, "yes, we did mess around including jacking each other off after swimming... And we had oral sex in the shower."

"Okay, Wilson. That's hot."

"It sure is easy to confess when I'm stoned. I wonder if the Catholic Church ever tried it? I tell you about Mason as easily as —Oh shit! I need to call him. He went to Woodmoor for me last night to spy on Norman."

"Oh?"

"Okay, Norman was meeting with the lawyer and —oh shit. Okay. You need to know this but tell no one. No one, understand?"

"Agreed. But what?"

"Here's the thing. There are two last wills and testament. One cuts me out, one doesn't. The second one I read is only a draft. But what if the lawyer brought the revised and signed document to Norman last night? I asked Mason to go to the house and use the intercom to spy on the meeting in case Norman's going to pull something."

"So, a phone call to Daniel Mason is in order when we get back to the house."

"Absolutely! And now ... oh wow. I wonder ..."

"What?"

"Maybe the bearer bonds … do you think Norman getting the ten thousand dollars changes what Norman is going to do? Johnny's prediction could no longer be what's gonna happen!"

"You think," Cyndy added, "what Johnny foretold won't happen? The only way to find out is to go to the source."

"Oh no." Kyle exclaimed and jumped to his feet.

"You have to talk to your brother Johnny."

"Fuck!" he kept exclaiming as he fell to his knees in the sand. "You're right."

"There's a first," she deadpanned.

He took a deep breath and exhaled noisily.

"Whoa, Kye, what is that about?" she asked.

"There's one more thing you need to know Cyndy." He said staring down at the sand.

"As much as I am in love with you, Cyndy, I am in love with Daniel Mason."

"I get it."

"I love you both very much and I don't know what am I going to do about it. Considering what I have experience in the past 72 hours, I know you are both very important to me. I love you both very much. It's not cocks and pussies and orgasms it's a connection. It's like you are the same person."

"Ever see us both in the same place?" She asked.

Kyle looked at Cyndy for a moment. Then he fell sideways into the sand.

He looked down the beach. The old man and woman had packed up their things and were departing. The little boy ran over to the girl's blanket. *Whoa. Brown bikini lady is playing cards with green Speedo guy. How cool is that? And that is so cute,* he observed as the little boy gave each of them a hug. *Sweet.*

The little boy then rejoined his grandparents. As they walked up the beach to the break in the snow fencing the students all waved. It was all smiles as the little boy and his grandparents waved back.

Kyle let out a long sigh, then sat up. "Well, I suppose if life were simple, it would be boring."

"Life with you is never boring," she replied, adding, "I missed that, I missed that a whole lot."

"Yeah. I missed you, too." he said standing up and brushing off some of the sand. "Right now, I am gonna grab some clean clothes and go talk to my dead brother."

"But the funeral home is in what, nine hours? You have to be there."

"So, I better hit the road real soon, and I certainly hope you will come along."

# CHAPTER EIGHTEEN

*KYLE VISITS WITH JOHNNY*
*Saturday Afternoon in Woodmoor*

Tunes from Abby Road played on the stereo as they crossed Delaware and cruised westward. There was no conversation. Things were uncomfortable since Aunt Rebecca insisted she go with them.

She started nagging them the moment they returned to the beach. She stopped them after they had changed and were walking out the door.

"I have unfinished business with Kyle. The ride will give us an opportunity to review a few things."

No matter what they told her she responded, "I understand." She then pressed her case again. She was desperate for him to help find "her inheritance" and she kept insisting every which way she could. He kept dodging her insistences to the point both were in foul moods when they got into the car. She hopped into the back seat. No matter how Kyle asked her to let them travel alone, she refused to budge from the back seat.

With the air in the car thick with disagreement, Kyle took off for the western shore.

Forty minutes into the drive, Kyle finally broke the silence.

"You know, now Dad's moved on, we're inheriting several hundred acres of prime pastureland in the upper county. We should become farmers. I was thinking we form our own government and secede from the States. Then start the biggest marijuana farm in North America. We'll be rich!"

Cyndy laughed and then asked, "can I marry you for your money and your drugs?"

"You betcha, sweet cheeks."

"You're sounding like Norman again."

Rebecca then chimed in saying, "we could make Norman king of the new country. That would please his megalomaniacal tendencies don't you think? He could then wage war on surrounding counties and grow his empire."

"The new and improved Norman conquest!" Cyndy added.

Rebecca began laughing. For some reason the concept seriously amused her. She kept repeating "King Norman" or "his royal highness, Norman." Then laughing a bit too loud she exclaimed, "that way he can make his staff kiss his ring as well as his ass!" And she laughed so loud she snorted.

Aunt Rebecca peppered Cyndy with questions about her paranormal research.

"How do you balance what you see as a medical student with your paranormal research? The things visible and the things invisible?"

"It's a lot to think about. When I'm in the ER and we have someone crash I can't exactly go into a trance and convince a spirit to come back to a damaged body. The biggest lesson is we have so little control."

"It's all predestined?" asked Rebecca.

"Not at all," Cyndy responded. "Predestination negates free will. We all control our fate."

"Then time is linear?" Kyle asked.

"Whoa, that's a leap," Cyndy responded.

"No, it's not," Kyle continued. "Predestination by its very definition requires time to be non-linear. We're simply following someone's scenario. So, if time were linear there is far more opportunity for the altering of fate."

"What if it were all true?" Rebecca chimed in.

Their discussion of the nature of the universe and time kept them entertained for a couple hours. Kyle cut it off announcing, "and on that note, we have arrived." He pulled into the driveway and up to the back of the house. "Here we are, sufficiently primed to go into a certifiably haunted house!"

And they did.

Once in the basement, Kyle explained what he saw and how he fell.

As he was telling his story, Rebecca went behind the bar and fixed herself a drink.

Holding up the Gilbey's Gin bottle she asked, "Anyone else?"

"No thank you," Cyndy answered over her shoulder as she was moving around and scoping out the room.

"Gotta stay clear-headed," Kyle responded.

"Let's get to brass tacks, then, "Rebecca began. "My grand-father promised me half of his savings, but John kept telling me to leave it alone. Kyle, you know I loved him and I am sorry he is gone." Another sip of her drink and then she continued in a very demanding manner. "God bless John, may he rest in peace, but I'm still here and I want what's coming to me, understand? Kyle? Kyle, answer me!"

"Aunt Rebecca, I understand —" Kyle began.

"No, I don't think you do. Nick and I visited with Grand-daddy back in the 1930's. He told me there were a thousand or more gold coins he kept put away for a rainy day. Far as I could find out, they were never touched."

She stopped speaking and removed the thin chain around her neck and held out toward Kyle. "This," she insisted, "this gold coin was one of many. Granddaddy told me so. Here, please. Please read it and tell me where the rest are."

"I can't do that."

"He told me the one coin he sent me was from a sack that held more than a thousand just like it.. He told me John and I should get them when he passed. John and me, understand?" she shouted. "Do you understand me, Kyle?" She was working herself into a fury.

"Please don't do this, Aunt Rebecca."

"We're in the shitter financially! We need that money, Kyle. It's hundreds of thousands and half is rightfully mine. I deserve to finally get it!" She took a gulp of her drink, set it down and came around the bar.

The energy in the room was charged with her anger. Cyndy noticed the basement was suddenly growing warmer and very humid. "Kyle —" she started to ask.

He held up his hand asking, "Cyndy, please?"

"You can help me, Kyle!"

"No. Aunt Becca, I can't —"

"I know you can!" she shouted as she tried to grab his hand and put the coin in it.

"No!" Kyle shouted backing away from her; his hands raised high. "I don't want to see that woman's face butchered by that shotgun blast! Please!"

That stopped her. "Then it's true!" Rebecca began, but stopped.

The air in the room had become noticeably humid and a stench seemed to rise from the floor.

"What is happening here?" Cyndy asked in a monotone.

Her wide-eyed expression caused both Rebecca and Kyle to turn.

The tall, bearded Nelson Wilson seemed to step out of the far wall.

Wolf-like, the apparition bared his teeth and charged across the room towards toward Rebecca who screamed and fell back against the wall.

For Kyle, it was as if time had slowed. Movements slowed, sound elongated. Rebecca's scream became a wail as she fell back, arms splayed, against the paneled wall. Cyndy was as still as a statue. All watched in horror. The disheveled man, his clothes torn and streaked with mud seemed positively real. As did the threat to her life as he charged at Rebecca with arms raised above his head as if he was aiming to strike her with something.

Rebecca closed her arms around her head and ducked. The apparition dissolved.

The room was still. Kyle, Rebecca and Cyndy stood motionless staring at the empty space. A sharp metallic "ping" cut the silence. Rebecca had dropped the gold coin.

More sharp metal sounds followed as the gold coin bounced several times. Once last "clink" and it settled on the cold floor. Silence.

Kyle and Cyndy rushed to Aunt Rebecca's side and each grabbed an arm as she started to slide down the wall towards the floor.

"I'm okay. Okay," she repeated as if in a trance. She stood up. They let go of her and she moved away from them and up the stairs. She was repeating "I'm okay, I'm okay" so many times that it was obvious she was not.

"Kyle?"

Stunned, he blurted out: "Pretty impressive boogieman, huh?"

"Enough to make anyone run up the stairs," she called over her shoulder as she rushed over to the bar. "I have so many questions!" she said as she grabbed the bottle of gin and headed for the stairs. "I will take care of your aunt." She tossed him a small velvet bag.

"We should go —" he started to say.

"Yes, we'll get her out of here as soon as possible. Use that rosary and do what you came here to do."

"Fly solo?" Kyle whined.

"Suck it up, kiddo. The scary part is over —or it's not." And with that, Cyndy was gone.

Kyle held the velvet bag as he wandered around the basement. He stared at an object or piece of furniture and let it trigger a random memory or two. He was like a child with an attention disorder. He couldn't focus on one item for more than a few seconds. At the bar, he noticed the guns in the rack. *Hmmm,* he wondered- *little shinier than I remember. The stocks seem polished. Someone recently clean them? Were they that way on Thursday? Who would do that?* He started to reach for the old Winchester. "Oh no," he stopped himself. "I don't need images of violence in my head right about now. Dead deer or bunnies- or people."

"But now" he told the empty room, "trance time." He chose a spot: the braided rug in front of the deacon's bench.

It had been years since Kyle followed any religion. But he believed that any ritual acknowledging a universal power summoned positive energy. So, he took the rosary from the little velvet bag and placed it on the deacon's bench. He recited The Lord's Prayer aloud. He then lay down on the rug parallel to the bench, closed his eyes and began to meditate.

He cleared his mind by focusing on the singular image of a candle flame on the inside of his closed eyelids. He felt its light and warmth embrace him. He appealed to the creator of all things visible and invisible.

"Please," he asked, "watch over me as I step into the gap between this world and the next."

He focused on the pure light and warmth of the flame.

He focused on the silence.

He could feel his heartbeat slow down as he experienced a familiar serenity. Along with it came a heightened awareness.

He was lying on the floor, he knew it. He was also able to sense everything in the house. He felt all the materials that made the structure and its contents. He felt connected to every atom of every item that composed all that he could see. And what a visual! The clarity was astonishing. Every detail of the room in his direct and peripheral vision were defined as if lit from every angle all at once.

Then he saw a light. He saw a shimmering light growing in intensity in the far corner of the room. It was not far from where Nelson Wilson first appeared.

He closed his eyes and concentrated on the light and the warmth it projected.

With new strength and courage, he held his eyes closed and made the next required move. He rose out of his body and into the unknown.

It was time to open his eyes. Not that it was a matter of opening his eyes. He was no longer in possession of his mortal form in which opening eyes was necessary for sight. It was no longer a matter of sight, sound, smell, taste nor touch. Awareness was all. It was a process of opening up; dropping all resistance and opening himself up to total awareness.

All senses combined.

For certainty, he confirmed he was still tethered to his mortal form by the familiar silver cord. It was an umbilical cord of pure energy.

"Kyle?" It was the voice of a young boy so familiar to him. "Kyle?"

The light in the corner started taking shape as it moved towards him. In a period of time shorter than thought, the boy stepped forward. His hazel eyes glistened.

Kyle reached out, as did the boy. Their hands grasped tightly and Kyle was enveloped in the care, understanding and love he missed since his brother was taken from him. A hatred for his brother Norman began to rise in him.

"Don't dwell on it, Kyle. Norman killed me and, eventually, he will have to deal with that. It's time for you to complete this work and to get on with your life."

For several moments the two boys were very still and calm and pleasant beyond any serenity known to the fleshy world.

"Did Dad get to see Mom?"

"'See' is not a word you'd use around here. You have to stop thinking three dimensionally. It has been some time since you have explored this level of consciousness."

"Can you blame me? You had such good news for me last time we talked."

"I told you the truth," Johnny explained with a slight laugh.

"Are you laughing at me? You're making me feel very defensive."

"Don't be that way, Kye. Just because I died doesn't mean I forgot how to laugh. It is arrogant to think laughter only exists on your side of the veil."

"That's good news, sure, but did Dad meet Mom or not? Jeez, Johnny, it's important to me."

"It was important to him as well. Theirs is more than a

recent connection. There are many links between them for many lifetimes."

"Is Dad okay? I want to know he is okay.

"Kyle, they are both very 'okay' as you understand it. We are all concerned for you. This is going to be very difficult for you. We know your fear."

"Then here's the big question, Johnny – Since I gave Norman all that money. Does that change things?"

"Norman is greedy. He wants everything."

"You're not answering my question."

"The answer, Kyle, is nothing has changed. You're going to have to stop him, even if you have to kill him- because if you don't, he will kill you."

Kyle felt a cry of protest forming in his throat. Then it dissolved as a new sensation, a feeling of warmth embraced him. There was nothing in his experience to which he could compare the sensation. He considered it for a brief moment. He felt someone touching each shoulder blade. The proper imagery formed in his mind: he felt he had grown wings and he could fly.

"And you, Kyle, "he heard a familiar and reassuring voice intone, "are no Icarus. And we are with you."

"Mom?"

"You are not alone, son."

"Dad? Holy-" But he could not find words. What he saw with his mind's eye wasn't the pathetic skeletal being he last saw at the hospital. He saw the vibrant woman she was before her battle with the cancers. His vision of his Dad was of the man whose face was far less etched by the challenges of time.

In that realm, there could be no embracing as we know it on

this side of the veil. A simple connection as two fingers touching could convey all matter of emotions. Holding his brother's hand and with his parents' hands on his back, there was a powerful connection. Kyle felt safe. He felt womb safe and very happy.

"I love you," was all that needed to be said.

That thought hovered in the air and enveloped all of them and sustained Kyle.

"You are not alone, son," his father told him as mother and father slipped away.

Their parting was not painful. It was what needed to happened at the moment and Kyle realized that without judgment nor regret.

"I will do my best, he reassured himself, but then asked, "Why should I go back? Why leave this euphoria? This deadly state is pleasurable."

"Here you are not alive nor are you dead," his brother reminded him "There is work we all have to do, Kyle. I'm here and you're there and there is work that has to be done."

"But I am tired of being without you, Johnny."

"I am with you most of the time. I am happy you have spent time with Mace."

He paused. "He needs to be honest with himself about who he is, and you will help him. Know I love you both and have always been with you."

"Johnny. Thank you. I like how this works. I feel closer to you than ever."

At that moment, from the light, there came three dark shades.

"Kyle, careful!" Johnny warned him.

Kyle suddenly felt very cold. Instinctually looked back to see himself lying prone on the floor by the deacon's bench. His body, prone on the oval carpet was now overshadowed by the dark figure stooping by his right shoulder. It was getting closer.

"Kyle, go back!"

"No, I —"

Just then, the rosary slipped off the deacon's bench and fell across Kyle's lifeless form's right arm.

The dark figure retreated followed by its two companions.

"See, Johnny?" Kyle chided, "Still charmed."

They were two spirits in the midst of a universe capable of crushing them to nothingness. Yet at this moment, they laughed. They laughed and the shades disappeared into a distance.

Kyle was in the basement he had so often feared. He was in the basement where he had had his most horrifying experience only days before. But Kyle was with his twin brother for the first time in twelve years. And for the first time in twelve years he experienced familiar caring, loving and wanting. He didn't want to return to the world. He also knew he could not avoid the responsibility that was once Johnny`s had now fallen upon his shoulders.

Kyle sighed.

"Kyle," Johnny began in a most reassuring voice, "you have the strength of legions now, remember? Mom, Dad, you and I were together. Remember the purity of that strength."

"I have the power to fly. I may need some reassurance. Can we talk again, Johnny?" he asked.

"It will happen," he assured his brother adding, "Take care

of Mason for me. Cyndy can help you with that. I love you both very much."

Kyle then sensed a letting go. Johnny withdrew. In less than a second, Kyle could feel the full weight of his body there on the basement floor.

He moved his head, looking side to side. He raised his knees to his chest a couple times to stretch his legs. Then he extended his arms and then placed his hands behind his head.

"Hmm. While down here I could find that coin and didn't I see something under the deacon's bench?"

He turned his head. On the floor to his left was a business envelope with a familiar logo and return address. He pulled the envelope out from under the bench and sat up almost at the same time. "Damn!" he exclaimed aloud as he read the typing on the envelope. "Last will and testament John Wilson, signed and witnessed December 26, 1971."

The empty envelope presented Kyle with somewhat of a puzzle. Could it have floated under the bench when I dropped the strong box, he wondered? No. That envelope only had a date on it. It must have been the draft copy I gave to Norman. This one is marked "signed and witnessed"-could one of them have dropped it when they met here last night?

So, he held the envelope and concentrated. He instantly heard threats; two men shouting; Norman and the lawyer.

"Okay!" Kyle wondered aloud with a long exhale of breath. "The second will was signed and that has pissed off Norman. That's gonna take further investigation, but for now-" and as he rose from the floor, he saw a glint of reflective light.

"Ah, there you are you little troublemaker."

Kyle knelt down and quickly picked up the gold coin and put in into the envelope without "reading" it. He then folded the envelope and stuffed it into his pocket.

He went upstairs and found Cyndy and Aunt Becca on the couch in the living room.

"She okay?"

"She'll be fine, I think."

"I'm right here, dear."

"And I think that's a damn good thing," he said with a big smile.

"Thank you."

"And now, ladies, it is time for all of us to return to the Eastern Shore."

# CHAPTER NINETEEN

## *A WAKE IS HELD FOR JOHN WILSON*
### *Saturday Evening in Henlopen*

As he drove away from Woodmoor, Kyle was dwelling on the situation. *I am going to have to kill Norman. It's either that or* — Kyle paused and then forced himself. *Or I will die.*

*Could it be my time?*

*I was there. "The other side" is pleasant. But I wasn't dead. Or was I? The silver cord was not severed. Is it the same once the cord gets cut? Should I let things play out?*

Cyndy's touch brought him back to reality. She had been sorting through Kyle's collection of cassette tapes. The stack of tapes on the console were about to spill over so she grabbed them. When she did, her hand brushed his leg.

*Then there is Cyndy.*

Feeling her hand on his leg; looking down at her long slender fingers; then gazing at her profile. *We're good together. I am not imagining that. Am I ready to leave her? Be apart again?* He glanced over at her again. She was smiling at him.

"Nice to be working together again, isn't it?" she asked poking him in the shoulder.

"Absolutely, Dr. Weaver."

Cyndy started humming and returned to her sorting.

*I can't give in to Norman that easily. No way. But how to stop him?*

Kyle continued sorting the possibilities for the next several miles. Cyndy considered the different cassettes.

Having availed herself of a couple of little blue pills, Aunt Rebecca was asleep in the backseat.

Looking at the sleeping woman in the back seat, Cyndy observed, "for a doctor, she sure is liberal with the drugs."

"Better living through chemistry she always told us," Kyle responded.

Gesturing towards the backseat, Cyndy told Kyle, "I've been thinking-"

"Dangerous habit."

"-of the Baltimore Street haunting. Thoughts?"

"Agreed. Plus complete written observations before anything is discussed." Cyndy added.

That would be their routine after any encounter: each type up a contemporaneous account. In this case, "Baltimore" was their code word for keeping information to themselves.

It was very difficult for Kyle to remain quiet in regard to the new evidence he'd learned. He was anxious to talk about his experience. He also knew talking it over with Cyndy would help clarify the possibilities. But his thoughts were shattered by "Back in the USSR" blaring on the car stereo.

"What the fuck?"

"-oops," Cyndy uttered as she adjusted the volume.

She turned to check the backseat. The old woman snorted slightly and adjusted herself against the back seat.

"Sorry, Kyle."

Cyndy had selected the Beatles' "White Album." Its mixed bag of songs played as Kyle and Cyndy discussed their post-college plans.

Kyle was happy to hear she is being considered by both GW and Georgetown for her next job. She could be in town for the next 3 to 5 years. Wouldn't be a bad thing.

They listened to the music for several miles and then Kyle spoke up. "Do you think we could get a place together if your residency is at a DC hospital?"

"Well, that's interesting. We could. But what about Mason?"

"Hmmm. We could move to France together and vie la ménage trois."

"Oh sure, Kyle. I haven't even met him and you're speculating about a three-way? Oh, please."

"Hey, don't knock it. San Francisco, 1968. I was taught by this hippie couple who were very fond of me."

"For real?"

He let that image hover and said no more.

She broke the silence. "You would actually want to resume our relationship after all these years?"

"Yes. Or we could be housemates and see what develops; you know, see how it plays out."

"You're serious."

"Yeah."

"Let me consider it."

"Okay," Kyle concluded. Then his mind went into overdrive. *What the fuck did I do? No. Stop. It feels right. Shut up and let her think.*

Except for unrelated small talk, they stuck to their own thoughts for the rest of the drive.

* * *

Rebecca woke with a start as soon as Kyle had turned off the car.

"Where?" she started to ask. "Oh. Well. Nice nap."

"Hold out your hand," Kyle told her. He opened the envelope and emptied the contents into her palm. "This gold coin is yours. You hold on to it."

"There's more, you know," she told him, trying to lock eyes with her nephew. But he looked away. "Please, Kyle, I need your help to find the rest of it."

"Let's put Dad to rest and then we will work on that, okay, Aunt Becca?"

"Promise?"

"You betcha."

Pleased with her nephew's vow, Rebecca got out of the car and headed to the carriage house where she and her husband were staying.

Cyndy was silent until she was certain the old woman was

out of earshot. "Did you just lie to her?" she asked Kyle without judgment.

"Well," Kyle began, considering his words. "She's in big financial trouble. I think I can help her out. But first things first. My dear dead brother Johnny pretty much told me the bearer bonds didn't do the trick. I need to stop Norman before one of us gets killed. I know it's possible."

"How?"

"I don't know but I'll think of something. I have an envelope that tells me the second will was signed and Norman wants it destroyed. There's no lawyer to stop him from doing it now."

"That's his plan?"

"So it seems. I need corroborating evidence. I can't move ahead on what I 'read' by touching this envelope. Last time I looked psychometry is not acceptable evidentiary procedure in a court of law."

"So, if Norman destroys this second will-"

"He gets control of everything. That's what the old will says. Cyndy, I know I'm not supposed to talk until I write it all down. But I gotta tell you it was pretty fucking trippy. I was with Johnny, Mom and Dad. This funeral is only a formality." Kyle stopped.

"What?" Cyndy asked.

The Harley Davidson motorcycle parked beside the drive distracted Kyle for a moment. "But," he told Cyndy, "I want to write it all down first. Contemporaneous reporting, right, chief?"

"You betcha. And I am so looking forward to reading it."

"Come with me. I am about to get the evidence I need to back up what the envelope told me."

He led her around the side of the house and through the side gate to the patio between the house and the pool.

"Who," Cyndy asked Kyle, "is the man on the raft at the far end of the pool?"

"That, my dear, is Daniel Mason."

"Mason as in Johnny's best friend and your former- the guy on the raft is Daniel Mason?"

"Something wrong?"

"Kyle, you have the best of taste, she whispered. "He's what my mom would call 'Marlboro man handsome'."

"He's more of a Newport kind of guy," Kyle observed with a grin.

"Men like him prove homophobia is mere jealousy."

They took one step in Mason's direction, but Trish stopped them. She grabbed their arms and turned them towards the house.

"It's about time to be going to the funeral home. Get changed you two."

"Right," Kyle responded, then added, "but give me-"

"No!" Tricia exclaimed a little too forcefully and started herding them towards the house. "It's mandatory you get there soon. The first half hour is for family only. Come on!"

"No problem, Trish," Cyndy responded and the two of them grabbed Kyle by the arms and pulled him toward the house. "Inside you go."

Kyle turned on the charm and slipped from their grasp explaining, "Sis, I will be up in a minute. Go. There's a business matter I need to discuss with Mason." Cyndy shot him a look, but he assured her, "banking business ladies. Money matters. I will be up in less than five minutes."

"It better be quick!" Trish admonished him, then she turned and went into the house with Cyndy.

Mason was toweling off at the other end of the pool as Kyle headed toward him.

"Mace!"

"Kye!"

"This is why I haven't been able to reach you? You're down here sunning your handsome self at the old homestead? You did get into the house yesterday, right?"

"In like Flint; used the intercom like you said caught Norman's conversation with the lawyer. Your brother is trying to pull a fast one on you, Kye."

"Dad did sign the new will?"

"The new will is official, but Norman tried to bribe the lawyer into destroying it. Norman offered him the third bearer bond as a 'bonus' but your lawyer refused. Fucking Norman got downright belligerent with the old man. I wish I had a tape recorder. But the worse part, from what I heard, I am pretty sure Norman could have prevented he old man's death."

"How?"

"Get this: they're arguing. The lawyer refuses to play along with Norman's scheme. I hear one of them shouting 'what the hell is that?' and there's a scream- Norman - yelling 'mother fuck!' Then it sounds like he's trying to get the old guy's attention; get him to say something, but gets no reply. Then I hear Norman on the phone. He only pretended to call the rescue squad the first time."

"The first time?"

"Yep. First call was a fake."

"How do you know it was fake?"

"No one calls 911 then ten minutes later calls them again and talks as if it's the first time he's reporting an emergency. He had to be faking the first call."

"Motherfucker. You say anything to him when you got here today?"

"No. It's eating away at me. I couldn't help save the man's life. But by the time I realized the first call was fake, it was too late. I sat still until everyone left and then I got out of there. We need to talk to him, Kyle" Mason insisted.

"No. Not until we have solid evidence."

"I was there. I know what he did. He let the old man die. We gotta nail him on that!"

"Norman's rotten enough to destroy your credibility first. He'd subpoena you and the photos and claim you're making all this up as revenge."

At that moment, the patio door slid open a little too noisily. "Kyle! Mason!" Trish yelled out them patio door. "I'm leaving soon with Vicki and the kids. Get a move on you two!"

"Fine!" Kyle called back to her. "I'm coming in now."

"No problem, Trish," Mason assured her. "We'll see you there. Guys take less time to prepare."

"Don't be a sexist pig, Mason. It doesn't become you," Trish answered making a face at them and then closing the sliding door.

Kyle turned back to Mason and explained, "We do nothing for now, okay? Trust me."

"Of course, I trust you."

"Did Norman say anything to you?"

"I'm invisible to him. But Trish and Vicki have been most welcoming.

"I'm glad you're here, Mace."

"Are you sure?"

"Huh?"

"That was Cyndy Weaver, right? This is awkward. I used your room to change and left my bag in there."

"Well, no time like the present. Come. I will introduce you. I need to change and get to the funeral home." Kyle started towards the house. "Let's go."

"You go. I'll give you and Cyndy time to change then I'll use your room."

"Fine." Kyle gave Mason a quick hug, and whispered to him, "make no mistake, I want you here. Got it?"

"Got it," Mason replied.

"Good," Kyle told him and then he headed into the house.

Mason thought for a moment. *Yep. He might want me here, but the question really has nothing to do with want. The question is who is he going to have in his bed tonight?*

\*\*\*

Kyle pulled into the funeral home's parking lot and discovered there were very few empty spaces.

"Wow, Cyndy exclaimed

"Yeah," Kyle responded. "Dad had a lot of friends."

Oh, the cars, certainly. But I meant these pages. Take them and put them away- I have one more nail."

"Kinda burned up the typewriter, didn't I?"

"Your typing has improved since law school."

"Did you record your notes?"

"Yes."

"You always travel with your cassette recorder?"

"Old habits." She smiled and blew on her fingernails. "I will transcribe it tonight for you to look over."

He watched her for a moment.

"What?" she asked.

"Thank you for coming."

"Sure."

"Okay." He said, then after a deep breath, he reassured himself. "I can handle this," he told himself as he got out of the car and went around to open Cyndy's car door.

He opened the door. She looked up at him. "I look okay, don't I? I mean-"

"Miss Weaver you bring a whole new sexiness to the little black dress. Trust me. You do."

And with that, Kyle held out his hand, which she took, and he helped her from the car.

She had taken a couple steps away from the car, but Kyle didn't move.

"Damn! I don't want to be in the same room as Norman right now."

"You want a valium? I brought some in case. An advantage of being in the medical profession."

Kyle was about to respond when he noticed Cyndy look over his shoulder. "We've got company," she whispered and reached out and loosened his tie and undid his collar button.

"Family?" he whispered back.

Kyle thought he felt someone approaching. The whiskey breath gave it away. "Norman and Susan?"

She nodded.

Turning to his brother, Kyle greeted him with a flat, "Hello, Norman."

"Brother Kyle," Norman gushed, "hell of a day, huh? We have to be strong for Vicki and Patricia, right?"

Kyle hugged Susan and told her, "Could you get him a peppermint or something?"

"I'm working on it," she replied adding, "I could use some help."

Backing away from Susan, Kyle produced a small plastic box and he pressed the box of Tic Tac mints into his brother's hand.

"That's our Kyle," Norman announced, "always looking out for his big brother. Thanks, buddy. Shall we go in?"

"We'll see you inside." Cyndy insisted as she fussed with Kyle's neckwear. "I have to fix Kyle's crooked tie."

With a shrug, Norman turned away and he and Susan crossed the parking lot and went into the funeral home.

"Is it my imagination," observed Cyndy, "or does he insist she walk behind him whenever they go anywhere?"

"He has to enter the room first. Asshole."

Cyndy re-buttoned his collar button and fixed his tie. The sight over her shoulder made him smile. "More family," he told her. "Extended family."

His tie all neat and straight, Kyle stepped back from Cyndy and announced, "Cindy, you know Alice, right? And new detective Michael Henderson as well?"

"Detective? Impressive. Congratulations Michael," she added, giving him a quick kiss on the cheek. "Hello, Alice, it has been a while."

"This," Alice observed as she gave Cyndy a hug, "could almost count as our four-year college reunion."

"Is reunion what you call it?" Cyndy observed "You have known each other since grade school, right?"

"And the four of us still talk to each other," Alice added. "But where is he? He told me we'd see him here."

"He?" Cyndy asked.

"Yeah, I would think he would be here," Henderson observed.

His words were almost drowned out by the harsh sound of a motorcycle entering the funeral home parking lot. The rider gunned the engine and then switched it off.

"Well that answers that question," Mike offered with exaggerated volume.

Cyndy realized who they were speaking of as he removed his helmet. "Oh my god," she breathed. "It's his Harley?"

"Yeah," Kyle chuckled. "How butch is that, huh?"

"He is so fucking male." She whispered into Kyle's ear.

"Hey, no secrets in the happy huggy wolf pack," Alice complained.

"What?"

"A name someone branded us with years ago," Kyle explained.

"'Cille dubbed you an honorary member," Alice added. "You remember, 'Cille, right?"

"Lucille, of course. Where's she nowadays?"

"Ancient history," Mike chimed in.

"Is there something-" Cyndy began.

"Cille broke Mike's heart when she decided she was a

lesbian and moved away to Pittsburg with some chick named Max. I healed it."

As usual, Mike shot her a look, but did not comment. He had long felt personal matters were only that: personal. But he would never correct Alice. It was love.

"The wolf pack plus one," Mason commented as he joined the group. "Too bad it's a sad occasion that brings us together."

Kyle gave Mason a big bear hug.

"Sorry old buddy, so sorry," Mason whispered in Kyle's ear.

"Thanks, Moose. Now, say hello to another dear friend of mine, Cyndy Weaver. Cyndy, my very good friend, Daniel Mason."

"Moose?" Cyndy had to ask.

Coach dubbed me 'Moose' because I wasn't as graceful as he wanted me to be in my approach to gymnastics."

"But you were awesome on the rings," Mike added. "But enough about him. Shouldn't we be going in?"

"Almost. I've got to ask Alice something," Kyle explained as he took her arm and steered her away from the group. "Visit among yourselves. We will be right back."

She took his hand in hers. "What is up my brother in the mystical arts?" she asked half joking.

"This psychometric thing- doing readings with touch- how do you turn it off?"

"Holy shit, Wilson, I knew you were psychic but you can do —"

"Stop, Alice. I need to know. I mean there is so much out there and most of it I don't want to know. Can I block it?"

Alice took both of his hands into hers. "When you touch

something or someone focus on the empty space between you and object."

"It's that simple?"

"Yep. Concentrate on the empty space and you will get nothing. Then again, you might start seeing auras."

"That's it?"

Suddenly he heard Mason and Cyndy laughing, and Michael joined in.

"What the-?" Asked Kyle.

Alice smiled. "Kyle, I saw this coming along time ago if you recall. There's a connection the three of you have that will confound everyone. Trust me."

"I can't even go there right now."

"You already have, Kyle."

"Is it going to have a happy ending?"

"Kyle the universe is, in many ways, a very uncomplicated place. It doesn't try to confound us. We confound us by layering on all kinds of meanings and shit if you know what I mean."

Alice felt more affection for Kyle than ever. She reached out and put her hand on his left shoulder. "It's all good," she told him.

Her smile turned in a very surprised expression and she immediately recoiled.

"What was that?" he asked her.

"I can't believe it. Mason is flirting with your girlfriend."

Kyle felt she was lying, but he let it go.

Cyndy was laughing when they returned to the group.

"Mason tells good stories, Kyle," Cyndy observed a little too casually.

"Most at your expense," Mike added.

"Not true! Well, yeah," Mason explained.

The small talk continued for a few more minutes until Kyle could no longer put it off. "Time to go in I guess."

\* \* \*

To some people the aroma off flowers can be a little over-whelming when you walk into a viewing room, but not to Kyle. Ever since Johnny's funeral, Kyle found the scent of flowers to be like a pillow of sorts. A very comfortable pillow is what came to mind when Kyle paused in the doorway to the viewing room. The place was very crowded.

Suddenly uneasy, he reached out and took Cyndy's hand in his right hand and Alice's hand in his left.

Alice leaned toward him and whispered, "He's not here you know. Just the shell he once used."

"He's with Johnny and Mom," Kyle responded. "We talked this afternoon."

"Go, Kyle. I always knew you could do it."

"Pretty fucking weird," he whispered, then added," neither of you let go of my hands and stay close. I don't want to touch anyone else's hands."

"Mace and I have your six," Henderson assured him from behind.

Kyle took a deep breath and then declared. "Let's proceed."

There were plenty of whispers behind hands as the group made their way through the crowd. Slowly, they reached the front of the room and Kyle's father's opened casket.

Trish was standing next to the casket making small talk with some neighbors.

"Our prayers are with you and the family."

"Thank you, Mrs. Fitzgerald, Mrs. Pearce."

The two women nodded silent greetings to Kyle and moved away to let the quintet join Trish next to the casket.

"Lot of flowers, huh?"

"You missed the half hour of family viewing. You owe me one, Kyle. I had to put up with those cousins of Vicki 's from Mississippi. They laid on hands and prayed wildly. I thought Henrietta was going to start speaking in tongues."

Cyndy spoke up. "My fault Trish."

"Stop." Kyle injected. "I will explain it to you later, sis, I know you'll understand. Geez, Dad looks so healthy."

"They do good work," Trish observed. She ran her hand across her father's cheek and then placed her hand on his two hands folded on his chest.

"He's so cold, Kyle. Take his hand."

"Trish," Kyle said after a pause and as he held tight to Cyndy and Alice's hands, "Give me time to get use to this."

Trish removed her hand from her father's clasped hands and Kyle saw the ring on his right hand. He knew the ring as one his father only wore on special occasions. It was gold and imbedded with a vintage twenty-dollar gold piece, a double eagle.

"Sure, Kyle, sure." Trish then moved away from the group and speak with some other friends.

Kyle looked to either side. Other than the wolf pack, no one was close. "Anyone close behind us, Alice?"

"Nope."

"Everyone seems to be keeping a respectful distance," Mike added. "You want us to leave you alone with your Dad?"

"Oh, no. Stay close, please. Cyndy," Kyle asked, "where is Aunt Rebecca?"

Cyndy glanced across the room. "Interesting. Aunt Rebecca just followed Norman out of the room."

"Good. I don't want her to see this."

Kyle stared at his Dad for a moment, then at the old man's hands and at the ring.

"Please, Kyle. A prayer first," Cyndy begged. "It will be less painful."

Standing there together, all five joined hands and recited the "Our Father" and on the "Amen," Kyle reached out and paused.

"Guys. Lay a hand on me and hold on no matter what, okay?"

Each whispered consent. Mason had his hand on Kyle's right shoulder and Mike had his on Kyle's left shoulder. Cyndy held his hand and Alice touched his arm, and for the second time that day, Kyle felt as if he had wings and could fly.

He grasped his father's dead hand being certain the ring with the gold coin nestled against his palm.

Kyle didn't move a muscle.

His four friends would later swear he wasn't even breathing.

It was difficult to remember to breathe. The images were coming at him so fast. He received the same images as this morning on the beach. As those receded, he saw the box, the initial hiding place and then marigolds. His father moved the box to the garden in their back yard under the marigolds when the new terrace was built. That's when he took this coin from the sack. And then there were emotions. Kyle understood his father's devotion to family and how much he cared for his grandfather. He pitied the old man and understood his tremendous loss.

Tears were streaming down Kyles face.

"It's okay, guys. Let go. I'm okay. Let go," he whispered and he leaned over and hugged his father.

*It may be a cold shell. He's not even here. But it's the thought of him I honor. I love you, Dad. And I know you love me. God be with you, and Mom and Johnny and the rest of those who have gone on ahead of us.*

He straightened up. Someone put a tissue in his hand, and he wiped his eyes and then turned to his four friends. "I'm good," Kyle assured them flashing his best boyish grin. "Saying goodbye to Dad." He then turned back to the casket, bent over and kissed his father's very cold forehead.

"I got this one, Dad," Kyle whispered into his father's ear.

He then turned and hugged his friends feeling he had spiked the landing after a very difficult vault.

"Come close like you're comforting me. Can you each hear me?" Four nods. Four affirmations.

"Good. I know what we need to do now. After the viewing and before the wake at the house, I need to speak with you. Cyndy and I are going to need your help tomorrow in Woodmoor. Cyndy, Mace, tell Alice and Mike everything you know. I want your word no one does anything until after we talk? Understood?"

Everyone agreed.

"I guess it's time for me to work the room," Kyle told them.

"You want us to stick with you?" Mason asked.

"No, I'm good. I'll let you say your goodbyes. I have to do the family thing."

Kyle patted Mason's hand, nodded to Michael, then gave Cyndy's hand a squeeze. He very gently took Alice's head in his hands. "Well, Alice, thanks." He kissed Alice on both cheeks. "Wish me luck."

"You'll do fine."

"Or not," Kyle added with a wink at Cyndy.

She winked back. "Oh yeah," he repeated. "I got this." And with that, Kyle turned to mingle with the rest of the mourners.

The next hour was a blur. Kyle circulated and spoke to the many people who had come to pay their respects.

At one point, Kyle saw Norman sneaking out of the viewing room and followed him. He caught up with his brother on the sidewalk as he was lighting up.

"Kyle! How ya holding up, little brother?" He exclaimed with a little too much bravado and he gave Kyle a hug.

"When we're done here," Kyle whispered to his brother, "you and I are going to get a drink and have a very serious talk."

"No worries, Kyle, you're going to be taken care of."

"Norman. I want to buy you out." He let go of his brother.

Norman broke the embrace and stepped back. He took a draw off his cigarette, studied his brother for a moment. and exhaled as he responded, "What an interesting idea, little brother. And with what assets? You have no cash."

"I have precious metals. Vintage coinage, you might say."

Norman took Kyle by the arm and lead him some ways down the brick walkway for a little more privacy. "Are you telling me," Norman hissed, "our batty old Aunt Rebecca is not making it all up?"

"I'm not sure what you're saying, but we do need to talk."

"I tell you what. Meet me at the house in Woodmoor at 1:00 tomorrow afternoon and we will discuss your ideas."

"I think you will be very happy with what I can give you tomorrow."

"One o'clock tomorrow it is."

"You and me, Norman. No one else, understood?"

"You won't bring your fan club?"

"You and me."

"I look forward to it, Kyle." He held out his hand. Kyle shook it firmly being sure to focus on the air between his brother's head and a nearby utility pole.

"Shall we return?"

"You go ahead. I want to finish this."

Kyle returned to the viewing room.

Norman was ecstatic.

*So, there is a stash of gold and that little shit knows where it is. Fine. I will get it from him. I will have it all. I better call Kent. This is going to go down like clockwork.*

Soon after the viewing room emptied out. Trish insisted she, Kyle and Norman say goodnight to their father together. They assembled next to the opened casket.

"I just need you two to be with me for this. He was a good father to us all, wasn't he?"

"He loved you very much," Norman assured his sister.

Kyle was once again amazed how Norman made an effort to say the right thing, and always sounded a little false.

*Sorry, Norman, you can't pull of sincerity. It's not in your blood.*

Vicki joined them beside the casket and handed each of them a long stemmed white rose.

"I'm pretty sure," she explained," we can agree none of us have been very religious. He'd be annoyed if we pretended we were and stood here saying prayers. But he would appreciate it if we left a remembrance. Each of us will leave a token of our love for John. He always loved the scent of roses."

She placed her rose across her husband's chest, whispering, "love for my love." Then she stepped back and quietly asked, "Now each of you, please? You don't have to say anything, but please give him your rose."

Norman placed his next. "Thanks, Dad. You're the best."

Trish was next. "I will never forget you Daddy."

Finally, Kyle placed the fourth rose. "Père au revoir." *(Until we meet again, father.)*

Kyle looked at Norman. *He's planning something.* Kyle thought. *But then again, so am I.*

# CHAPTER TWENTY

## *ALL TOGETHER NOW*
### *Saturday Night / Sunday Morning in Henlopen*

Kyle caught up with Cyndy, Alice and the guys in the parking and immediately asked Mike, "So did Mace fill you in?"

"Yeah. I could arrest Norman's ass for blackmail, however it would create all kinds of trouble for Mason."

"Sure enough. Besides," Kyle continued, "come tomorrow I am certain you'll get him on a lot more. We're going to get a confession on tape."

Mike, remember how you and Johnny used to play Hardy Boys and spy on people in the rec room?"

"You guys took those books too seriously," Alice chuckled.

"Alice," Mike responded, "might I remind you that you and Lucille and Nancy Drew were inseparable?"

Alice turned to Cyndy. "It was cute," she explained, "I would be Nancy, Lucille would be Nancy's 'boyish friend George.' Makes sense in retrospect, doesn't it?"

It took a moment, then Cyndy got it and laughed out loud.

"Sorry, Kyle," Alice explained. "This is getting a little to Brutus & Cassius so I thought I would try to lighten things up a little."

"Right," Kyle continued. "Cyndy and Alice are going to use the house intercom and get everything on tape. Mike, you and Mace are going to stake out in the workshop."

"The knot hole?" Mike asked.

"Exactly," Kyle affirmed. "It's still there."

"Oooo, that's murky," Cyndy interjected.

"The workshop," Mike explained, "is not paneled. The rec room is paneled. Johnny and I rigged a large knot in the knotty pine paneling so we could remove it and spy on the action in the rec room."

"In their Hardy Boys wannabe days." Alice added.

Cyndy and Mason laughed quietly. Henderson turned away for a moment. Alice adjusted her shawl and coughed as if stifling a laugh.

"Guys!" Kyle continued, "Norman is going to be early; we have to be earlier. Mike, Alice, you meet us at the house in Woodmoor at 11:30. Leave your car blocks away. Cyndy and I will drive up. Mace, you ride your Harley on up to your place where Cyndy and I will meet you. The three of us will go to the house in Woodmoor. We good?"

"Quarterback sneak! hut hut hut!" shouted Mike.

They all did a poor job of stifling giggles. -

Kyle looked from one to another of his friends. Then, facing Cyndy, he sternly asked, "What are you doing giving them a joint at a time like this?"

"Don't get on her case man," Mason spoke up. "It was my idea."

"Yeah," Mike chimed in, "it's no different than going back to the house and tossing back a few beers or mixed drinks."

Kyle looked at Mike. "You're smoking? You want to be bounced off the force?"

"Get down off your seriousness. No one's going to turn me in."

"Cyndy. Mace. Did you tell them everything? Everything? Johnny's prediction?"

"I thought that was- you want them to know about Johnny, too?" she asked defensively.

"Yes!"

No one spoke. The pained look on Kyle's face inspired silence.

A Good Humor truck's bells pierced the evening's twilight as it worked the housing development near-by.

The others waited for Kyle to speak.

The sound of the ice cream truck bells receded.

Mike Henderson spoke up again, and in a calm and soothing tone asked, "What's this about Johnny?"

Kyle took a deep breath, then spoke.

"Johnny warned me when Dad died, Norman's business dealings would destroy the family. Johnny told me, 'you are going to have to stop him, Kyle, even if you have to kill him. -because if you don't, he will kill you.'"

"Holy shit," Mason whispered.

"Kyle, this kind of thing," Mike asked, "It's not cast in stone, right?"

"I am working very hard to alter events to prevent —"

"Predestination meets free will," Alice observed flatly.

"Now you know, guys. Now you know why it is difficult for me to 'get down off my seriousness' as you put it, Mike."

"Sorry, buddy."

"You're my closest friends. I am asking you to help me set up Norman, so he confesses everything. After that, we rely on the rule of law to shut Norman down and alter Johnny's prediction."

"Count on me," Mason insisted.

"And me," Cyndy added.

"We're in," Mike and Alice answered almost simultaneously.

"Thank you." Kyle responded with a sigh.

With arms folded across his chest, Kyle became very still. *I need to think ...*

Suddenly, Alice put her palm against Kyle's forehead and pushed. "Snap out of it! Your sister is counting on you to be at the house ten minutes ago. Move your ass!"

"Good. Good plan," Kyle agreed. It was his turn to laugh. "Alice, sometimes I think you can read people's minds."

"Who says I can't?" Alice responded then added a high-pitched cackle which made everyone laugh.

"Perambulation is in order. Let's move out!" Mason commanded.

They all headed down the road to Henlopen.

\* \* \*

After what seemed like an endless couple of hours of hospitality, the house was finally emptying out about 11:00. Trish retired. Norman and Susan disappeared and Vicki and her cousins handled the cleanup. This allowed Kyle, Cyndy and Mason a moment to say good bye to Alice and Mike and then they settled by the pool.

Mason was very curious about "this trance mediums and ghost hunting thing." So Cyndy told him a few stories from their years researching paranormal activity.

Kyle was only half paying attention to their conversation. He couldn't stop thinking Mason was flirting with Cyndy. But he became too antsy to sit with them.

Kyle started down the road toward the beach. *Mason and Cyndy are getting along so well. How could I want anything more? How can I choose between two people I love so much? Do I have to choose? No. Deal with Norman first. Should I dig up the garden and get the coins? Should I have them in the house when he arrives? I will be at the bar in the rec room with a stack of over a hundred thousand dollars in gold. He's got to go along with my plan.*

Suddenly Kyle got a chill. A shiver started in the small of his back and snaked up his spine with such intensity his shoulders shook.

At that point he didn't want to be alone. He turned around and walked back toward the house. *Get Norman to the house in Woodmoor. Get him talking. Offer him the deal. He's either going to take the money and leave me alone or he's going to try to push me out. If I don't neutralize Norman, the rule of law will do him in. We can do it.* Then that little voice in his head reminded him.

*Aunt Rebecca. I will take care of Aunt Becca as soon as I get Norman handled. Then I will deal with Cyndy and Mason. Oh shit.*

* * *

Returning home and finding no one by the pool, Kyle went to his room and found the door closed. He knocked and heard Cyndy.

"Who is it?" she asked.

"The boogeyman," Kyle insisted.

The door opened. Mason and Cyndy were standing there dressed in Speedos and t shirts.

"Whoa, don't my clothes look good on you?"

Cyndy spoke first. "I hope you don't mind, but we sorta dove into your supply of summer uniforms."

"Going for a swim," Mason added.

"You disappeared," Cyndy offered a little defensively. "I figured you wanted to be alone."

"Huh." Kyle uttered, looking them both up and down. *How can they be so fucking relaxed when I am so fucking mental right now?"*

"Care to join us?" she asked.

"Feel like talking this out?" Mason offered.

"I dunno," Kyle mumbled. "We have to be in Woodmoor by noon we have to leave here by 7:30. I need sleep."

"A swim will help you sleep." Mason continued. "Clear your head."

"My head is fine!" Kyle snapped. He kicked off his shoes and removed his socks.

"Whoa, Kye. Buddy."

294

*I am so into myself right now, I'm detached. They want to help me and I want to drive them out of here. What the fuck, Kyle? Talk to them!*

"I know," he explained. "I'm sorry. I am being a crabby asshole, okay and I am having trouble dealing with everything, but I want you guys here. Stay with me tonight. Stay with me. Please."

He sat down on the bed, cross-legged and dropped his head into his hands.

Both Cyndy and Mason reached for him at the same time, but Kyle flinched and scrunched up into a tighter ball. "No," he snapped. "No touching right now."

"Sure."

"All right, buddy."

Cyndy and Mason looked at each other. She gestured toward the door. "I have to brush my teeth," she said. They both got up left the room.

Out in the hallway, Cyndy saw the bathroom door was ajar, so she pushed it open and asked Mason, "Won't you join me in my office?"

"Is this to be a consultation, Dr. Weaver?"

"Get in here smart ass." She closed the door and locked it. "All right. What's your plan? I don't want him to be alone tonight and neither do you. I don't want to force him to choose between us. Do you love him?"

"That's kind of direct."

"I am very direct. Do you love him?"

"I don't have a plan and yes, I love him and I am afraid to force him to choose, okay? After what he did for me yesterday,

I'd do anything for him. I have a huge fucking desire to see he gets through tomorrow and we put Norman away."

"But you're afraid."

"Jesus, Cyndy, you're not? Norman can be a nasty motherfucker. I'm afraid of the same thing you are afraid of: after tomorrow Kyle won't even be around for either of us to lose. I lost Johnny. I don't want to lose Kyle. Does that answer your question?"

Cyndy threw her arms around Mason, pulled him very close and held on tight. "I am so sorry, Mason. I am so very sorry. I didn't want to hurt you. I wanted to know for sure how you felt because I love him very much."

She held on to him and he held on to her.

"I understand. I love him, too."

"I pushed a little too much there," she confessed. "Sorry."

Cyndy stared at Mason for a moment and then asked, "are we good?"

"We're good. I don't think he should be alone tonight. The way he's into his head tonight this isn't about sex, this is about helping him get through the night."

"I agree. One more thing Mooseman, I have an agreement with Kyle and I want the same with you. We tell the truth even if it gets awkward."

"Would you rather comfort Kyle all by yourself?

"Cyndy, I'm a gentleman. I would never tell a lady she is not wanted."

She punched him on the shoulder. "None of that evasive crap, Mooseman!"

"It's not evasive, it's polite." *Damn. I am actually starting to like this woman.*

"Fuck polite!" she hissed at him. "Do you want me to leave?"

"Yes! There. I said it. Happy? I didn't want to hurt your feelings." He rummaged through his shaving kit and withdrew his toothbrush and toothpaste.

"I would prefer to have him to myself." And with that, he began brushing his teeth.

"Thank you," she told him as she found her own toothbrush and helped herself to his toothpaste.

"Feel better?" he mumbled, his mouth full of toothpaste.

"Yes."

"Good."

"But I am not leaving," she assured him and began brushing her teeth.

"Can't say I am surprised about that," he told her and then spit into the sink and continued brushing.

The two of them brushed their teeth as they watched each other in the big mirror. They finished, rinsed and spit. She grabbed a hand towel and dried her toothbrush, and then her mouth. She then reached over and dried his lips with the towel.

"Kyle was right," Cyndy observed staring into Mason's eyes. "Your green eye is brighter than my green eye."

"He told you that, did he?"

"Mason." Cyndy asked, "Would you ever want to fuck me?"

"Alright, now that's-"

"Mooseman, if we are going to help the man who is the most important guy to either of us- total honesty, remember?" Mason nodded. "Would you?"

Mason smiled. *Now I can understand why Kyle loves this woman.*

For a moment, Cyndy admired how handsome he was and forgot she was trying to drive home a point. *Damn, but he is so hot. Stay focused, Weaver and stop being distracted by a pretty face and a full Speedo.*

"Fess up, Mason?"

"That's for me to know and you to find out. You said tell the truth. That's the truth!" he whispered with a big shit eating grin on his face. He reached over and drew her body against his. He made an effort to crush his cock up against her. Then he kissed her passionately until both needed to pause to catch their breaths.

"Now that," Cyndy intoned, "I didn't see coming."

"Neither did I," Mason confessed, then turned and left the bathroom.

She grabbed his shaving kit and followed him. "In case we need this."

They entered Kyle's bedroom.

No Kyle.

"Abducted by aliens?"

Then Kyle popped up from under the bed. "Peek-a-boo!" He was dressed in his summer uniform and was holding a hash pipe. It was obvious from his eyes he had started without them.

"I needed a sleep aide." He handed the pipe to Cyndy and positioned himself in the center of the bed.

"I don't want to talk, I don't want to fuck and I don't want to be left alone, Kyle explained. "Finish that pipe and then come to bed."

Cyndy picked up the cigarette lighter from the dresser. She lit the pipe, toked and then handed it to Mason. As he inhaled, she went over to the door, locked it and turned off the lights.

When his eyes got used to the dark, Mason, moved to Cyndy and handed her the pipe.

They stayed leaning against the dresser and finished the bowl.

Eventually Mason whispered, "left side or right side? Ladies first."

"You first. I need to change."

Mason got under the covers on Kyle's right side. Cyndy removed her t-shit and her swimsuit and got one of Kyle's swim briefs from the dresser. She put them on along with one of Kyle's t-shirts.

As she crawled into bed next to him, Kyle stretched out his left arm and drew Cyndy to him. He did the same on his right; drawing Mason close to him as well. His two friends each laid an arm across Kyle's stomach and held him.

"I feel safe."

No one moved or spoke.

For so many reasons for all three of them, holding and being held was exactly what they needed that night.

* * *

The sun was cutting through what was left of the night when Cyndy woke up and sleepily glanced at the men in bed with her. What a warm feeling, knowing she was with two people she cared about and enjoyed being close to. It wasn't about sex this time. It was a different similitude; a different connection than she had ever experienced. At that moment she wanted to kiss them both, but she couldn't move and what was stranger was she got the unescapable feeling there was someone else in the room.

She opened her eyes to find a boy standing at the foot of the bed. It was Kyle but it wasn't Kyle. It was Johnny.

She stared at the boy who was staring at her.

"Help him," she wanted to say. "Help your brother Kyle!" But she could not speak. "Hello, Cyndy," he said in almost a whisper. "We have something in common, you know. We love them both very much."

The boy moved around the bed to a point where he was standing by Mason's shoulder. He looked down at the two men in bed with Cyndy and smiled. He put his hand on Mason's shoulder, leaned in and kissed his cheek. Though still asleep Mason smiled, inhaled deeply and sighed.

Cyndy had so many questions. *Does Mason know? Is he dreaming about Johnny? Am I dreaming? Johnny, can you hear me? Are we going to lose Kyle? Tell me what to do.*

"No, you're not dreaming."

Cyndy's startled expression amused him. He giggled then put his finger to his lips asking her to not to say anything. "No. I can't read your mind. I know that's what you're thinking because it's what anyone would be thinking." He stroked Mason's cheek with the back of his hand. "Coarse. Still so handsome. He likes you a lot. Who can blame him?"

The boy walked back to the foot of the bed looking from Mason to Kyle and to her.

As he moved around to Cyndy's side, she sat up. She was too intent on getting an answer to her question. *Tell me what to do.*

As he came closer, she could feel a radiating warmth.

Johnny smiled at her. "You are going to be very good for each other." He leaned toward her.

*Tell me what to do.*

His presence was no longer extraordinary. The wonder had diminished enough for her to notice details. He wasn't breathing, yet there was the scent of fresh rosemary. He never blinked.

*Tell me what to do.*

He leaned closer, kissed her on the cheek and then whispered in her ear, "take the shot."

And with that, he was gone.

Cyndy fell back on her pillow and stared at the ceiling. *Take the shot? What shot?*

She rolled over and embraced Kyle. At the same time their bodies made contact, Cyndy felt a deep sorrow move from deep inside, engulf her and grow into an over-powering sob. Never before had she felt so powerless.

"Hey, whoa. Whoa, whoa-"

"I don't want to lose you."

Mason sat up. "Are you okay?"

"No!" she sobbed.

"You're safe, Cyndy." Kyle explained in a very soothing tone. "You are safe with us. It's okay. You are safe."

Instinctually, Mason reached over and rubbed Cyndy's back. Neither man was sure of what to say next.

Mace tried to excuse himself, saying, "I will let you two -"

"No! You have to stay," Cyndy insisted. She grabbed Mason's head in both hands and kissed him with enough force to open his mouth so she could massage his tongue with hers.

Breaking the kiss, she told him, "That was from Johnny. He loves you so much."

Mason looked to Kyle as if for approval. "We have to talk, but I have to go." Mason added, jumping out of bed and leaving the room.

"Me, too!" Kyle added starting to get out from under Cyndy.

"Don't leave me alone. One at a time, please." And she laid down on Kyle and held him. "Oh my god, I got hysterical. I don't know what to tell you. Hold me."

Kyle reached over and grabbed a box of Kleenex off the bed table. "Here, let me." and he took a couple tissues and tried to dry her face.

"Oh hell," She complained, "mascara all over your t-shirt. I must look like Morticia Addams." She sat up and began wiping her face using multiple tissues.

"Let's say you have a certain Harlequin look to you."

"Wow, both of us making literary references and the sun's hardly shown its face."

"Your face is lovely no matter what," he crooned hoping to sound as loving as he was feeling at the moment. "Better now?"

The door opened and Mason stepped back into the room.

"Johnny was here," she blurted out.

"Oh shit. Hold that thought and I will be right back!" Kyle exclaimed as he leapt out of bed.

Mason closed the door and walked over to the bed, Cyndy couldn't help but notice a protrusion in his Speedo. "Here.

Please?" Cyndy asked holding up the sheet in invitation for him to join her.

Mason got into bed and took her into his arms. "You feeling better?"

"I am having so many feelings right now I haven't the slightest idea if better is one of them. Just hold me."

They lay there quietly for a moment.

"Johnny was here. He kissed you on the cheek and you smiled."

"You and I had the same dream."

"What dream was that?" Kyle asked reentering the room. He walked around to the other side of the bed and got under the sheet with them. "Tell me about my brother Johnny."

"Johnny was here. He told me the three of us are good for each other. It was like he gave us his blessing. I tried to ask him if I could save you from Norman, but all he would tell me was 'take the shot.'"

Kyle reached over and embraced them both. "Could be whiskey," he cracked.

"Stop that!"

"Have you ever even handled guns?" Mason asked.

"Yes, I have but it doesn't matter! Let's not go to Woodmoor today. Or ever," Cyndy pleaded, "Mason tell him. His life is too valuable to both of us. Kyle, you have two people who love you so much we are willing to share you. You want to risk losing that? Stay out of Woodmoor."

"Cyndy, I have to do this for my family. I love you both and if you love me you will go with me. Whatever happens, let's promise we will look after each other."

"Kyle!" Cyndy started.

"No, Cyndy. It's what I have to do."

"How much time before we have to leave for the western shore?"

"Little under an hour."

"Then let's make it count," Cyndy responded. She then wiggled around so she was on her back. She took a deep breath then reached over and placed her hands on the front of each man. She leaned over and licked Mason's ear lobe then kissed Mason on the lips.

"Mace," Kyle explained, "you need to know something about sex with Cyndy."

"I know," he gasped as he broke contact with Cyndy. "Tell the truth even if it gets awkward."

Cyndy then spoke up. "Kyle, teach us what that hippie couple taught you in San Francisco."

He smiled.

What followed was very athletic, and pleasurable, shared love-making.

# CHAPTER TWENTY-ONE

## *JOHNNY'S PREDICTION COMES TO PAST: THE FINAL CONFRONTATION*
### *Sunday Afternoon in Woodmoor*

As she lay in bed Sunday morning, Rebecca reconsidered her situation. She resolved to make one more attempt to gain Kyle's help. Another walk to the beach would be in order.

Arriving at the main house for breakfast, she was disappointed to find Kyle had left hours prior. "To take Cyndy to Dulles Airport," she was told. She also learned Norman had gone to Woodmoor where he was to meet up with Kyle.

"They are meeting at the house," Trish explained, "to go over a few things. You'll have plenty of time to visit with them tonight."

Rebecca excused herself, told her husband she needed to take care of some business. "I need to see the boys," she told him. "I am off to Woodmoor."

Nick had a bad feeling about it and asked to go with her, but Rebecca was adamant about going alone. He let her go.

* * *

Kyle and the others reached the house in Woodmoor when Rebecca was about halfway there. As planned, Cyndy and Alice took their place in Kyle's second floor bedroom. They switched on the home intercom system. Mason and Mike Henderson made themselves comfortable in the basement workshop.

Kyle got a tarp and a shovel from the tool shed and considered where to dig. He took a moment to study the flowers in the terraced beds between the driveway and the patio.

*Marigolds. I saw marigolds. Nice pun, Dad. But it would be a shame to dig up all those flowers. The strong box or treasure chest or whatever wouldn't be too deep in the ground. The shovel is about ten or twelve inches. Use it as a probe?*

He started in the center of the first terrace and pushed the shovel into the ground every eight inches or so. He reached the far end and had detected nothing. He so he returned to the center and began working his way in the other direction. The fourth time he thrust the shovel into the soft earth the blade stopped about three inches short. He probed again about two inches over. Definitely something hard.

Up on the second floor, Cyndy was keeping an eye on the back yard and driveway. Alice was lounging on the bed reading an old comic book she had found on the bookshelf when Cyndy hissed at her.

"Alice. Check this out."

Alice joined Cyndy at the window and they watched Kyle.

He had put a drop cloth on the patio, removing flowers from part of the garden and placing them on the tarp. His digging in the dirt was surgical as he extracted several spades full of earth and placed them on the tarp. After several minutes of digging, he stopped.

"Think he's found it?" Cyndy whispered to Alice.

"Without a doubt," Alice answered.

They watched as Kyle knelt down and extracted a metal box from the ground. He set it on the wall, opened it and removed a canvas bag. When he opened the canvas bag, he glanced inside and then looked up at his bedroom window and smiled.

The ladies watched as Kyle replaced the metal box, the dirt and the marigolds. He then gathered up the tarp and shovel and returned them to the tool shed.

"He's going to leave the sack on the wall?" Cyndy whispered to no one in particular.

"It's not as if aliens are going to come and snatch the gold, "Alice cracked. "They only come here to mine magnesium and lithium."

Cyndy looked at Alice and then decided she wasn't even going to ask.

"This will be very interesting," Alice observed.

"Interesting?" Cyndy turned off the intercom and turned to Alice. "Honest to god, Alice, stop being so calm! Kyle could get killed! Has everyone forgotten that?"

"No, but shifting into drama queen mode isn't this group's style. You don't know for sure the worst is going to happen."

"Do you know it is not going to happen? Do you have a read on situation?"

Alice turned away and went back to the bed. "It's only speculation," she lied. Truth is, she had a very strong premonition,
and it wasn't all good. It wasn't all bad because the end justified
the means. But she wasn't happy about what she had seen during
her meditations earlier that morning.

Cyndy watched Kyle take the canvas bag and disappear
around the side of the house. She let the curtains fall closed
leaving enough of a gap for her to keep an eye on the driveway.

Cyndy switched the intercom back on.

"Okay basement dwellers, here's your chance. Kyle's about
to come through the basement door with a small fortune in gold.
Do we knock him cold and head for the Spanish Main?"

Over the intercom, they could hear the guys congratulating
Kyle.

"Check this out, gentlemen. It's the real deal. The Applegate
Treasure!"

Cyndy shot Alice an inquisitive look.

"A Hardy Boys reference. *The Tower Treasure.* Didn't you
watch "The Mickey Mouse Club?"

"You watched the Mickey Mouse Club?" Cyndy asked her.

"Didn't everyone?"

They turned toward the intercom.

"Hand me that serving tray." Kyle was heard to say. "Yep.
Good. Okay, here goes."

There was a clatter; Kyle was pouring the coins out of the
bag and onto a metal serving tray.

"Whoa!"

"That's incredible!"

"Shall we count it?"

"Start with stacks of ten, "Kyle instructed. "Awesome, isn't it? See those brown spots on the bag? S'not rust."

"Blood splatter," Mike observed.

"Yes, it is," Kyle responded. "There's a gruesome story about why this money stayed buried for so long. If we get though the rest of the day, I'll tell you all about it."

As the guys were counting the gold coins, Cyndy kept her vigil by the window. Alice continued reading the X-Man comic book.

"So Cyndy," Alice whispered. "How did it go after we left last night?"

"Okay," she replied trying to sound positive.

"No. *How* did it go. Who wound up with Kyle? You or Mason?"

Cyndy looked at Alice for a moment with her hard to read poker face.

"Ah," Alice concluded. "You both did. Very cool." and she went back to reading the comic book.

"Kyle didn't want to be alone. He wanted us both with him," Cyndy explained. "We slept together, but we didn't *sleep* together last night."

"You comforted him. Cool." Alice paused a moment and then asked, "Ever do a three-way?"

"All the time. How do you think we keep the doctors awake during those long night shifts at the hospital?"

"Okay!" they heard Kyle shouting into the intercom in the basement.

"Let 'em talk," Mike chimed in

"Yeah, it's getting interesting," Mason added.

"Back into the workshop you two. Norman will be here any minute. And you two upstairs, please remember you have to be silent. The odd thing about the intercom unit in my room is you don't have to depress the talk button to be heard. Anything you say can be heard all over the house."

"Stay on mission and maintain radio silence." Mike ordered them. "Got it?"

"Roger that, red fox leader. Recording team out."

Alice whispered to Cyndy, "You and two doctors or two nurses and one doctor? Or-"

"Silence means not talking Alice!" Kyle shouted.

"Oops!" Alice responded, then added a very sheepish, "sorry, Kye."

"Cyndy?" Kyle asked. "Any sign of Norman?"

"The big-assed Lincoln will be hard to miss. Wait. Okay, gang, this is it. Norman is coming up the drive. I will start recording as soon as I hear him enter the house."

"Thanks," Kyle responded. "No more talking. Don't respond. I will say it for all of us. Good luck everyone."

No one responded.

*Radio silence.*

Cyndy started the cassette recorder and wondered why Alice was so damn calm. *How can she just lay there and read a comic book?*

Mason and Mike Henderson pulled the knot from the wall and tested their line of vision. Kyle's back was visible as was everything to his left. The glass racks at the left end of the bar, the gun rack and the sofa. If Kyle wasn't standing there, they would also be able to see the stairs and the other side of the room. Not a full view of the basement, but enough.

Mason heard a "click," then caught Henderson's eyes as he looked up from his service revolver. He had unlocked the safety and was replacing the weapon in its shoulder holster.

The reality of how dangerous this could get finally hit home for Mason. The hair stood up on the back of his neck.

Kyle positioned himself behind the bar.

Before covering them with a bar towel, he took another look at the gold coins. Some coins remained in a heap, some in little stacks of ten. As far as he knew each little stack of ten coins was worth ten thousand dollars. There were fifty stacks at last count and they were only halfway through the pile.

*What is it about gold? In this quantity, the mere appearance inspires a need to own it. Is it chemistry? Or is it what it represents; the sense of superiority, the ability to buy things. Oh shit, the canvas bag. I don't want to touch it, but think, Kyle: empty space, empty space.*

And with that mantra, he was able to place the canvas sack behind the bar. He heard the patio door open on the first floor so he covered the coins.

"Norman?" Kyle shouted, then lit a cigarette.

"Yes, Kyle," his brother answered. "Ready to talk business?" he asked as he came down the stairs.

Kyle poured Norman a scotch.

"I'm surprised to find you in the basement. Aren't you afraid of the boogieman?"

"You're not?"

Norman smirked and took the offered tumbler of Chivas.

"Not now," Kyle explained. "I know what he looks like and who he is. When I saw him the other day, I was frightened. I ran up those stairs, tripped and fell backwards. I hit my head on the floor. Apparently, that did something interesting to me. I can read things."

"Aunt Becca told me about it. I thought she was batty."

"You saw him. Want to know who he is?"

"What are you talking about?"

"He is our Great-grandfather's brother Nelson. He was running away with his brother's wife and a stash of gold that didn't belong to him. Nelson tried to shoot his brother. Instead, he killed their other brother, Derrick, and his sister-in-law. That's his shotgun in the rack over there. Without access to more shells, he charged at his brother aiming to club him with the shotgun. But great-grandfather stopped him with a serious punch to the gut. Nelson fell —died from internal injuries. He's still looking to get revenge."

"How much weed have you been smoking brother?"

"Come on, the game is over. I know what you've been up to. We can forget all about it if you agree to my offer."

"Your offer?"

"It starts with this," Kyle explained, uncovering the gold coins on the serving tray.

Norman tried to keep a poker face but failed. He smiled the broadest smile Kyle had ever seen him smile. "Our batty old aunt was right. It is real."

Upstairs, Cyndy and Alice were glued to the intercom.

Cyndy thought she heard something out back. She looked out the window and saw a young man standing on the patio. He took a gun from his belt, checked the clip; replaced the weapon in his belt. He then walked around the house. She grabbed a pad and pencil off Kyle's desk. She wrote a note to Alice: "Man gun —basement."

Alice grabbed the pencil: "Warn Kyle. Blow plan."

Cyndy read Alice's note. She shook her head.

Alice wrote "Mike armed."

Neither Kyle nor Norman heard Kent let himself into the laundry room. Mike did but there was no way he could tell Mason nor warn Kyle.

"You see little brother, you spend so much time chasing after things that aren't real. This," he continued, grasping a hand-ful of the coins and letting them spill out of his hand, "this is real. What it can do is real."

"I agree. So, you take all this, a million or so and start your own business. You agree you and Trish each get twenty-four percent of the construction business. I get fifty-two percent and I run the company. All the other stuff in the will goes to whom-ever Dad says it goes to."

Norman shook his head. But before he could speak, Kyle picked up the envelope he had put on the bar.

"Take the deal and we forget everything you have done or were about to do. That includes the fifty thousand dollars Dad advanced you for a supposed land deal in Jersey. We could zero balance it." Kyle paused. Norman did not respond, so he contin-ued. "This gold would be all yours. I'll make sure Aunt Rebecca is taken care of."

"Well, well, well, aren't you the guy in the white hat?" Norman said with a smirk.

"I'm no hero, Norman. I'm trying to keep the family on an even keel. No one needs to know about your illegal shit."

"What do you mean?"

"Blackmail, manslaughter, and bribing Federal officials."

"Kyle, you are now being silly, not to mention delusional. Let's stick to business and keep your fuck buddy out of the equation."

"Take the money, Norman, and nothing is ever said of any of this ever again. You have my word."

"A pretty good deal Kyle, but-"

"Norman," Kyle continued gesturing with the envelope. "I learn information by touching objects. I can read things. This envelope used to hold a signed copy of Dad's revised last will and testament. You now have it and plan to destroy it, don't you?"

"Yes, I do."

Kyle made a show of holding the envelope in both hands as if giving a "reading." He focused on the empty space between him and Norman and spoke. "When Rosenberg was about to give you a revised will, you refused to take it. You told him to destroy it. You told him you would give him a bearer bond worth five-thousand-dollars to do it. But your discussion was interrupted. Something happened. It's not quite clear, but I can hear Rosenberg yell for you to 'look out!' The two of you saw something, didn't you? Something so frightening the old man had a heart attack, right?"

"Right again, Kyle."

"You could have saved Mr. Rosenberg's life, but you didn't

speak with the 911 operator until you were sure the old man was dead. Is it true?

"Does it matter?

"Did you wait to call 911 for real?"

"Also, true," Norman affirmed downing the rest of his scotch and walking over to the gun rack. "Come around the bar, Kyle, I'd like you to use your magical powers and 'read' something else."

Kyle came around the bar as he inquired, "Why? Is sharing the family business with me such a bad thing that you would let Rosenberg die? Why?"

"Because it is my turn. I put in my time, understand? I earned it," he explained as he took the old shotgun down from the rack. "You got to spend years supping from the family trough with no strings and no obligations. Then dear old Dad gives you an equal share with me? That's fucked up, Kyle. This is my time. It is my turn to be on top."

"You're going to shoot me?"

"Shut up! Kent? Kent, are you out there?"

"Yes, sir." Kent responded, entering the room

"Check it out. My very talented brother does the most interesting parlor tricks." He tossed the vintage shotgun to Kyle who caught it.

Nelson turned and took the four-ten Remington off the rack.

"Yep, this was Norman Wilson's. Three people died not far from this very spot because of greed. His wife, Amelia, bled to death in a puddle of water. Can't imagine why he kept this shotgun."

*So I could use it today. Brother against brother.*

Norman made a show of clicking off the safety on his shotgun. "You know, Kyle, there are thousands of gun accidents in this country every year."

Kyle started to grab the shotgun by its barrel and wield it as a club to disarm his brother.

Kent drew his pistol. "Don't do that, sir."

Kyle ran his hand over the weapon as he observed. "Ah. I see. An antique shotgun misfires and kills the assailant trying to rob his brother." Kyle backed up and positioned himself at the bottom of the stairs. *Maybe I can get up the stairs and out of the line of fire?*

Kent countered Kyle's move by walking towards the lounge chairs near the pool table. He aimed at Kyle.

Kyle looked down at the shotgun and ran his hand long the barrel. It was an easy read. Both barrels were sealed with dense epoxy resin "Clever Norman. I pull either or both triggers and the explosion will rip the near end of the barrels open. That'll force the stock at me with such force that it will take off my head."

"How about that? Always an A student, Kyle. It's time you were reunited with your twin- also someone who didn't know when to shut up."

"What are you talking about?"

"He gave me so much shit that night."

"You killed Johnny?"

"He killed himself. He punched me, I punched back. The stupid little shit fell and tumbled down the hill. Not my fault!" Norman raised the four-ten to his shoulder and aimed it at Kyle.

"You are now going to shoot me because you don't want me taking the family fortune."

"And if I don't?"

He heard a click-click. Kent advanced a round into the chamber of his gun.

"Do it, Kyle!" Norman yelled.

BLAM!

Norman discharged the shotgun at the ceiling about half-way between the two of them.

"Do it, Kyle!" he shouted.

What happened next went very fast and several things happened at one time.

Henderson entered with revolver drawn: "Down!"

Kyle heard the command.

Kent fired shots.

Kyle took one round in the shoulder, screamed, dropped the shotgun and fell on the stairs.

Henderson shot at Kent hitting him twice.

As he fell, Kent got off another round. It caught the back of Henderson's calf. Henderson dropped to his knees, but he kept his revolver trained on Norman.

Mason grabbed Kent's gun and tossed it.

Mike yelled "Put the weapon down."

Norman heard, but kept his shotgun aimed at the spot once occupied by Kyle.

Alice and Cyndy raced down the stairs. Alice maneuvered around Kyle and went to Mike.

"Apply pressure!" Cyndy shouted and she pressed a tea towel against Kyle's bleeding shoulder.

"But," Kyle protested, "Norman —ow!"

This last was because Cyndy pulled him up to look at his back. "Straight through soft tissue and out the back. Good." She moved behind him and cradled him between her legs pressing down on the towel. "Norman, I am going to —" but the expression on Norman's face made her look to her left.

Mason was standing, back against the wall.

Alice and Mike stared.

The specter of Nelson Wilson charged across the room towards Mason. It stopped where Kent lay dead. Nelson suddenly dissolved into the floor next to Kent.

Cyndy got up and set Kyle on the stairs. "Stay still." She ran behind the bar.

"No!" Alice shouted.

Cyndy snatched up the phone. "Norman's in shock," she explained. "He's not going to do anything more. I'm calling 9-11."

"I'm Dr. Cyndy Weaver. There's been a fight and we have two GSW's and one man dead-"

But no one is watching Cyndy as she gave the address and confirmed it with the 9-11 dispatcher. All eyes were on Kent. A little unsteady, the young man rose to his feet and stood there starring at Norman.

He was not an apparition, a mist with shape you could put your hands through. Nelson Wilson fully occupied Kent's dead body and the young man's hair was turning dark and long and filthy. His face seemed to partially decay right before their eyes.

"Norman! Kyle! Are you down there?" they heard Aunt Rebecca shout from the kitchen.

Before anyone would respond, Nelson/Kent let out a blood curdling shriek. Then screamed, "Jonathan!"

Rebecca came halfway down the stairs then stopped: "God almighty!"

The creature who was the risen Nelson walked slowly toward Norman. He stopped and picked up the shotgun Kyle had dropped —his shotgun.

His raspy voice sent shudders through everyone's spines. Raising the shotgun by its barrel, he stalked Norman shouting, "Jonathan, you will pay for what you did to me!"

Norman backed away, and in a voice not his own said, "Nelson, you brought it on yourself. You're lazy! Always expecting something for —"

But he was unable to finish. Nelson bashed Norman's head hard with the butt of his shotgun.

Looking old and decrepit, Norman was sprawled on the floor being spat on by the ghost. It turned, shouting at Kyle, "Brother Derrick you betrayed me! You will pay for it, you coward."

It staggered toward Kyle. "You pile of horse shit! I should rip your tongue out and feed it to the hogs." It reached out and took Kyle by the throat. Kyle's eyes were bulging.

"Drop him!" Mason screamed as he charged at it.

Kyle's murderous ancestor grabbed at Mason's arms. He seemed about to break his hold, but Mason's anger gave him incredible strength. He tightened an arm lock on its neck. A loud crack. A broken neck.

Mason went to the stairs, swooped up Kyle and carried him to the couch.

Cyndy shouted: "Pressure on the wound!" She was about to join them when Rebecca screamed. Cyndy turned around and saw Nelson/Kent beginning to stand. It would have been funny if it weren't grotesque. He got to his feet, but the broken neck left his head lolling around. His eyes were open and his head swung around as he took a step then another. His lips moved but he could only produce guttural sounds.

Alice yelled, "Cyndy! The shotgun!"

Cyndy leaned down and picked up the four-ten shotgun. What she saw next made her freeze.

Nelson groaned in a vicious tone, spastically grabbing at his head.

"Cyndy," Kyle shouted. "Take the shot!"

Cyndy raised the shotgun to her shoulder. "Everybody down!"

She fired into Nelson's face. She fired the last two shells; one into his chest and the last into his abdomen.

Cyndy ordered, "Alice, get those throws and cover these guys up, will ya?"

Alice covered Kent with the lap robe off the deacon's bench and covered Norman with a ratty blanket.

"They will question us one at a time. Each of us tells the truth as you saw it," Mike instructed.

"And play them the recording!" Alice shouted. "We have the recording!"

"Wait!" Mike exclaimed. "It will come in handy, but for now, don't let anyone have the tape. It could get lost. We'll take it to a professional transcriber tomorrow and sit with them as they type it up. We get it professionally transcribed and notarized then turn it over to them."

"Got it." Alice stopped at the stairs. "But first I think Auntie is in need of something very strong. Gin, if memory serves." Alice headed for the bar.

"Thank you dear," Rebecca intoned still staring at the small pool of blood on the floor.

"Please, Cyndy, bring Aunt Becca over here," Kyle asked Cyndy. "And Mason, get the gold coins. Put them into the canvas sack —it's under the bar. Then lock them in the lock box under the bar. Here's the keys. Quick! Before anyone else arrives. It will be safe for now —shit, the antiques!"

Mason headed to the bar as he explained, "no problem. All import papers on the boxes have all the correct stamps and seals. Totally legit."

Cyndy guided Aunt Rebecca over to the couch. Alice met them there with a tumbler of gin.

It took an effort, but Kyle sat up and patted the sofa beside him. His Aunt was dazed. She mechanically took the glass from Alice. "Thank you."

"You're welcome. I'm going for the tape." And with that, Alice went up the stairs.

"Put the cassette in your pants," Henderson yelled after her. The cops are going to search this place."

"Gotcha!" Alice yelled back and then disappeared up the stairs.

"It's a little more paranormal than anyone should have to witness wasn't it, Aunt Becca?" Kyle asked. "Have a drink."

The old woman lifted the glass and started to drink, but Cyndy stopped her after the first gulp. "It's not water!" she shouted.

"Can you understand me?" Kyle asked his Aunt. Then he turned to Cyndy and asked, "Do you think she had a stroke?"

The gin brought Rebecca back to reality. "Stroke? Not likely. Oh, that hit the spot. I do think we need to get a priest in here to clean this place. I always told my brother there were extra people hanging around his house, but he never believed me."

She realized Cyndy and Kyle were looking at her funny. "What? I'm okay. Okay?" and she drained the tumbler. "Can I have another?"

"Only if she promises not to drive home!" Mike shouted.

"Are you kidding. She's going with us to the hospital," Cyndy explained. "I'm still not convinced."

"Back off, dearie. Remember? I am a doctor!" Rebecca announced with some indignation.

"Yeah? Well so am I and we both know you should get looked at."

"Oh, all right," Rebecca caved. "But I still want another gin!"

"I'll get it," Mason told them, then disappeared behind the bar.

"Please focus," Kyle cut in. "Do you remember the gold coins?"

"Yes."

"Gold coins that belong to you. It will take several days, but you will get what your grandfather promised you."

"You found my money?" she asked softly. Tears welled up in her eyes. "You found my money grandpa promised me?"

"Here," Mason said, offering her a fresh glass and a couple napkins.

"Thank you, Mason," she said then sat back in the couch and sipped her drink smiling and crying all at the same time. "I knew you kids would help me. I knew it! What a day this has been."

"At least one good thing can be said about this," Kyle observed.

"What's that, Kye?" Cyndy asked.

"Finally, a story where the faggot doesn't off himself or get killed."

"Down here, gentlemen!" Alice announced as she led paramedics and several police officers down the stairs.

\* \* \*

Weeks later, Kyle, Cyndy, Mason, Alice and Mike were seated in the large conference room in the Rockville, Maryland courthouse building. A small tape recorder was on top of all the file folders, banker's boxes and envelopes of evidence on the table.

Across the table sat the county police captain, an FBI agent, a Federal prosecutor and a judge. There was no stenographer to record their interview.

From the cassette recorder, all could hear Kyle's voice stating, "Finally, a story where the faggot doesn't off himself or die."

The judge reached over and pressed the "off" button.

"Click."

He then gathered the pages of the transcript before him, straightened the small stack neatly and passed it to the police chief.

Everyone was silent for a moment.

"Your honor, if we take this to trial it is going to be a total circus." explained the federal prosecutor. "Detective Henderson worked with everyone here and created a comprehensive description to accompany the audio tape. It is an extraordinary story that is difficult to disprove for a variety of reasons – the first being they all passed polygraph tests."

"They all passed?"

"Yessir," confirmed the FBI agent.

"Thank you. Well. This is the most outrageous case I have ever encountered," the judge explained, shaking his head. "I think for all parties concerned it is concluded.

"On Monday when I issue my official ruling whether or not the state should proceed, I will need all of this evidence in my courtroom. Without it, there can be no trial. Thank you for your time everyone. See you Monday."

On Monday, the court convened. Oddly enough, the evidence had been lost and would never be found. Case closed.

# CODA

## *THEIR GIFTED OFFSPRING*
### *A Weekday Morning in Bermuda*

Within eight years, Cyndy, Mason and Kyle began a family and wrapped up their business on the mainland. They purchased a closed elementary school with several acres of land and moved to Bermuda. The main house gave them plenty of space to raise a family with the help of a couple nannies. They refurbished the school building, a large carriage house and several smaller cottages. In 1985, Alice, Michael Henderson and their children moved in. All continued to pursue a very laid-back existence with home schooling in normal and psi studies.

Cyndy's writing of their experiences attracted like-minded scholars from around the world. They had many international visitors. They learned to enjoy cricket matches and soccer games on that very British Island. They kept horses and chickens, and they raised vegetables. It was important to all that they stayed connected with mother earth.

Mason supervised the installation of a four-lane lap pool and became "P.E. teacher." The parents believed physical development would enhance mental abilities. Mason also learned to read auras and to embrace Buddhism.

Was it a "happy ending"? No. Not with three such dynamic individuals raising a family. It was never horrible nor was it ever boring. As Mason would say, "it's okay."

## Late Summer 1991

In her bedroom office, nineteen-year-old Denise Wilson has finished the second draft of her new novel. She leans back in her big leather office chair and smiles. "Finally done. I will print out this last bit and get the manuscript to Aunt Alice for proofing."

Her twin brother, Dennis, examines the laptop screen from over his sister's shoulder. He reads out loud, "finally a story where the faggot doesn't off himself or die.' Can you use that word? S'not very P.C."

"It's true to the times. Another example: 'off himself' instead of 'suicide.' Both are normal for 1973. Verisimilitude, brother, verisimilitude."

"Ooooooh —S.A.T. word!"

Denise did not respond but glared at him over the top of her wire rimmed eyeglasses.

"Oh zing!" Dennis cried and fell back onto her bed grasping at an invisible arrow in his abdomen.

"Could I look more condescending? I have been practicing. Mom says silence is more powerful than words."

"The Cyndy Weaver stare. I know it well. But you shouldn't use 'faggot,'" he explained. He then folded his legs into lotus position and sat ramrod straight with his hands posed on his thighs. "This isn't 1972 it is 1991 and saying 'faggot' is as bad as using the 'n' word."

"Control P. Enter. There. Too late. When this is printed, the entire manuscript is going to Alice for proof reading. Would it offend you if someone referred to you as a 'faggot'?"

"You're asking the wrong person. I don't care. I am comfortable in my being. Like Dad Kye and Dad Mason, I am neither homo nor heterosexual. I'm sexual. And why don't you email the novel as an attachment?"

"Alice prefers words on paper."

"Good point. Me, too. My book of shadows couldn't exist without paper. Which is- whoa-" he exclaimed. His body rose about a foot straight up off the bed causing him to lose his balance and fall on his right side.

For a moment, everything in the room was still except for the sounds of the printer. Denise and Dennis fixed their eyes on the elongated lump in the bed.

"It seems," Dennis observed, "that your bed has a nasty new growth." And, with that he lifted the quilt and dove under it to tackle their visitor. "Gotcha!"

"No tickling!" shouted the boy under the covers.

From the voice, Denise could identify the "lump in the bed." It was her seventeen-year-old brother John Wilson, III or as they all called him "J3."

The two boys rolled to the floor, taking the quilt with them.

"You two are going to re-make my bed, you know!" Denise shouted.

"Nice of you to make an appearance, little one," Dennis remarked as tossed the quilt back up on the bed then slapped his baby brother on his naked behind.

"You could at least cover up," his sister chided.

"Yeah, one of the disadvantages of traveling into empty space is your clothes seem to dissolve. I'm still wondering where they go —still working on that."

"Johnny, put some clothes on, will you?"

"Don't give him any, Denise!" Dennis cried. "Make him cross campus in his adorable birthday suit!"

"Too late," J3 bragged. He opened a dresser drawer and retrieved a pair of black biker's pants and a Boston Red Socks baseball shirt.

"You're putting clothes in my dresser nowadays?"

"Always prepared, that's my motto! And Denise, by the way," he added as he pulled on the uniform shirt, "it was a 4-10 shotgun, not a 10-4 shotgun. You have to correct page 379- s'only place you made the mistake."

"I wish you wouldn't watch me from empty space when you do your dimension trippy thing."

"Hey, I'm a nut for family lore," he added as he slid into the spandex shorts and adjusted his privates.

"Nice package, little bro."

"Thank you. It was a gift. But sis, why did you stop writing once they stopped Norman? A lot happened after that. They cleansed the house and even little Lucy finally arrived on the other side. I liked that."

"Well, J3," she explained as she placed the book's pages into a large padded envelope. "And *we* happened after that. They discovered new talents, children happened. This school for the mystical arts happened."

"They prefer to call it an ashram," J3 corrected her.

"Right. It keeps the authorities from snooping around," Dennis added.

"This ashram happened after that and everything becomes rather paranormal, doesn't it? It gets a little trippy as Aunt Alice would say. I don't think people are ready for the details about our extended and talented family."

"Oh, come on." Dennis chimed in. "They eat up Star Wars and other sci-fi bullshit, and Anne Rice was on the best seller list again last year. If they believe vampires and witches and The Force, they'll love our family."

"Marvel comics. The fan boys eat that stuff up. They would cream their cargo shorts if they ever discovered us, an actual tribe of mutants."

"So why did Mom and Dads bring us up on this island? We're very careful that no one sees us as we are?

Suddenly a lump appeared in the other twin bed.

"Sammy, is that you?" asked J3.

Sammy, a scruffy-looking 17-year-old boy, poked his head above the covers. "Hi guys. You got some clothes I can borrow? I gotta go with J3 to see Dad Kyle."

"Something about Sammy's Dad being in trouble again."

Explained J3. "Here, use these." And he tossed a pair of running shorts, a Speedo brief and a t-shirt to Sammy.

He disappeared under the covers and quickly dressed.

Denise laughed. Little brother, you always plan ahead, don't you?"

"My OCD comes in handy. Especially with Sammy and me traveling as we do in empty space."

"Sammy!" shouted Denise. "When are you going to teach the rest of us how to get in and out of empty space? We want to be travelers, too!""

"In time," he explained jumping out of bed.

"Well, sibs of my heart, we must leave you," he grandly intoned with a deep bow. "Our father, Dad Kyle, beckons us." And off they went —using the door this time.

"Such a drama queen," chuckled Denise.

"It happens," Dennis added, "when your nanny is a former musical theatre major. Come on, sis, we don't want to be late for afternoon yoga."

They slipped on their sandals and headed out. Their afternoon routine would include yoga, meditation and then lap swim.